A Pumpkin
and a
PATCH

USA TODAY BESTSELLING AUTHOR
JENNIFER PEEL

Dedication
To Beckett: the cutest pumpkin in the patch.

A special thanks to:
Audrey Monson for the pumpkiny-est song ever!

One

EVERY PERSON HAS THAT ONE defining moment in their life. The one they will be known for, good or bad, for the entirety of their life. And it doesn't matter what they do from that moment on; even if they save a woman from choking to death—which I did, thank you very much—that one moment will come back to haunt them. Repeatedly. Take me for example, once said woman could breathe, she said, "You're the *Reece the Rogue Pirate* girl." That's right. *Reece the Rogue Pirate* is what I will always be remembered for. For fifteen years, half my life, that's been my identity.

Josie Peterson ceased to exist, replaced by the stupid story I wrote as a high school freshman about the object of my desire. You may be wondering what a rogue pirate is. Because by nature, pirates are unprincipled, dishonest, and roguish. Let's just say you can blame my teen obsession with *Pirates of the Caribbean*, mainly Orlando Bloom, and my newfound love of regency novels that cursed year. At the time, it had only seemed right to couple both my loves into one thrilling story, hence the term rogue pirate. It hadn't helped that Reece Cavanaugh bore a striking resemblance to Orlando Bloom. As a senior in high school, the guy could grow a goatee on his ridiculously chiseled face. Not to mention his dark, tousled hair and his olive skin that glistened in—or out of—the sun. It was nearly incomprehensible that a teen boy could look the way he did.

Of course, it meant he wasn't only the object of *my* desire but of every girl within a hundred-mile radius of my hometown, Carson City. Where I still live today. If I were smarter, I would have moved and changed my name, but no, I wanted to stay close to my parents and my cousin Jenna, who is more like a sister and definitely the best friend a girl could ask for. My older brother, Oliver, not so much. He is, after all, the reason for my life's predicament. He thought it would be hilarious to not only read my torrid story over the school's PA system during the morning announcements, but also to hand out copies in the hall to every passerby. Thanks to him, I never wrote in my journal again and have a deep distrust of people, especially myself.

As if that humiliation and an eternity of mocking weren't enough, I somehow got grounded for a month. Apparently, my parents thought I had too much "carnal" knowledge after they read my masterpiece. They'd grilled me for hours on end to see where I had gained such knowledge. Uh, hello, a free trial of HBO. To this day, cable and streaming channels are forbidden in my parents' home.

The irony of it all? Reece did grow up to be a pirate. Well, lawyer. Same thing. The cherry on top was his hand in trying to steal my treasure, as any good pirate would. That's right, I was currently staring at the man I had done everything in my power to avoid up to this point in my life. We are talking army-crawling-in-department-stores and hiding-behind-a-Chiquita-banana-display avoidance tactics. In case you're wondering, he grew up to be every bit as sexy as my story had made him out to be, hence the grounding when I was younger. Thankfully, I no longer dreamed of sailing the seven seas with him. A lifetime of mocking will sour you on someone. Unthankfully, he was representing my louse of an ex-fiancé, Trevor, who could afford a better lawyer than I could. Worse, Reece recognized me. I saw the recognition in his caramel-brown eyes and the tiny smirk on his face. Really the one caramel-brown eye. You see, Reece wore a patch. The story went that he had a terrible accident as a child and lost an eye. For some people it would be a tragedy, but for godlike creatures like Reece, it only adds to the allure. And oh, did he have *all* the allure, just like in my infamous story.

I sat tall across the conference room table from Reece and Trevor and tossed my chocolate-red hair over my shoulder, signaling I wasn't going to be intimidated by the two. Inside I was a hot mess, wishing I were anywhere but Reece's office . . . or that there was a banana display to hide behind. But, duty called, and as unpleasant as it was, I had every intention of keeping the four-carat halo diamond stunner—worth forty thousand dollars—that was now sitting in the middle of the table in the same Tiffany box Trevor had proposed to me with at this time last year. My favorite time of year—fall. It was all so perfect and cutesy, just like I had dreamed my engagement would be— a hayride on my family's pumpkin farm, warm apple cider, and hot kisses, thanks in part to HBO. There were things a girl didn't forget no matter how long it had been since she'd first witnessed them. What a waste of "carnal" knowledge.

Now looking at Trevor, I shuddered to think that I almost got stuck with him until death did we part. Sure, he was as handsome as ever with his textured sandy-brown hair and perpetually tanned skin, complemented by heartbreaking blue eyes that lived up to the adjective. Trevor might have broken my heart, but not my spirit, which was why we were facing off with our lawyers. Well, his lawyer and my sweet sister-in-law and the only reason I still claimed my brother. Kitty practiced law on the side while chasing toddlers. One might think I should have chosen a better attorney, but Kitty was more than capable. And she was cheap—as in she accepted my offer to babysit my niece and nephew any time or place for eternity in exchange for representing me against my scummy ex, who was trying to sue me to get the engagement ring back.

I would have happily thrown the ring back in his face, but

we'd gotten far enough into our engagement that I had booked and bought all the things. We're talking the château in Aspen Lake for the reception, the band, my five-thousand-dollar wedding dress, all because Trevor insisted on it. To marry a Kensington meant something, he would say. It meant my parents and me taking out a loan. A loan I intended to pay back with the ring. And hopefully I could use the extra to help my parents out a bit.

The past year had been rough for my family, who own the biggest pumpkin farm in the state. The big barn that housed the corncribs had burned down. Insurance was only going to cover part of the rebuilding cost. And Dad had been hurt trying to put out the fire. His broken leg had only just healed. And, as luck would have it, two of the tractors died. Then, to add insult to injury, Trevor decided marrying a third-grade teacher was beneath him. He'd highly "suggested" I put my master's degree to better use. I mean, how would it look to his colleagues at his fancy strategy consulting firm where they were wining and dining the top CEOs, not only in the country but around the world? He was horrified that he would have to tell people my parents were pumpkin farmers. At least if I had some high-powered career, he could spin that. He was all about the spin. How did I miss that? It was the eyes. Those hypnotic babies had me in a trance for far too long.

And sadly, I thought maybe if I married someone like Trevor, people would forget I was the *Reece the Rogue Pirate* girl.

Kind of hard to forget now that Reece kept opening his mouth like he should say something to me—you know, other than that the ring didn't belong to me as it was a "conditional gift." I hadn't seen the guy since high school. Well, I had seen him plenty—I just made sure he never saw me. And I had never once spoken to him. Weird, considering I wrote a mini novel about us sailing the high seas together while he ravished me. Yes, I used the word *ravish*—repeatedly. My parents made me explain that one. I told them I only meant that Reece filled me with delight. They didn't buy that meaning either. So, I wasn't sure what else he would have to say to me. Maybe he wanted to tease me mercilessly like all his friends had done back in the day, and continued to do when our paths crossed. Or perhaps he wanted to see if I could speak, as I was a functional mute around him. Even today when we'd entered, he'd tried to shake my hand while saying hello, and all I could do was stare at him with my mouth hanging open. More than likely, though, he wanted to tell me he was as off-limits now as he was then. Per the grapevine, he was divorced. He didn't need to worry on that front. I was over men. All. Of. Them. This time I meant it.

"Your client, Mr. Cavanaugh," Kitty argued, "is in breach of his contract with Miss Peterson, as he ended the engagement. This entitles my client to the ring." For her only practicing law on the side, she sounded pretty dang smart. I mean, I believed her. "And," she added, "one can argue that the condition of the gift was that she say yes to the proposal, which my client did." Kitty slammed her pen on her notebook like she was doing a mic drop.

I sat a little taller, with a take-that air.

Reece debonairly grinned my way, unfazed by Kitty's bold declarations. "Kitty," he practically purred her name. "You know very well most courts agree that the condition is marriage."

"But the courts also take into consideration who broke off the engagement," Kitty countered.

"Not in this state." Reece popped his brow like a pro.

Meanwhile, Trevor folded his arms smugly.

Between the two men, there was enough arrogance in the room for us all to choke on—both their egos and Trevor's cologne. I always told him he went overboard on the citrus scent. At least he was clearing out my nasal passages along with my bank account.

"That's not necessarily true." Kitty glared. Well, she tried. She was all of five two with the cutest pixie cut framing her face and flawless skin, making her look twenty years old instead of thirty-three. She was intimidating no one.

"I don't think you want to test that theory." Reece gave her a hard stare.

"Perhaps we do." Kitty smiled.

"Listen," Trevor jumped in. "I'm willing to pay for my half of the deposits. But it's time to move on." He flashed me a condescending smile. "It was fun while it lasted. Now that I'm engaged to Brenda, we—"

"You're engaged already? To your secretary?" I spluttered. I didn't even know he was dating anyone, much less Brenda. This was more of a sucker punch than when he broke off the engagement a few months ago. Now the suddenness of it all, and the lame excuse about my job and family's farm, was making more sense.

"Administrative assistant," he corrected me, while tugging on his collar. What a slimeball. She was ten years younger than him and used emojis instead of names in her phone's contacts. And not to be rude, but I was pretty sure she didn't even know how to spell *administrative*.

"That's much better. Much classier than a teacher. You are such a cliché." I glared. The glare I'm told that can make you wither in shame.

Trevor did squirm in his seat.

Reece's head whipped Trevor's way. He surprisingly gave him a deadlier glare than the one I had conjured up. From the looks of it, he was just as surprised by this admission. "I need to speak to you now," he demanded in a steely voice.

Both men stood and marched out of the posh office and into the hall. Everything, from the Italian leather chairs we were sitting on to the fine art on the walls, spoke to Reece making at least a few hundred dollars an hour.

Kitty patted my hand under the table. "You okay there?"

"I'm peachy," I groaned, while lowering my head to the table.

Kitty stroked my hair. "Sorry, Jo Jo." That's what my three-year-old nephew, Charlie, had started calling me, and it kind of stuck. "You're better off without him."

"I know. He was probably cheating on me, and I had no idea. I'm such an idiot." Hot shame brewed in my belly. Why had I trusted him? I knew better. It was all the dang wooing. Trevor knew how to woo. We are talking notes on my car window, long walks, a listening ear, learning all my favorite things ... he'd even helped out on the farm. He never even teased me about *Reece the Rogue Pirate*. Ironic how he hired him as his lawyer in his final act of revenge. Ugh. I should have known Trevor was too good to be true.

"He's the idiot. I mean, you're the prettiest pumpkin in the patch. Literally." She cracked herself up.

She was referring to the role I played every weekend at the family farm from mid-September to Halloween. I would take up my duties this year starting next week. Just me in my pumpkin costume reading to kids in the patch. *Patch* meaning the cute little playhouse near the bunnies. The stories were written by me. They were all about the adventures of Priscilla Pumpkin and the magic of Halloween. Why couldn't I be known for those stories? My parents were at least happy I knew how to write more than "smut," as they called it. My fifteen-year-old brain was pretty imaginative, but if they thought that was truly smut, they should probably get a free subscription to HBO again. Then they would see I was an angel by today's standards.

"I just want to get out of here. How much time will I do if I take the ring and pawn it?" I asked.

Kitty pushed the ring out of my reach. "Hold on there. Your parents will never forgive me if you go to jail."

"Are you kidding me? They love you more than me. You are the only *procreator* in the family." As my mom loved to say.

"That's a word for it. I was thinking more along the lines of toddler wrangler and diaper changer."

I raised my head and gave her a small smile. "It's not a bad gig."

"No, it's not." She gave me a knowing look. "Someday, it will be your turn."

I rolled my eyes. "Not unless I get a lobotomy and forget all the trouble men are."

Kitty glanced at the door. "I would say Trevor is in trouble with your pirate."

I scrunched my nose at her. "Don't make me hate you."

"Oh, come on, that was some fantastic writing. I wish your brother would take some pointers. That whole scene where they get stranded on the beach." She fanned herself. "I can taste the salt water when you describe that kiss. How did it begin? *His tongue skimmed my lips like the water tickling my toes before it crashed into my mouth like a tidal wave threatening to drown me eternally in a passion so deep, I would gladly breathe only his breaths for the rest of my days.*"

My cheeks burned while I groaned. "Please don't repeat that drivel to me."

"Drivel? Oh, honey, I'm pretty sure that line alone is the reason Charlie was conceived."

I held up my hand. "Okay, that was more than I needed to know. And what are you even doing with a copy of that story? Oliver swore to my parents he burned all the copies he had left."

She gave me a sheepish smile. "Well . . . we didn't want to say anything, but someone posted it online several years ago."

I jumped out of my chair. "What???" How had I missed that?

"Calm down." She grabbed my hand. "If it makes you feel any better, the comments are ninety-nine percent positive. People LOVE your story. You're like an inspiration. By the way, your fans would love a sequel."

No way was that ever happening. I couldn't even watch *Pirates of the Caribbean* anymore or read any books that mentioned the word *rogue*. This day was getting better and better. "I can't believe you kept that from me."

"We were just trying to protect you."

"Gee, thanks. Anything else you want to tell me? Maybe that dark chocolate is now deemed unhealthy for you?" Not that it was going to stop me from drowning in it later.

"Well . . ."

"Don't even say it. Let me live in my fantasy world for just a bit longer."

"Your fantasies are hotter than mine. Can I come live there too?" She wagged her brows. "I have to say, Reece does make for good material. Wowzer."

"Kitty, please stop. After today, if I never see him again, it will be too soon. Maybe I will move."

"Sorry, you can't. You promised me an eternity of babysitting, and I fully intend to take you up on it."

"Oh, fine. Just don't quote any more of that forsaken story. Deal?" I took my seat again.

"Is in my head okay? Because dang, girl, sometimes momma needs a pick-me-up."

I couldn't help but smile at her. "I guess, but don't do it around me. I'll know." Like right now, judging by her dreamy smile, I was pretty sure she was thinking about the lines that came after those she'd just spouted. Let's just say there was a lot of sticky skin and sand to go around. It was no wonder my parents had grounded me. Even I was feeling a little heated thinking about it.

Before she could respond, the two men who made my life feel like a living hell walked back in, looking none too happy. They were both red in the face and refused to even look at each other. Which unfortunately meant they were looking at me.

Reece sat down first, three chairs away from Trevor. "My client," he strangled out, "has agreed to pay for the cost of all the deposits, your dress, and any fees associated with the wedding, in exchange for the ring."

I turned toward Kitty to see what she thought of this twist. I mean, it wasn't all I hoped for, but it would mean being able to pay off the loan my parents and I had taken out. Though I had to wonder what brought on Trevor's change of tune.

Kitty pulled me to her, in probably an unprofessional manner, and whispered for my ears only, "This is a good deal. Reece is right; this state doesn't care who broke off the engagement. P.S. I think your pirate just became the hero."

I grimaced and pulled away from her. Reece Cavanaugh was no hero in my book. Well, not my book, because actually in *my book*, he really was the hero, which was ridiculous. I mean, could a rogue pirate really be a hero? I probably hadn't thought that through very well. I chalked it up to being only fifteen. But that was neither here nor there.

"Are we in agreement?" Reece Cavanaugh smiled at me. The same crooked smile I had written about so many years ago. We are talking a heart-stopping, chocolate-melting, roll-around-on-the-beach kind of smile.

I gripped my chair and closed my eyes. I was surely losing all sense of reality. Reece Cavanaugh would never smile at me in such a way, especially under the circumstances. He probably smiled at everyone like that. I peeked my eyes open to find he was still smiling at me, but this time his head was tipped to the side. He was probably wondering if I was having a mental episode. The odds were in favor of that diagnosis.

"Josie," he spoke my name. It was the first time I'd ever heard him say it. It was just as I'd imagined it in my story: sweet and sensual, like only he was meant to say it.

Oh. My. Gosh. I was definitely having an episode. I jumped up. "Great. That works. I have to go," I blurted at the speed of light. Burning with an embarrassment to rival the day my story was read over the PA system, I ran out of the conference room, not sure where I was going. Kitty was my ride. All I knew was I couldn't stand to be in the presence of Reece Cavanaugh another moment.

Once out of the office, I stopped and leaned against the hallway wall, trying to catch my breath, vowing then and there to never have another run-in with the man, or any man for that matter. I would no longer be held captive by *Reece the Rogue Pirate.*

Two

"OH, HONEY, YOU NEED TO stop furrowing your brow like that. You don't want to get W-R-I-N-K-L-E-S." Jenna spelled it out like it was a four-letter word while she fixed a wrap around my hair. As the best person in the world, she'd offered me a free facial massage following my ordeal at the law office.

As appreciative as my skin was going to be, I was more grateful I had her to talk to. We had a special bond. You see, our mothers were sisters who married brothers, which made us cousin cousins. It was like inbreeding, but the legal and non-gross kind. Whatever it was, Jenna and I were stuck together like Gorilla Glue. Our moms even got pregnant at the same time. I'm only three days older than Jenna. My family is a little quirky, to say the least. Don't even get me going on all the Peterson traditions. Let's just say I already had my ugly Christmas sweater picked out and it was only September. I was determined to win this year. Or get electrocuted, judging by how many lights were on it.

"I don't care if I get wrinkles," I whined. "I may even stop using sunscreen to speed up the process." Who did I have to look good for anyway?

She gasped and covered my mouth. "Don't even joke about that. I'll stab you if you ruin your perfect creamy complexion."

11

She only got violent when it came to skin care. Other than that, she was the sweetest person ever. Prettiest, too, with her light-brown hair and the Peterson green eyes. The combination was striking.

"Just make sure you use a butcher knife and it's fatal," I teased, sort of.

She patted my cheeks. "No can do. Peterson family rules state there is no dying during pumpkin season."

"Fine, come November first, all bets are off."

She laughed and turned on some soothing music.

Meanwhile, I lay there practically naked under a blanket on the aesthetician bed waiting for my heavenly treatment. I took in the swanky surroundings, boasting an indoor waterfall and fresh rose petals wherever you walked. Once again, I found myself more than thankful for Jenna. No way on my teacher's salary could I afford this spa in Aspen Lake. Really any spa for that matter, even though I worked for a private school. I constantly had to remind myself that being a teacher was more of a calling than a profession. I did love my students, but sometimes I wished I got paid more to love them.

Jenna took her seat behind me. "Sorry, no dying during the holidays either. I mean, our moms' pumpkin pie alone is worth living for."

This was true. Even if Jenna and I were salty they wouldn't share the recipe with us yet. Apparently, that was a rite of passage we'd be initiated into upon turning fifty. Not sure why they chose that particular age. It was probably some weird family tradition I wasn't aware of.

"Okay, fine. I'll live, but I might eat an entire pie by myself on Thanksgiving."

She smoothed my long, curly hair. "Good. Not to sound like my mom, but you need to put some meat back on your too-skinny bones."

It was all the stress. I never thought I would ever be too upset to eat, but thanks to Trevor, I found it was more than a possibility. I wondered how many other things I would find I was wrong about. "I can't believe he was cheating on me," I whispered.

"Ugh," Jenna growled. "For that I may be willing to sell my soul to the devil to curse him."

"He's not worth losing your soul over." At least I could be thankful I never gave him mine. Maybe my heart, but I held back my soul. That should have said something to me.

"Maybe instead of having Cami crop him out of your engagement photos, have her turn him into a clown or a dog."

Cami was a local celebrity in Aspen Lake and a mutual friend. She'd become famous for hilariously cropping her ex-husband out of their wedding photos after she caught him cheating on her. That led her to starting the wildly popular Holiday Ex-Files. She has quite the following and is known for her snarky posts about single life, even though she's now happily remarried and pregnant. She also runs a local Ex-Filers chapter that's a charitable support group.

I recently joined and was helping with the Halloween Bash that donates all the proceeds to a nearby women and children's shelter. You know, because I'm not already ridiculously busy helping my family with the pumpkin farm this time of year. Not to mention having to help with the school fall carnival, all the field trips, lesson planning, teaching said lessons, wiping noses, putting Band-Aids on owies, breaking up the occasional tiff, and talking over fifteen boisterous students. Make that fourteen because sweet little Giselle just moved away. Along with her went her mom, the best room-parent coordinator ever. Now I was stuck without one, as no one else would volunteer.

I was exhausted thinking of it all. I didn't even have time to be lying here, but I closed my eyes anyway, hoping Jenna could work her magic on me and make me forget for one hour I wasn't such a loser. For some reason I had this idea that if I got married and moved into Trevor's house off Aspen Lake, I would no longer be *Reece the Rogue Pirate* girl. That finally people would see Josie.

When I didn't answer, Jenna responded, "I know what you're thinking, and you aren't a loser." She knew me too well. We did share an overwhelming amount of DNA. "Look at everything you've accomplished—a master's in education, Teacher of the Year two years in a row, and let's not forget, you come running anytime one of us needs you. If that wasn't enough, you're gorgeous. I mean, who has naturally chocolate-red hair paired with green eyes? I don't think that's fair." She squeezed my shoulders.

"You're one to talk, Miss Prom Queen and most likely to become a cover model for *Vogue*."

"Was that a category in the yearbook?" She laughed. "Regardless, you're awesome. You have to quit letting that story define you. You should be proud of that story—it's an online sensation."

I sat up and turned around, making sure to keep the blanket over the girls. "You knew about that too? Why didn't you tell me?"

"For this reason." She waved her hands up and down. "I knew you would freak."

Freaking out hardly covered it. I rubbed my forehead, feeling a major headache coming on. "Why won't that story just die?"

Jenna patted my arm. "Well, there's something about a hot pirate. Speaking of which, you haven't mentioned how it was seeing him today."

"Purposely." I smirked.

"Come on. I have dived behind banana displays for you."

She, more than anyone, had been privy to my ridiculous tactical maneuvers when it came to Reece Cavanaugh. Why couldn't I have been born one year later? Then he would have already graduated from high school and I would have never seen him swagger down the hall like he owned the place, capturing my young, fragile heart without a clue. Nor would I have felt the need to pour my soul, burning with unrequited love, out onto the pages of my journal, feeling as if that was the only relief available to me. Even at that tender age I was smart enough to know the student body president and most popular guy was never going to notice gangly me, who hadn't yet grown into all her limbs and was still sporting braces. I hadn't even learned how to tame my hair.

Despite having grown into my limbs, having perfectly straight teeth, and possessing the ability to do some killer hairdos, I was still the pirate girl.

"It was awkward, obviously," I offered.

She wrinkled her cute button nose. "I could have guessed that. Give me more, woman."

"What more is there to say?"

"Oh, I don't know. Maybe something along the lines of how he still makes your blood pulse and rage like the white waters of the Congo River."

I cringed all over. "Don't repeat lines of the story to me. Between you and Kitty today, I'm definitely getting a lobotomy."

"Why?" she laughed. "That was some fabulous writing, especially for a fifteen-year-old. Maybe you should try your hand at another love story. I bet you could really rev some motors now." She nudged me.

"Absolutely not. I will be sticking with Priscilla Pumpkin, thank you very much. Besides, I might give my dad a coronary if I write anything steamier. And our mothers may start that petition again to get HBO banned. Do we really want to see them on the local nightly news holding up signs that say *Honk Your Horn If You Hate Porn?*" I mean, I didn't like porn either, but I didn't need to stand on a street corner and shout about it. Especially if I had a daughter who had already been humiliated enough. I should probably get some therapy.

"Good point," Jenna admitted. "But . . . you could use a pen name. I hear there is good money in self-publishing. Think of it. Noble schoolteacher by day and madam of seductive romance by night."

I rolled my eyes. "You're crazy. And knowing my luck, my brother would find out and give copies to everyone he knows, including the school administrators and parents, and I would find myself unemployed. Which still wouldn't top the humiliation I lived through in high school." The private school I worked for was all about their image, and I didn't think *madam of seduction* fit the bill. "Not even Reece Cavanaugh being witness to my ex-fiancé's bombshell today could compare to the hell I lived through in high school." Why him, though? Out of all the lawyers in Nevada, it had to be him. He must think I'm the ultimate loser.

"Oh, Jo Jo." She patted my head. "I wish I could take away everything that happened to you in high school, even today, but all those experiences made you who you are—a kindhearted and passionate teacher who always watches out for the kids she loves."

I tried to be. I never wanted any student to be bullied or mocked mercilessly the way I had been. I'd begged my parents to homeschool me, but they'd said I couldn't run away from it. It would give me character. It gave me something, all right— unhealthy coping mechanisms.

I lay back down and squeezed my eyes shut, though not because I was going to cry. I hadn't cried in years. Not sure I could anymore. My tear ducts retired after all the overuse in high school. No, I just wanted to shut the world out.

Sweet Jenna knew me well enough to let me be for a minute. She started the treatment by gently cleansing my face, neck, and chest with a cleanser that smelled like orange blossoms. I breathed in the invigorating scent and tried to relax under Jenna's skillful touch. It was easier said than done. What a day.

"Soooo," Jenna whispered, "I know you probably don't care, but word on the street is that Reece's ex-wife is in rehab, and he now has full custody of their daughter."

I really didn't care. I had done everything in my power over the last fifteen years not to know anything about Reece Cavanaugh. But I suppose I was curious, seeing as his ex-wife

16

was the epitome of perfection. I mean, at least what I had seen of her from behind the banana display a few years ago. Besides, I knew Jenna was obviously bursting to share the news. How could I deny her the pleasure? "What street have you been on?"

"Uh, hello, I work in a spa; I hear all the juicy gossip. And Reece Cavanaugh's ex-sister-in-law, Evie, is a client here. Apparently, Reece has been trying forever to get custody of his little girl." She spoke in conspiratorial tones.

I did know enough about him to know he had a darling daughter. Not sure of her age, but she was the most angelic little thing I had ever seen—you know, from behind something or other. I had lost track of all the things I had hid behind to avoid Reece. But from what I could remember, she had lots of dark hair like her mom and dad, and big emerald eyes. She looked like a fairy come to life. Just one more reason for me to dislike Reece. I wanted a daughter of my own so bad I could taste it.

"Interesting," I said nonchalantly.

Jenna made soft sweeping motions across my cheeks while ignoring my less than enthusiastic response. "Anyway, according to Evie, her ex-brother-in-law is a real class act, paying for his ex-wife to go to rehab even though she's the one who left him."

"Why did she leave him?" fell out of my mouth before I could stop it.

"I knew you were interested!" Jenna cackled.

"I'm not," I defended myself. "I'm just making conversation, and I know how happy this makes you. It's all for you." That was my story, and I was sticking to it.

"You are such a liar. But . . . I will proceed. So"—her excitement level went up a few notches—"Nicolette, the ex-wife, apparently just decided one day she was done being a wife and pretty much a mom, too, but didn't want to look bad, so she wouldn't give full custody to Reece up front. Even though she mostly left Andi—that's the daughter—with her parents when she had her."

"That's sad."

"Right? But it gets sadder." Jenna was now being not so gentle as she pressed her fingers into my chest. The story must have been really juicy. "Not only was she basically ignoring her daughter, but she would leave for days, and no one would know where to find her. She was usually with some guy on his yacht or at a nightclub, getting high."

"Oh my gosh. That's awful."

"Yeah. But get this," she whispered, as if we weren't the only two people in the room, "your rogue pirate—"

"He is not my pirate. He's not my anything," I complained.

"Okay, okay, keep your panties on. I mean that," she laughed.

Considering it was all I had on under the blanket, I planned to keep it that way.

"Anyway," Jenna continued, "Reece, *not your pirate*, marched right into an LA nightclub and scooped her up and took her straight to rehab, begging her to get better for their daughter. Isn't that the sweetest?" She sighed. "Kind of romantic too."

"Yeah, sure, if you think *Traffic* is a romance."

She waved her hand in front of my face. "I get it. You're over men and love."

"I'm more than over them. I've buried them." Like alive.

"Ooh, like buried treasure, to dig up later." Her tone intimated that she thought I wouldn't be able to stick to my plan. She had no idea how serious I was this time. Yes, this was not my first foray into swearing off men for eternity, but this time I meant it. Really. Truly.

"No, more like dead corpses never to be unearthed."

"You're hilarious." She smushed my cheeks. "We shall see how long you last this time," she sang.

"FOOOREVER," I exaggerated, but meant every syllable.

"If you say so." She didn't believe me at all. "But, I do have to say this. It's kind of weird how Reece keeps popping up in your life lately."

18

"He's not popping up in my life," I vehemently disagreed. "And now that I know which law firm he works for and that he's willing to take on scum-of-the-earth exes as clients, I can totally avoid him. Especially since I will never have another ex."

"Which could mean the next man is the one."

I rolled my eyes. "I love you, but you're hopeless. If any man pops up in my life, I'm going to Whac-A-Mole all over him."

Jenna laughed hysterically. "I would love to see that."

"I'm getting a mallet ready just in case." This time I meant business.

Three

"GOOD MORNING, DARLIN'," LIBBY DRAWLED, as I walked into the front office Monday morning. Only she could get away with calling the staff *darlin'*. Anyone else would probably have been written up. But our local southern transplant was not going to let anyone change her ways. And honestly, who didn't love to be called *darlin'* by a cute little grandma? She reminded me of Betty White during the *Golden Girls* era, complete with snow-white curly hair and a permanent smile on her face. It was hard not to be happy around her.

I leaned against the receptionist desk she was seated behind. "Good morning, Libby. How was your weekend?"

"It was finer than a frog's hair."

I loved her southern sayings. "That good, huh?"

"How about you, darlin'?"

"I helped my family on the farm this weekend. We're getting ready for opening day this Friday." And I binge-watched fifteen hours of a Turkish soap opera I was addicted to, but no one except Jenna needed to know that information. And not even Jenna could, because it was our thing, and I wasn't supposed to be watching it without her. But I needed a binge coma. Besides, it was educational because I had to read the subtitles and I now knew plenty of Turkish words. And maybe I was half in love with the main character, Can Divit, real name Can Yaman. He was going to be the only love of my life moving forward.

"I can't wait to take my grandbabies when they visit me next month."

"I bet you're excited to see them." Most of her family lived in Tennessee. She'd moved to Nevada a few years ago after her first husband passed, and she remarried what she called her hunk, a hunk of burning love. She was known to say she married for love the first time, but this time it was all about the looks and money. I did have to say her husband, Pete, was an attractive older man. And she only worked as the school receptionist because she claimed it made their sex life better. I guess due to the longing to see each other. I didn't really want to know. I mean, she was older than my mom, and as a rule, I tried not to get involved in the intimate details of my coworkers' lives.

"I've made a countdown." She beamed.

"Well, please make sure to bring them by. I would love to meet them."

"Sure thing, darlin'." She grinned.

I peeked around the corner toward the administrative offices. "Is Mr. Nelson in? He said he wanted to meet with me this morning." I was a little sick about it. Mr. Nelson, the principal, had texted me that weekend. He had never done that before. I texted back asking if I was fired. I was joking, but serious. I mean, if he was going to fire me, I would rather just know so I could have stayed up all night bingeing my show instead of only half the night. His response was a simple *no*. It didn't leave me feeling all warm and fuzzy.

Libby didn't answer me. Instead, she began fanning herself as if a fierce hot flash were consuming her.

"Are you okay?"

"Oh, honey, look what the cat dragged in." She pointed toward the school entrance. "He's as hot as a two-dollar pistol."

I turned to see who she was talking about. I expected not to be impressed, seeing as one, I was so over men, and two, I had just spent many, many hours of my life lusting after my Turkish boyfriend. Yes, I said lusting. My mother would blame HBO.

Well . . . unfortunately, I was proved wrong. The man in question was more beautiful than my TV boyfriend. "Holy shiz." I dove behind the receptionist desk like I was taking shelter from an incoming missile attack. I crouched next to Libby, feeling as if I were having my own hot flash now. I fanned myself. "No, no, no, no. What is he doing here?" I mumbled to myself like a raving lunatic.

Libby was staring at me wide-eyed. "Darlin', you're acting crazier than a run-over cat. Should I call somebody?"

I rubbed my chest, feeling like maybe it wouldn't be a bad idea to dial 911. I was pretty sure my heart wasn't supposed to pound like it was Thor's hammer. "Um . . ." I didn't know what to say. All I could think about was the fact that Reece Cavanaugh had just walked into my school. Was it not enough that he stole my engagement ring from me? Or, you know, ruined my adolescent life? Why did he need to be here? Worse, I was pretty sure he caught a glimpse of me before I did the worst impression ever of an actress in an action movie. I would not be surprised if my dress flew up. Oh well—in that case, people would know that, even if I was mental, I at least was stable enough to wear panties. *Which panties did I wear today?* Please let them be something silk and lacy, not the big cotton ones my mom put in my stocking last year. Not sure why she still felt the need to buy me under-wear every year for Christmas. Actually, of course I knew. It was tradition.

Libby smoothed my brow delicately as if she were afraid to touch me. She probably didn't want to catch my crazy. "You feel a little warm. Should I call the nurse?"

Yes, yes. Call her. I could use a sick day right about now. Before I could articulate a thing, a familiar voice said, "Hello, I have an appointment with Ken Nelson."

Oh no he didn't.

Libby forgot all about me and smiled like she was starring

in a toothpaste commercial at Reece who was going to get whacked like a mole. "Hello, darlin'," she purred. "You must be Reece Cavanaugh," she said his name as if she were pouring syrup out of her mouth, all sticky and sweet.

"Yes, ma'am." He did too good of an impression of a southern gentleman.

"I like your manners. Oh yes, I do."

Oh my gosh. She was probably older than his mother. Not that I knew his mother, because why would I want to know the woman who bore the most beautiful creature on earth who was meant to torture me for the rest of my days? No thank you.

"Well, thank you, Libby," he responded.

"Reece," a booming voice filled the front office area.

I stilled, not knowing what to do as my boss, Principal Nelson, entered the picture. How did I find myself in these sorts of situations? It was one thing to dive behind clothing racks and fruit displays—this was a whole new level.

"Ms. Peterson?" Mr. Nelson said, before I could formulate a plan.

I turned from my crouching position and stared up at my intimidating boss, who I was told was just a big teddy bear inside. But he looked more along the lines of the grizzly variety this morning, with his pinched expression and dark eyes lasered in on me.

I had at least a few functioning brain cells left—very few, mind you. I slapped a hand over my eye. "I lost a contact," I lied. I indeed do not wear contacts. What was wrong with me? It was then I realized I should have gone with *"I lost an earring."* Crap.

"Oh, let me help you." Mr. Nelson knelt and started looking around.

Reece peeked over the receptionist desk, and dang it if we didn't lock eyes. Or eye. I wasn't sure what the proper term was, since he only had the one. A gorgeous one, mind you. Either way, the eye contact came with a crooked grin as if he knew I was lying.

My face erupted in lava, splotches trailing down my neck all the way to my abdominal region, where the hot molten mass stirred in my belly. I tore away from his gaze and faced my boss, who was doing his best to help me find the nonexistent contact.

"Mr. Nelson, it's fine. It's disposable anyway." Like my job.

"I want you to be able to see." He was obviously concerned.

"Believe me, I can see just fine." See that my career would be ending, that is.

"Are you sure?" He stared into my lying eyes.

I stood quickly, hoping he didn't notice that neither of my eyes had any inkling of a contact in them. I smoothed my navy pocket shirtdress, sure my knees would give out. I could feel Reece's gaze.

Libby was wobbling her head back and forth, trying to assess me.

Mr. Nelson stood and brushed off his suit pants. He towered ten inches above me at six feet, four inches. He had played basketball at UNLV. He would have gone into the NBA except for a knee injury.

"Ken, it's good to see you." Reece came around the desk and held out his hand.

Mr. Nelson took his hand and pulled him in for a bro hug. "Good to see you, man. How is your mom?" he asked, like they were good buddies.

"Doing well. She's upset you and Denise haven't been by for dinner in a while."

Uh, why did Reece know my principal's wife's first name? And why were they having dinner together?

Mr. Nelson chuckled. "Tell her soon. You better be there too."

"Of course." Reece patted his back before he stepped away from the bro embrace.

I gripped the desk, feeling as if somehow I was missing something important. Something that wasn't going to be to my liking.

"Shall we meet in my office?" Mr. Nelson nodded toward the hall where all the administrative offices were located.

"Sounds good," Reece responded, before he flashed me a grin.

I scrunched my nose. There was no reason for him to smile at me. The ring stealer.

"Ms. Peterson, will you please join us?" Mr. Nelson asked.

Oh, no, no, no. I put a finger to my ear and rubbed. Surely, I'd heard him wrong. Why would I need to meet with Reece Cavanaugh in my principal's office? My ex-fiancé suing me to get his stupid ring back had nothing to do with my job.

"My students will be arriving soon," was all I could think to say. I couldn't outright tell my principal no.

"It won't take long." Mr. Nelson marched off as if he were the general, and, as his soldier, I had no choice but to follow him.

Reece waved his arm out. "Ladies first."

I wanted to say some very unladylike things; instead, I skirted around Reece and tiptoed after Mr. Nelson.

Reece fell in by my side as we walked down the hall together. "Sorry about your contact." His smile spoke volumes. He knew I was lying.

"It's fine." I stepped away from him. He smelled like my dreams, and I didn't especially care for it. You know, the dreams where I was rolling around on the beach with him and he smelled heavenly, like the first rain of spring. The distance didn't help. His scent was stuck in my nose like I was a freaking bloodhound. "I still have one good eye left," I blurted without thinking, because of that dang scent of his. "I mean . . ." I'm an idiot.

"I have one good one too." He chuckled.

I covered my face with my hands. I wasn't referring to his patch at all. In no way was I an ableist. In fact, I had always admired, from afar of course, how he'd seemed to persevere despite his challenges. How could I ever define him by an impairment? He played every sport in high school and went on to do great things. Unlike me. Being around him made me feel as if I were the gangly girl back in high school, so insecure. My only friend was Jenna back in the day. Beautiful, popular Jenna who always stood up for me and made sure I had somewhat of a social life during those four years of misery.

While I burned in my private hell, I noticed the outright drooling of those we walked by, even from Vice Principal Rawlings, who was very married, mind you. Yes, Mrs. Rawlings, I see you there clutching your chest like Reece just stopped your heart. I had been there before. Maybe she would go home and write some torrid story about him now too.

Mr. Nelson waited by his door with a smile, which was unusual for him. He was more of a let's-get-down-to-business kind of man. He expected great things from his teachers and students and ran a tight ship, as he would say. Perhaps his smile could be attributed to the attention his friend Reece garnered. I still couldn't believe they were friends. Had I known, I would not have taken this job. Maybe that was a lie. It was an honor to teach at Highland Academy. It was a top-ten private elementary school. The waiting list to get in was so long, people put their newborns on it. I would have been a fool not to take the job.

Mr. Nelson waved us in. Reece gestured that I should enter first. I slid past him, holding my breath, hoping not to get any more whiffs of the ridiculously handsome man. It didn't help much; his scent was ingrained in my olfactory system. I tried my best to focus on something else, like Mr. Nelson's cozy leather chair that swiveled behind his fancy hardwood desk and the glistening monitors on it. I had to remind myself that the real rewards in education came in the classroom. Who needed a six-figure income and the ability to take bathroom breaks whenever you wanted? Not me.

"Please have a seat." Mr. Nelson pointed at the two high-backed chairs in front of his desk. Chairs that were too close to each other for my comfort. But did I leave well enough alone? Oh, no. I picked my chair up and moved it. Yep, right there in front of my principal, I moved the furniture in his office.

Both men blinked abnormally, as if they couldn't believe their eyes. How I wished their eyes were lying to them.

I gripped the back of the chair, wishing I could crawl under it and die. "Uh, I read this article recently that suggested chairs be at least thirty-six inches apart, so they aren't too close but you can still converse naturally." I was turning into such a liar, liar, pants on fire. I loathed myself for it, as I hated liars . . . a.k.a. my ex-fiancé.

Mr. Nelson's brow furrowed. "Hmm. Take a seat."

Reece pressed his lips together in a sneaky smile that said he knew I was lying again. Maybe that was his lawyer superpower, or maybe he was just the devil.

I plopped into my seat, clasping my hands together, begging myself to behave normally. Whatever that meant. At this point I would just take not acting like a nutjob.

Mr. Nelson took his seat and got right down to business. "Ms. Peterson, I would like to introduce you to Reece Cavanaugh; his daughter will be joining your class."

"No, she won't." I laughed . . . maniacally. Seriously, this was not happening. This was some kind of practical joke, right? Maybe this was Trevor's final, final revenge. But really, there was no way the rogue pirate's daughter could be in my class. I mean, it was unethical, seeing as her father and I had a very steamy fictional encounter.

Mr. Nelson's lips curled into a scary snarl. "Excuse me."

I blew out enough air to make a 747 take flight. I was two seconds away from losing my job. "What I meant was, you two are obviously friends, and I want to make sure his daughter receives the best we have to offer. And there is no better teacher around than Aline." She was my partner in crime and the only other third-grade teacher. Next to Jenna, she was the best friend I had.

Mr. Nelson tipped his handsome black bald head, which was now starting to accumulate sweat beads. "Ms. Peterson," he gritted out, "as much as I appreciate your modesty, you are one of the best, if not the finest teacher in this school."

27

I slapped a hand against my chest. "You really think so?" Wait, I wasn't supposed to be flattered here.

He sat up tall and cleared his throat. "I'm beginning to have my doubts."

Join the club.

"If you wouldn't mind," Reece interjected. "It should be noted, Ms. Peterson and I are acquainted already. She and I went to high school together."

Ugh. Why did he need to mention that? It's not like we ever talked. Sure, I had semi-stalked him and then written a lust-filled story about him, but that hardly made us acquaintances.

"I wasn't aware of that." Mr. Nelson tapped his fingers on his desk, probably wondering if he should notify Human Resources he was putting me on administrative leave.

"Josie's always been a kidder," Reece added.

Was he taking a swipe at my story? Here's a newsflash, buddy: that unfortunately was all real.

I whipped my head in his direction, daring to look at him. It was probably not the smartest thing. Holy moly was he beautiful. That stubbled jawline was the eighth wonder of the world. "Yeah, you know me. Just a kidder."

His right brow quirked like a freaking Turkish drama actor.

"Well, good." Mr. Nelson clapped his hands together. "I'm sure Andi will grow and flourish under Ms. Peterson's care."

"I have no doubt." Reece smirked. "In fact, if it would be all right, I would like to see the classroom and speak further with Josie, I mean Ms. Peterson, about some things she should be aware of in regard to Andi."

"Absolutely. Just get a visitor pass and Ms. Peterson can show you around." He gave me a pointed look, painting a very clear picture. If I said anything contrary, I should start polishing my résumé.

I stood, calculating in my mind how long I could financially survive without this job. It amounted to all of about two seconds, given the fact that I had spent all my savings on a wedding that never happened. Too bad I liked to eat and pay for my Turkish TV streaming subscription. I blame that Can Yaman. Show the devil around it was.

"Follow me, Mr. Cavanaugh."

Four

AFTER PASSING THE SECURITY DOORS, we clicked down the hall together while students began trickling in. I was still waiting for someone to pop out of a door and tell me this was all just a joke and I had won a prize on some reality show, or even a mental evaluation. That was a thing, right? Please tell me that was a thing.

"Josie, or Ms. Peterson. What should I call you?" Reece interrupted my unrealistic thoughts.

"Whichever." I couldn't think straight. If I had my wish, I wouldn't like him to address me at all. Wait until I told Jenna this. She was going to flip. I hurried my pace.

He easily kept up with his long legs. Legs I had once dreamed would be wrapped around me. Oh. My. Gosh. This was so, so wrong.

I sped up.

He kept pace, chuckling now. "Wow, you really don't like me, do you?"

I halted, skidding in my leather wedges, something in me snapping. "Well, let's see, you and your friends made my life a living hell in high school, and you just stole my engagement ring. A ring that I needed to—never mind." He didn't need to know my family's personal situation. "Anyway, I guess you could say I don't like you." I marched off.

He followed. "I like honesty. So, if we are being honest, I did nothing of the sort in high school, and I didn't steal anything. By law that ring wasn't yours."

"Whatever helps you sleep at night." I walked into my beloved classroom. My happy place filled with bright colors and inspirational sayings on the wall like, *Today a Reader, Tomorrow a Leader*, near the cozy reading nook in the corner.

"I have no issues with my conscience, Ms. Peterson. While I may not always like how the laws are written or must be applied, I always adhere to them."

"You're just a saint." Whoa. I wasn't usually so snappy. And never, ever to a parent. But it was as if the years of building resentment toward him begged to be unleashed.

Reece folded his arms, making me take note of his dark tailored suit that fit him to a T. "I would never claim to be such, but I do my job, and I expect you to do yours where my daughter is concerned." Ouch. I bet he was a worthy opponent in a courtroom.

My mouth fell open. He was putting me in my place and doing it well. I didn't particularly care for it. "I, like you, take my job seriously and have loved every student who has walked through that door." I pointed toward my classroom's entrance, wishing he would walk right out of it.

His arms fell to his side as he released a deep breath. "My apologies. I didn't mean to imply I thought you would do any less than your best. You come highly recommended, and it's why I requested Andi be in your class."

Say what? He requested me. And who was he hearing these things from?

"Oh," I breathed out. "That's nice. I guess." I sounded like a dolt.

That charming smile of his appeared. "You guess?"

"Yeah." I shrugged, acting like more of an idiot. "Anyway, what would you like to discuss?"

He stepped closer, doing me no favors. He and his

intoxicating scent needed to keep their distance. "First, I would like to say, Trevor didn't tell me the whole story when I agreed to take his case. If he had, I wouldn't have represented him."

My face flushed at the mere mention of Trevor. "It's neither here nor there." It was the last thing I wanted to talk about—you know, other than the pirate thing.

"Understood." He nodded.

"So, this is my classroom," I said, flustered, hoping he wouldn't bring up the stupid story of which he was the star. "I like to place my students in group settings, to facilitate collaboration as they learn how to cooperate. I also have active and quiet learning areas, as you can see." I pointed to the reading nook and educational games area. "I'm a huge proponent of student-led learning and discussion. My focuses are on reading, writing, problem solving, arts, and arithmetic."

Reece surveyed the room with interest, even walking around and picking up some of the books on the shelves. He held up a copy of *Tales of a Fourth Grade Nothing*. "I loved this book when I was a kid."

"Me too. You can never go wrong with Judy Blume."

"I'm glad to see so many classics on your shelves. I look forward to reading more of them to Andi now that she lives solely with me."

"Is this a recent change for her?" I asked, like the attentive teacher I was, pretending I had no clue about his current situation.

"Yes." He placed the book back on the shelf. "It's one of the reasons I wished to speak to you."

"Okay."

He leaned against the wall and folded his arms as if he were posing for *GQ*. "Andi's mother and I shared custody until recently," he said, as if it grated on every one of his nerves. "That's no longer the case. That said, the reasons leading to the change are of a delicate nature. I've been doing my best to protect my daughter from it all."

"How is she adjusting to the change?" I asked, admittedly impressed with how much he seemed to care for his daughter.

He tilted his head from side to side. "To be honest, I don't think well. She's been quiet, not like herself."

"I'm sorry to hear that. I will be sure to pay special attention to her behavior and let you know if I see anything unusual or that concerns me." By letting him know, I meant by email. I would be talking to him as little as possible over the next eight months of my life. Summer break couldn't come soon enough. It was like high school all over again: me living for the holidays.

"I appreciate that."

"Can you tell me how she fared academically at her last school?"

He rubbed the back of his neck. "She's a bit behind. My ex-wife, well . . . she . . . well, let's just say she had other priorities. I did what I could when I had her on the weekends."

I knew what some of those priorities were, and even though I didn't know Andi yet, it broke my heart she had suffered for it. "I'll do some assessments and let you know my findings." Again, by email. "I can work with her to fill some of the gaps."

"Any extra help you can give her would be greatly appreciated."

"Of course. My students will be arriving any second now." That was my way of saying, *"See ya later, alligator."*

"Yes." He pushed off the wall. "Thank you for letting me take some of your time this morning. I look forward to getting to know you better."

I tilted my head.

"You look confused, Ms. Peterson."

I think I was well past that stage. "Uh, no. I was just thinking we won't really get to know each other all that well." Why did I say that out loud?

He stepped closer with his brow furrowed, as if he were the confused one now. "You will be teaching my daughter."

I stepped back until I was up against the whiteboard. "Yes. Yes, I will. And you can email anytime you have any questions."

"Email?" he questioned, as he moved even closer. Close enough that I could see he had magically acquired more stubble than he'd had just moments ago. How was that possible, and why was he so sexy?

"Yep. Email." I swallowed hard.

"Right. Because you don't like me." A hint of a smile lingered in his words.

I clasped my hands together, trying to avoid direct eye contact, but his gaze owned me like my thirty-year mortgage. It was like we were playing out a scene from my stupid story. You see, the rogue pirate and the heroine, a.k.a. me, didn't hit it off right away. I mean, he did kidnap me—I mean her. Kind of like what his eye was doing now. He was totally hijacking me. Next thing you knew he was going to say, *"You don't like me now, but believe me, love, it's only a matter of time before you'll beg me to own you, body and soul."* Yep, that's why I got grounded.

I wrung my hands so tightly, trying not to think about what happened next in the story. The part where he pulled her to him and they began to breathe as one, as his fingers danced down her bare arm, leaving a trail of raised skin. In that moment, she knew her life would never be the same. No man had ever affected her in such a way. Except she wouldn't give in so easily, oh no. She was going to make him beg for her. And beg he did.

Oh. My. Gosh. I needed to get my head out of my head.

"Uh, it's nothing personal," was all I could say, while having more-than-personal thoughts about him. Why did he have this strange pull on me? Maybe my mom was right: HBO is evil.

The corners of his mouth pointed downward. "I think it's very personal when you don't like someone, especially when perhaps you've misjudged them."

"Who says I h-have?"

"I do."

I stood tall, though I felt weak in the knees. "Of course, you would think that. Regardless, it won't affect Andi. I will love her and do my best for her, as I would any other student."

"I'm sure you will." He inched ever closer. "But . . . I have a prediction."

"What is that?"

"You're going to like me."

Oh, no, no, no. That was never going to happen. It was impossible. "I don't think so."

Judging by his smirk, my negativity didn't faze him at all. "We shall see. Good day, Ms. Peterson." He strode off, only to turn around at the door. "By the way, in high school, if I heard someone making fun of you, I put a stop to it."

I bit my lip, not sure I believed him. How easy for him to say something like that now.

"I quite enjoyed that story," he added, before leaving without another word.

I stood there with my mouth hanging open, staring at his retreating figure as he walked down the hall, stealing all the air. For years I had prayed he never read it. I had even convinced myself he hadn't. Now he had just verified my worst nightmare.

"Knock, knock." Aline walked in, all dolled up in a colorful midi dress. The Brazilian beauty queen had curves for days, the silkiest dark hair, and brown eyes as deep as the chocolate I loved so much. Oddly enough, she married the fairest man of all time with red hair and freckles. His genes were strong, as all three of her kiddos looked just like him. Nate was the luckiest guy around, and it was clear he knew it by the way he worshipped his wife.

"Ay, ay, ay, who was the guy who just left?" Aline wagged her perfectly arched brows.

"Um," I could barely manage to say. The air around me still felt thin.

She stepped closer and waved her hand in front of my face. "You okay there?"

I shook my head. "I'm not sure."

She looked back and forth between the door and me. "Did I see a patch? Is that the—"

"The pirate? Yeah." To know me was to know the story.

"Did he come in here to ravish you?" She laughed.

"No." I scrunched my face. "Worse, his daughter is going to be in my class."

Her eyes widened. "Oh querida."

"Right?" A sudden brilliant idea popped into my head. "I'll trade you the Wittmore twins for her." The Wittmore boys were, in a nutshell, little terrors. They were either going to grow up and rule the world or go to prison. There was no in between for them. Don't get me wrong, we loved them, but they'd made every teacher in this school cry. Except me, who couldn't shed tears. But they'd made me come close.

"Don't tempt me. Darlings Trager and Teagan thought it would be hilarious yesterday if they flicked earwax at each other and then ate it."

I put my hand over my mouth, sick to my stomach. "I didn't need to hear that."

"Imagine witnessing it." She turned a little green. "And don't forget, I probably send out an email once a week apologizing to the other parents because their child learned some colorful words or how to make a baby from the beasts, I mean *sweet, sweet*, boys."

I laughed.

"You only laugh because they aren't in your class." She gave me a pointed look. "Do you want to trade now?"

I rubbed my temples. "Is there an option three?"

"How bad can it be to have her in your class? Most of the time we only see the parents a few times a year for back-to-school night and parent-teacher conferences. Back-to-school night is over, so you're safe there."

"This is true. But even the thought of seeing him twice a year makes me feel queasier than your earwax story. I just told him I don't like him."

Her brow raised. "Well, that was bold."

"I know," I groaned. "I don't know what came over me."

"Maybe . . . it's all the built-up sexual tension, because deep down you want to live out that story with him." Her gorgeous eyes danced with amusement.

There was no sexual tension. Like none. Okay, so I found him sexy. Who didn't? "Don't tell me you read it too?" I squinted.

She fanned herself, telling me all I needed to know. I rolled my eyes while she laughed.

"You didn't deny wanting to live out your fantasies with him." She nudged me.

"I thought the eye roll spoke my denial loud and clear." And hello, it was no longer my fantasy. The only fantasies I had now were of me eating dark chocolate and watching Turkish soap operas until my eyes burned red. I was totally fulfilling that dream tonight.

She eyed me carefully, pointing her finger all over. "I'm not buying it, querida. I think this will be good for you. I will keep the beasts and let you tame yours." She evilly laughed and pranced out of the classroom.

Uh, excuse me. I wasn't going to tame anyone, especially Mr. Reece Cavanaugh. I didn't like him, or any men for that matter. And there was the little issue that he was now the parent of one of my students. That was a big fat no-no at the school. It wasn't a policy per se, but everyone knew it was an unwritten rule. Tad Fellows, the last teacher who dated a parent there, was no longer teaching. Let it be a lesson that no matter how good a student's mom thinks you look in a tight pair of jeans, if you give her child a well-deserved failing grade, she will not take kindly to it. As in, she will come to the school and write horrible, intimate things about you on the whiteboard before trying to break into your laptop to change said grade. It wasn't pretty. Ever since, Mr. Nelson had made it clear he deeply frowns upon any fraternization among teachers and parents.

He had nothing to worry about. Mr. Cavanaugh and I would never fraternize. Ever.

Five

"OMG. WHAT THE FREAK? I'M dying." Jenna grabbed ahold of my shoulders and shook me.

"Shh," I begged. We were at the farm, helping to get ready for opening weekend, and everyone in our family had ears like a bat. Especially the sisters. A.k.a. our mothers. The sisters who somehow believed Reece was a real pirate who had ravished me. It didn't matter how many times over the years I had told Lottie and Dana, a.k.a. my mom and Aunt D., I had made it all up— they had it in their minds I couldn't have gained my carnal knowledge strictly from HBO. Their theory was that Reece and I had rolled around somewhere together. If only. I mean, not now obviously, but back in high school I would've loved to have taken a tumble with him in the barn and rolled in some hay. Now that I think about it, hay isn't all that sanitary and it sticks places that aren't all that sexy. I learned that the hard way with Trevor. Grrr.

Jenna pulled me back around the cider stand where we sold the liquid gold by the gallon or warmed in lidded paper cups. The would-be supermodel pushed me against the cedar wood— forcefully, mind you. She was strong when she got excited.

"Ouch," I complained while taking in a deep breath. There was something about the farm that made me want to breathe in

38

deeply and take in the scents of my favorite time of year. The earthy smells of freshly dug-up dirt mixed in with cinnamon and apples. I could never get enough of it. Which I guess is why I've never moved away. This farm is home, and as crazy as my family is, they're my people. Especially Jenna, even if she was acting a little *Looney Tunes* at the moment.

"Tell me everything," she demanded.

"I don't know what more I can say. His daughter is in my class. She starts tomorrow." My stomach was in knots over it.

"But you talked to him."

"Sort of." I twirled some of my hair. "I kind of lashed out at him, which makes me even more embarrassed to be around him."

"Ooh. I like it." She tapped her fingers together in a devious way. "What did you say?"

I stared past her at the large empty space where the corncrib barn used to be. It still felt like a sucker punch. We had no idea how the fire started. Visions of my dad all sooty and limping out of the blazing structure made me shiver in the warm evening air.

Jenna waved her hand in front of my face. "Earth to Josie."

I shook my head, trying to get the awful images out, desperately avoiding the other images of Reece from earlier that day. "Um. Sorry."

Jenna looked behind her and let out a sigh. "We'll build it back." She, like me, loved this place. Not only did our childhood memories live here, but so many other children's fall memories included our farm. It's exactly what made the place magical. Just ask anyone who grew up coming to Peterson's Pumpkin Patch. It was why generations of families came back every year.

"I know," I agreed, hoping she would forget about Reece. That was wishful thinking.

She focused back on me. "So, spill."

"Jen, what else can I tell you? You know, besides the possible need for a Xanax infusion to get me through the next eight months. Is that doctor still hot for you?" I teased.

"There are a lot of things I will do for you, but illegal prescription drugs are not one of them." She laughed.

"So, the handsome doctor still wants you."

She batted her eyelashes. "Maybe, but I'm thinking about it. He doesn't have the zing I'm looking for. And knowing my luck, he'll be emotionally unavailable, you know until I help him get in touch with his feelings and then he breaks up with me . . . Annnd," she exaggerated, "marries the next woman he dates."

We both had bad luck when it came to men. "Yeah, well, I'm over the zing."

"Uh-huh." She patted my head. "You're one Turkish man away from going all zingy."

"Okay, you got me there." I grinned. "But seeing as I've never met anyone from Turkey, I think I'm safe."

"I'm wondering if Reece doesn't have a little Turkish blood in him. I have a feeling he's a total alpha roll."

Alpha roll was a term Jenna had come up with. It was an alpha male mixed with a cinnamon roll. Meaning he was the perfect mixture of a take-charge man with a heart of gold who would do anything for those he loves, especially the woman he loves. Like Jenna would say, he is hot and ooey gooey and you want to sink your teeth right into him. I wouldn't be biting anyone.

"It doesn't matter if he is or isn't. All he is to me is a parent of one of my students. Besides, I don't like him. Even if he thinks I will."

Her eyes widened. "What? Did he say that to you?"

"Yep; then he had the audacity to tell me he liked that forsaken story," I groaned.

She tapped her lips. "This is so good."

I scrunched my face. "How do you figure?"

"Look at this like exposure therapy. I think it's time you finally confronted this. Confronted him. You know, maybe then you can stop diving behind displays."

"Ugh." I closed my eyes. "I dove behind the receptionist

desk at school when he walked in this morning. I'm pretty sure he saw me and possibly my panties."

Jenna snort-laughed, like a honking snort. She may have coughed up a lung, too, from the sound of it.

I opened my eyes to see her doubled over trying to catch her breath. "Thankfully, I was wearing a lacy pair."

She clutched her chest, finally getting ahold of herself. "That's something to be thankful for."

"Yes, I'm so grateful the panties fairy took mercy on me." I oozed more sarcasm than was necessary.

"Panties fairy? Is that like the tooth fairy? Because I could seriously use some good new undies. Do I just stick an old pair under my pillow?" she teased.

"Ha ha, you're hilarious."

"I totally am," she sang. "At least this way you know Reece has been informed you're a pretty-panty girl."

"I can't believe you just said that." I couldn't help but snigger. "Why does Reece need to know about my underwear choices?"

"Did I hear that right?" My mother, who usually spoke in dulcet tones, ripped the air with her question, startling Jenna and me, just like the time we'd been caught sneaking out, thinking we could somehow get away with driving to Vegas to see a concert and returning home without our parents wondering where we had been for hours upon hours.

I clenched my fists and turned around to find that not only was my mom standing there, but so was Aunt D. How they could still sneak up on us, I would never know. Maybe we would get those powers when we procreated.

There stood the sisters, both still tiny things who were a few days past needing to dye their brown hair, judging by their gray roots, which I would not be mentioning. Lottie and Dana prided themselves on how young everyone thought they were, even though they were well into their fifties. Like, their sixties were calling their names. Another thing I would not be mentioning.

41

"Hey, Mom. Aunt D." I smiled.

Mom narrowed her hazel eyes at me. "Did I just hear you say Reece Cavanaugh saw your panties in high school?"

"Absolutely not." How many times was I going to have to tell my mother the story never, ever happened.

"It was today, Aunt Lottie," Jenna was more than happy to fill her in.

I whipped my head in her direction, giving her the evilest of eyes, to find she was already smirking.

"I thought we told you to stay away from that boy?" Mom scolded.

I whipped my head back in Mom's direction. I was going to need a neck brace. "Mom, for one, Reece is not a boy. For two, I'm a grown woman, if you haven't noticed, and I can see whomever I want. Last but not least, I want nothing to do with him."

"Then why is he looking at your panties?" Mom tapped her foot on the dusty ground.

"Yeah?" Aunt D. added for emphasis.

"He's not."

"His daughter is in Josie's class now." Jenna was getting way too much pleasure out of this.

The sisters' mouths fell open in sync. It was seriously scary.

"Charles," Mom shouted for Dad, after she came to and closed her jaw. "Charles, come quick. The pirate is back."

I turned around and banged my head on the cider stand. "He's not really a pirate."

Jenna grabbed my arm. "Don't do that. You're too pretty to get splinters in your forehead."

"It might be worth it. You can take me to urgent care then," I said out of the side of my mouth.

"You know the sisters would come," Jenna whispered back. That was true. Ugh.

I watched as my dad and Uncle Craig moseyed on over from the barn where they kept the farm equipment. Dad was still sporting a pretty good limp. Both wore looks of *Please, let's just get this over with. We have work to do.* I could see in Dad's glazed eyes flashbacks of Mom on the news with her anti-porn posters. While Dad never appreciated my pirate story, he at least hadn't turned into a zealot over it. He'd even let me out of my grounding a few days early for time well served.

The brothers, as we called them, arrived tall and lanky, heads of gray and weathered faces. Our moms called them silver foxes. I tried not to think about it.

Mom turned to Dad as if her worst nightmare had come true. "Charles, the pirate was looking at our daughter's panties today at school."

Dad's eyes, Peterson green like mine, bulged.

Jenna started giggling uncontrollably while her parents gave her the eye.

"Oh. My. Gosh. No one was looking at my panties. And the man is not a pirate!"

"Oh," Dad said. "Well, that's settled, then."

"No, Charles. It's not. The pirate's daughter is in her class now."

"Mom," I whined, "please stop calling him that. Some people might find that offensive."

She slapped a hand against her chest. "I would never offend anyone." Said the woman who literally chased a man down in his car and told him he was going to hell after he'd told her he loved *Game of Thrones.*

By now the entire family had arrived. Oliver, my traitor brother, was carrying Lila, my one-year-old niece, on his shoulders. Kitty was holding my nephew Charlie's hand; well, until he saw Grandma and rushed to her. I was still a little disgruntled about Oliver naming his firstborn Charlie. He knew I wanted to name my son that to honor our dad. And he also knew I didn't want my family to be any weirder than it already was, so I would never duplicate the name. You see, Jenna's older sister is named Olivia. That's right, the sisters thought it would be cute. They had tried desperately to have Oliver and Olivia at the same time, just like Jenna and me, but the stork did not grant them such a wish. Olivia came well over a year before my brother.

Olivia and her all-too-perfect brood meandered over too. I wasn't even sure why they came. She, her husband, Reginald the Pretentious, as Jenna and I called him, and their three perfectly well-mannered children, ranging from two to six, never seemed to get their designer clothes dirty or have a hair out of place. They basically just walked around the farm telling everyone else what to do. The two-year-old, Jonathan, had even told my nephew that he should get potty trained already. I was sure he had heard that from his parents.

So, there we all were, one big fat happy family, while my mom did what she did best—overreacted.

"I always knew there was something sneaky about that kid. Why won't he just leave our poor girl alone?" Mom lamented.

It didn't help when Aunt D. added fuel to her fire. "I know, it's like he's obsessed with her. I want to know who he paid to get into the overpriced school she teaches at."

Our dads stepped back, knowing this was not going to good places and it would be best if they could make a quick getaway. If only I had such an option.

"We should do an inquiry," Mom suggested. "Talk to the school's board of directors."

I held up my hand as if to say, *Stop, for the love of it all.* "Okay, ladies."

The sisters looked down their noses at me. They never appreciated when we called them anything but terms of endearment.

"Mom. Aunt D.," I sang sickly-sweet. "Please, listen to me. Reece Cavanaugh is not obsessed with me. He—"

"Well . . . I kind of got this feeling last week in his office that he might be into you," Kitty interrupted me. "He sure smiled and gazed at you a lot."

44

I shot her the kiss-of-death stare. "Don't make me hate you."

Kitty laughed.

"*Hate* is a bad word," Lucas, Olivia's oldest, informed me.

"You're right, Lucas."

"I know," he responded, like only Reginald and Olivia's child could.

"Anyway, I need everyone here to listen to me once and for all. Reece is not a pirate; I repeat, he is not a pirate. And his daughter got into my class fair and square. Her name has been on the list forever. Most importantly, there never was anything going on between us, and there never will be. Got it?"

Everyone except Jenna stared blankly at me, blinking like I was speaking a foreign language.

"Then how did he know about the heart-shaped birthmark on your abdomen?" Mom asked.

I turned around and began banging my head again on the stand, while flashes of that stupid story played in my head. Reece was brushing his warm lips across my birthmark, making me gasp. We were taking cover in a cave, hiding from my uncle, the person who raised me and, unbeknownst to me, was the most ruthless pirate on the seas. Reece whispered while I trembled from his touch, *"My love, may the last words I ever speak in this life be spoken with my lips upon your heart."*

Yeah, I wrote those words.

I've regretted them ever since.

Six

I PACED AROUND MY CLASSROOM, not knowing what to do with myself. Andi Cavanaugh was joining my class today. I had thought about calling in sick but knew Mr. Nelson would be none too happy about it. It was bad enough I would have to explain to him one day why I wasn't wearing contacts. I might have to take a personal day to get "LASIK surgery." I should probably write myself a note about that.

Once I was done pacing, I rearranged my desk at the back of the classroom for the fiftieth time. I picked up the insulated cup one of my students gave me last year that read, *Teaching is a Work of the Heart.* I set the cup down and rubbed my chest. No matter what, I knew I would give Andi my heart, as I had each one of my students.

"Ms. Peterson," a voice so smooth startled me.

I steadied myself before turning around, only to grip my desk.

There he was, looking like the rogue-pretending-to-be-a-gentleman from my story. He wasn't wearing a cutaway coat with tails and a cravat wrapped around his collar, but his dark tailored business suit sufficed. It was sexy enough to have me thinking about how the rogue pirate arrived at the ball, zeroing in on me dressed in a cream low-cut gown showing off my heaving breasts. Yep, I used those words. And I wondered why Mom and Aunt D. thought I had carnal knowledge of Reece.

It probably didn't help that in the story, the rogue pirate secreted me away to the gardens for a moonlight stroll and a scandalous kiss. He was a handsy rogue, and I was overzealous.

My face flushed, thinking of it all. I needed to snap out of it. I wasn't living in a fantasy world where all Reece wanted was me by his side for eternity. I didn't even like him, regardless of how he was smiling at me, as if I were the young woman at the ball who captivated him.

But I knew instantly I would love the most beautiful little girl I had ever seen, with her emerald-green eyes and dark hair done in a perfect French braid, who stood clinging to her father. She was dressed in one of the school uniforms—a navy mock-layered dress with a white collared shirt. Most girls chose to wear the khaki pants and polo shirt, but somehow the dress suited her.

On the other side of Reece was an elegant older woman with shorter slicked-back gray hair tucked behind her ears. She was stunning and shared the same caramel eye color with Reece. Whoever she was, she offered me a warm smile, which I returned. Anything not to look at Reece.

As they approached, I knelt, ready to greet Andi. Thankfully, I wasn't in a ball gown that showed my heaving cleavage, but my black pencil skirt hiked up a bit, showing my toned legs. Kickboxing really did a body good. And there was just something about knocking the crap out of a punching bag. At least it wasn't my lacy undies showing. *Note to self: wear slacks tomorrow.*

Andi turned more into her dad the closer they got.

"Good morning, Andi," I said as sweetly as possible.

She peeked at me, her lip twitching as if she were thinking about smiling.

"I'm so glad you're joining my class. I'm Ms. Peterson." I held out my hand to her.

She stared at my hand; her gorgeous eyes filled with trepidation.

I patiently waited, smiling.

Reece knelt next to her when she didn't move an inch from his side. "Honey, I promise you, you're going to love it here. Ms. Peterson will take good care of you. I hear she doesn't bite," he teased her.

She giggled and my heart melted. There was something about her—what I didn't know, but for some reason she was calling to me like no other child ever had.

Reece pivoted to face me and unexpectedly took my hand.

Uh . . . did anyone else feel the earth move, or was that just me? Maybe Reece? His widened eye grabbed ahold of mine as his grip tightened, deepening the connection. Not only did the ground move, but a bolt of electricity went through me, making every inch of my skin raise, just like I had imagined and written into the pages of my torrid story. And just as I had written, I swore I saw strands of golden gossamer weaving a web around our clasped hands, bonding us together in an inexplicable way. To say it freaked me out was an understatement. I tried to pull away, but Reece wasn't letting go.

"Josie," he whispered, then cleared his throat. "I mean, Ms. Peterson."

Yes, yes, we needed to be as formal as possible. This was bizarre. Either that or I was hallucinating. We are talking LSD-level hallucinations.

"Mr. Cavanaugh," I responded, ridiculously breathy. What was wrong with me? Technically, I didn't even know this man.

"Please, call me Reece."

I shook my head.

"We'll work on that." He smirked, before addressing his daughter. "See, honey, how nice it is to shake Ms. Peterson's hand? Do you want to try?"

Yes, Andi, for all that is good and holy in the world, take my hand so that your father will release this hold he has on me.

Meanwhile, the woman Reece brought with him flashed me a crooked grin, almost as if she knew there was some alien-level weirdness going on between Reece and me.

Andi bit her lip, thinking about it.

Reece was in no hurry to let go. In fact, his thumb lightly brushed my skin, making me feel lightheaded. "She has smooth skin, and she smells nice," he tried to coax his daughter.

"Reece," the woman scolded. "I think you're embarrassing Ms. Peterson." I was guessing she was his mother.

He wasn't embarrassing me. I was doing a good enough job of that on my own. All I could think about was that blasted story and how every time the rogue pirate would touch the heroine, she felt as if she were drunk on rum. It was exactly the way I felt now, and I couldn't say I disliked it. Believe me, on principle I wanted to, but I had never felt so woozy from a touch. Not to mention, he smelled divine. My nose was like, *Yes baby, come to Mama.* Did he bottle up spring rain and splash it on himself? Whatever it was, he needed to stop.

"Am I embarrassing you, Ms. Peterson?" He kept ahold of my hand.

"Are you trying to?" I zinged back.

"Not in the least. I'm only trying to show Andi how nice you are."

Right. He was doing this for his daughter, not because he wanted to whisk me off to his private island in the middle of the Caribbean that no one knew about. Or at least that's what he'd thought in my story. My lecherous uncle found us there. But oh, what fun we had on that island before we were besieged and had to fight for our lives.

Yikes; I needed to get my imagination under control. I yanked my hand out of Reece's and once again offered it to Andi. "I promise, I don't bite."

She giggled while slowly inching her tiny hand toward my own.

I waited patiently until she met me halfway. When I took her hand, the earth didn't move, but my heart about burst. What was it about this family? "It's very nice to meet you, Andi." I gently shook her hand. "I hope you're ready to have some fun today and learn a lot."

She nodded.

"Good." I let go of her hand before I wanted to keep her. I was pretty sure that was illegal and would get me fired. With a deep breath in and out, I stood, straightening out my curve-hugging skirt. I did my best not to look at Reece, who stood as well. Instead, I held out my hand to the elegant woman who was carefully examining me. "I'm Josie Peterson."

She took my hand. "I'm Molly Cavanaugh, Andi's grand-mother. It's a pleasure to meet you. I've heard nothing but wonderful things about you."

I wasn't sure from whom. Certainly not Reece. "I hope not to disappoint you, Mrs. Cavanaugh."

"It's Ms., dear, but you can call me Molly."

I was seriously a dolt. "I'm so sorry, I just assumed—"

"Don't apologize. It's understandable. But it's just been Reece and me since he was a little boy. I thought it only fair he should have my last name." She winked.

I liked her spunk. But for some reason I had pictured Reece with a doting mother and father, living a picture-perfect life. How did I not know he was raised by a single mom? Not to say life couldn't be picture-perfect with only one parent. I just assumed things I shouldn't have. "I agree." I tried to cover up my faux pas.

"I wanted you to meet my mother." Reece paused.

He wanted me to meet his mom? I think we skipped all the relationship steps. The first step being that we were never going to be in a relationship. You know, except in my mind and on the paper I burned. I angled my head. "You did?"

"Of course," he said casually. "She'll be picking up Andi from time to time."

"Rigghhht . . ." I swallowed down my stupidity. Why would I even think Reece saw me as anything but his daughter's teacher? "That's great. So great," I rambled. "Family support is great." How many times could I say great?

"It is," Reece chuckled, as if he liked seeing me unhinged.

"Well." I clapped my hands together. "Let me show you where Andi's desk is so she can get settled in. The other students should be arriving soon." Please let them all arrive like now. "I start every class off with a brainteaser on the board." I pointed at the whiteboard where I had written, *The more there is, the less you see. What is it?*

Andi read it out loud, albeit quietly, to herself. Then with hardly a thought, she said, "Fog."

"Very good." I was so impressed. I thought for sure this one might take all day for one of my students to get, if anyone did.

Reece beamed at his daughter. "She takes after her dad."

Molly rolled her eyes.

I liked her.

I ignored Reece and focused on Andi. "I have a few brainteaser books in the reading corner you can borrow."

Her eyes lit up as if she liked the thought.

Molly sidled up to me. "I saw you on the news last night. You are a darling pumpkin."

My cheeks pinked. I didn't like the attention, but one of the local stations offered to do a piece about the farm right before opening weekend. They wanted me to don my pumpkin costume, citing that it would add warmth and character to the story. I couldn't refuse, as it was highlighting the tragedy of the fire and that we would be taking donations. It killed my dad and uncle Craig to ask for any sort of help, but no one had been able to come up with anything better.

"Oh, thank you."

"I'm impressed you wrote those children's stories," Molly added.

Reece stepped closer, interested. "You write children's books?"

I tucked some hair behind my ear. "Not really. Just some stories I read to kids on the weekends at my family's pumpkin patch."

"Sounds like something Andi and I should check out."

That wasn't a good idea. I could only imagine what Mom and Aunt D. would do if he showed up. I went to say something, but Reece asked Andi, "Would you like that, honey? Do you want to go to the pumpkin patch and have Ms. Peterson read to you?" Her enthusiastic head nod had me keeping my mouth shut.

"It's a plan, then." He squeezed Andi. He was awfully adorable with her.

I tried not to think about how adorable it was, because it made me think of how adorable the rogue pirate was when he would pick wildflowers for his lady love and tuck them into her hair. Or how he made her a necklace from seashells. Seriously, I needed to stop.

"When does the patch open to the public?" Reece asked.

"This weekend." I swallowed hard, hoping he was busy.

"Perfect."

That's not the word I was thinking of.

"It's a shame about the barn fire." Molly patted my arm. "I'm so glad your father is recovering."

"Me too. It's been kind of a heartbreaking year, but hopefully after this season we'll be able to rebuild. We always bounce back somehow," I said, as chipper as possible.

"I'll be sure to stop by and make a donation." Molly smiled.

"That's very kind of you. Thank you." I tried not to be embarrassed by it. Petersons had their traditions—and pride.

Reece pressed his lips together, tightening his jaw, as if something were bothering him. How odd.

I ignored him the best I could and showed Andi to her desk. I placed her near who I thought were the sweetest girls in class, Hazel and Penelope. I hoped she would find a friend in both.

While Molly helped Andi unpack her backpack full of school supplies, Reece asked, "May I speak to you for a moment?"

What was I going to say? No? That's what I wanted to say, but it didn't seem like good form in front of his mom and daughter. "Sure." I stepped a few paces away from Andi and Molly.

"I didn't know about the fire," Reece said in disconcerted, hushed tones.

I wasn't sure why he seemed so bothered. "Why would you?" You know, other than it was all over the local news when it happened.

He ran a hand through his luxuriously thick hair. Yes, those were the adjectives I used in my stupid story. "I'm sorry, I've been caught up in my own world lately. Is that why you wanted the ring? To help your family?"

"What does it matter?" I couldn't keep the bitterness out of my voice.

"It matters to me." He let out a heavy breath. "I'm sorry."

"You were just doing your job."

"Perhaps I can see now why you don't like me." The corners of his mouth twitched.

"I'm glad we cleared that up." I gave him a hint of a smile before I started to walk off.

"Ms. Peterson." He gently grabbed my arm, making me feel all sorts of woozy again. What was it with his touch?

"Yes?" I could hardly say for my head swirling.

He leaned in, close enough that I could practically taste his spearmint breath. "I'm still going to make you like me."

"Good luck with that." And heaven help me.

Seven

WITH THE LAST KIDDO GONE for the day and car line duty over, I sank into my chair and reached for the Cherry Coke on my desk that had been calling to me all day. I'd been addicted to the stuff since I was a toddler. At least that's what my mother says. Seeing as she's addicted to it, it's safe to assume she's telling the truth. Not sure what it was about it, but I took my first sip and let the carbonation and sugar soothe my nerves. I loved being a teacher but always felt the need to unwind after my nonstop days.

The day had been more nerve racking than usual considering the morning I had with Reece Cavanaugh. I wasn't sure why he was so determined to make me like him. It was impossible. I was afraid if I liked him, it would open the door to more torrid fantasies. Fantasies I knew I could never live out, which would mean I would find myself writing another tawdry story. And let's just say I have a bit more carnal knowledge than I did fifteen years ago. I refused to be the reason my father had a heart attack and my mother got arrested for storming HBO's headquarters. Besides, I was over men, except the Turkish ones I obsessed over.

I took another sip of my drink and breathed deeply for a moment. I still had work to do. Least of which was begging the parents in my class to volunteer as the room-parent coordinator. This would be my third attempt. I was getting desperate.

I flipped open my laptop and cracked my knuckles. I was going to write the ultimate plea.

Dear Parent or Guardian,

Thank you so much for entrusting me with your most valuable asset. I count myself blessed to be able to learn and grow with your child each day.

I was laying it on thick. But a girl had to do what she had to do. And I wasn't lying.

As you know, we have a lot of exciting field trips and class parties planned throughout the year, not to mention the upcoming fall carnival that has been a Highland Academy tradition for twenty years. This community event could not be as successful as it is without the help and generosity of the great families who attend our illustrious school. This year our class is in charge of the photo booth. I'm in need of one parent to coordinate this effort and activities throughout the year. This parent would be bestowed with the honorable title of Your Most Royal Highness to the Educational Professional. It is a title most revered and comes with the undying gratitude of said Educational Professional, a.k.a. me. And for a limited time, two dozen homemade pumpkin spiced doughnuts and as many gallons of apple cider as you can drink will be bestowed as a token of appreciation upon the esteemed volunteer. This offer expires at midnight, so be sure to claim this once-in-a-lifetime deal now.

Sincerely,

Ms. Peterson

I read over what I wrote and smiled to myself. Surely someone would have mercy on me. I said a little prayer before clicking send.

Next up on my list was going over Andi's reading and math assessments I'd given earlier in the day. I smiled thinking about the quiet, thoughtful girl who stayed as close to me as she could during lunch and recess. I didn't mind in the least bit, but I hoped she would find comfort around her peers in the coming days. I'd noticed Hazel trying to make strides with her. Andi was wary, but I could see she was thinking about it. I believed she thought about a lot of things, which was why she was so cautious. Her eyes spoke of so much more going on in her head. I could only imagine that her mother's situation was a major concern for her. And it's never easy to attend a new school. Poor thing had a lot going on.

The results of her assessments weren't surprising. Her comprehension was excellent, but her spelling and vocabulary could use a little help. Her math skills were more on par with a second grader. It was nothing overly concerning, given the school year had just begun. I could easily catch her up or recommend a tutor if need be.

I supposed I should email Reece my findings. I didn't want to, but it was the responsible thing to do. And I guess the right thing to do. I clicked on my email portal, praying some benevolent parent had already responded to my plea. I wasn't hopeful, but a girl could dream. I logged in to find I had a response, all right. Just one.

Reece Cavanaugh's name stared at me. Oh no, no, no. Surely he didn't volunteer. When would he even have time to fulfill such an obligation? You know, in between stealing people's treasure?

My hand shook while scrolling over to read his reply. I closed my eyes and clicked. When I braved opening them, I squinted, like that would help lessen whatever was going to happen. FYI, it didn't.

Dearest Ms. Peterson (Or can I call you Josie yet?),

I've always wanted to be called Your Royal Highness, so I'm your man. When do we get started?

All the best,

Your Most Royal Highness

I slammed the laptop lid down before I thought about how cute it was, because this was so not happening. He was not my man. He was not my anything. You know, except the long-ago object of my desire. I rested my head on the desk, wondering how I'd found myself in such a situation. One thing I knew for sure was that he was not going to become my Royal Highness— I mean room-parent coordinator. I was just going to pretend I didn't see his email and then go home and offer up a burnt offering or something in hopes of another parent stepping up to the plate. Yes, yes. That was a good plan.

"So how was spa life today?" I asked Jenna over the phone while I strolled through the grocery store late at night. Late meaning nine. I was in need of all the chocolate products. Everything from chocolate ice cream to chocolate syrup that I might just drink straight from the bottle. I was trying to talk myself out of it, but so far I hadn't come up with any compelling arguments not to. At least I had been smart enough to only grab a basket to carry around instead of a cart. Who knew what kind of mayhem might have ensued?

"Let's just say"—Jenna cleared her throat—"that I had to give a facial massage to a man who had to be part gorilla. I've never touched so much hair in my life."

"Ooh. Gross. You win for worst day."

"Did you have a bad day?"

I picked up a bag of chocolate-covered blueberries, thinking some *fruit* would be a good idea. "I wouldn't necessarily say it was bad, but I'm currently at the store trying to decide which goes better with chocolate ice cream: chocolate-covered blueberries or pomegranates."

"Let me guess. Reece? And by the way, pomegranates have more vitamins."

"Pomegranates it is." I tossed the bag in my basket.

"So, you never answered. Is Reece the reason for your late-night shopping trip?"

"Yes," I whined.

"Did he see your panties again?"

"Worse. He wants to infiltrate every aspect of my life. He's even planning on coming to the pumpkin patch this weekend. The sisters are going to lose it."

"Oooh. I'm glad I have the weekends off during pumpkin season. Our moms coming face-to-face with the pirate. I'm going to record this."

"You have to quit calling him the pirate." I continued to stroll down the aisle while perusing the Halloween candy. I had a little more room left in my basket, and I might need some protein—like peanut butter cups.

"Have you ever asked him if he minds being called that?"

"Of course not."

"Well, he might like it. Maybe you could role-play."

I could picture her wagging her brows. "Oh. My. Gosh. Stop it."

"I'm just saying. You should think about it."

That was the problem. I had thought about it in great detail, and then I wrote it all down. "I'm hanging up now."

"Come on, you know you love me."

That I did, but I didn't get a chance to tell her. I looked down the aisle just in time to see the bane of my existence walking past. "Shiz."

"What?"

"He's here," I whispered, as I rushed toward the caramel apple display at the end of the aisle and crouched behind it. I needed to see if I could ascertain where he was headed. If I had to, I would abandon my fifty thousand calories and make a run for the exit. Though I would be irked about it. I was salty that he was in this particular store. I had already quit shopping at Trader Joe's because I'd seen him in there once and literally held up a bag of oranges to hide my face while I walked out. Now he was invading my favorite mom-and-pop shop.

"Are you talking about Reece?"

"Shhh. Yes."

"He can't hear me. What are you hiding behind?" She could hardly contain her laughter.

"Caramel apple display," I said with no shame.

"You teach the guy's daughter. I think you can quit hiding behind things when you see him in public."

"I don't think that's a good idea." Then I would actually have to talk to him. I craned my neck to see if I could spot him. "Dang it. I lost visual of the suspect."

"Jo Jo, I love you, but you might want to think about getting some help to overcome this little problem."

She wasn't wrong. "Maybe I'll go home and shock myself. What's a good voltage?" I teased.

"I was thinking more like counseling."

"I'm way beyond that."

"Who are you looking for?" the sexiest voice in existence crooned.

"Oh shiz," I squeaked into the phone before I fumbled it. I could hear Jenna asking if I was all right while I played a game of hot potato with my phone, trying to prevent it from crashing to the floor. Meanwhile Mr. I-Shop-in-My-Dress-Pants-and-Button-Down looked on, getting way too much pleasure out of this. I barely got control of my phone before it dropped. "I'll call you back," I mumbled to Jenna before blinking up at Reece. I swore I heard Jenna say, "He sees you, doesn't he?" Yeah, he did. Me in all my glory, squatting down in my tiny athletic shorts and sports bra. Did I mention I had just come from the farm, where I had worked out before coming to the store? My dad had hung up a punching bag for me in the loft of the barn where we kept the tractors. So, I was a little sticky and sweaty on top of being an idiot.

"Hello, Ms. Peterson." His smile should have been illegal.

"Um . . . hello." In case you're wondering, I did not stand.

Reece cocked his head, and if I wasn't mistaken, he perused me like I did bags of chocolate, his eye landing on the heart-shaped birthmark on my abdomen. "Did you lose another contact?" That was a low blow. "Would you like some help looking for it?"

I narrowed my twenty-twenty-vision eyes at him. "I'm good, thanks. Enjoy your night."

He stepped closer and looked into my basket. "You're here for some essentials, I see."

"Uh-huh." Move on, buddy.

"Me too."

Somehow, I didn't see him buying a basketful of chocolate. My guess was he had abs of steel under that fit-me-right shirt of his, which was unbuttoned just enough for me to get a peek at what looked like a smooth, sculpted chest. It had me feeling even more heated than I already felt. I had dedicated practically an entire chapter to his chest in my story. I was sure the real-life version would live up to, or maybe even exceed, my expectations.

"Okay," I said, hoping he would get the hint and skedaddle.

He did not take the hint. "Would you like some help up?"

"No. I'm good down here." I mean, it was a great workout for my legs, which were already on fire after kicking the snot out of the punching bag earlier. It was like one big squat. I probably wouldn't be able to walk come tomorrow.

What he did next, I didn't see coming. He crouched down next to me, giving me a good whiff of his intoxicating scent. He was evil.

"What are you doing? I'm sure you have better things to do," I said, annoyed.

"Not really." His eye penetrated my own.

I squinted, hoping to lessen the effect. It didn't help. "Uh, where's Andi?"

"At home, sound asleep. My mother's watching her." He cleared that up nicely.

"Good."

"Despite what you may think of me, Ms. Peterson, I like to think of myself as a devoted and responsible father." There was some bite to his tone.

"I have no doubt that you are." I felt terrible for insinuating anything else. "Well, I'm sure you want to get back to her, so please don't let me keep you." Surely, he would leave now.

Nope.

"I have some time." He flashed me a crooked grin. He knew he was torturing me and liked it. "Besides, don't you think we should discuss my Royal Highness duties?"

I shifted, not sure how much longer my legs could hold the crouching position. "You know, I'm weighing all my options." More like, I was going to be doing some burnt offerings when I got home.

"So, a lot of parents volunteered?" He seemed disappointed.

"Well . . . not exactly."

"What does *not exactly* mean?"

I felt as if he were cross-examining me.

I bit lip. "It means . . . well . . ."

"I'm the only one who volunteered, aren't I?" He cut right to the chase.

"Technically"—I blew out a big breath—"yes."

"But you don't like me . . ."

Wow, was he ever blunt.

My legs gave out, and I fell on my butt in both a literal and figurative sense. "Ouch," I couldn't help but say as I stretched out my legs.

"You okay?" Reece reached out to help me.

I waved a hand in front of me. "I'm fine."

He sat right next to me on the not-so-clean floor in his expensive dress pants.

A couple started to walk down the aisle but thought better of it after giving us a strange look.

I looked over at him. "What are you doing?"

"I'm trying my best to be friends, but you're making that difficult."

I dipped my chin toward my chest, wondering if this guy was for real. "Why do you want to be my friend?"

61

"First of all, you are my daughter's teacher. By the way, she couldn't stop talking about you after I got home. Thank you for making her feel so welcome."

"It was my pleasure. She's the sweetest thing."

"Something we agree on." He paused. "I would like for us to agree on more."

I exhaled loudly. I guess I was just going to have to lay it all out, no matter how embarrassing it was. "I appreciate that, but we have a weird history, which I totally take the blame for, so can you please just leave well enough alone?" I pleaded. "My life has been plagued by you. Again, not your fault," I was quick to add.

"*Plagued?* That's a strong word." He seemed amused.

"It's the truth. You don't know how ridiculed I've been because of the stupid story I wrote about you."

He rested his hand on my knee, and I can't say I didn't like it. "I don't think it was stupid. Honestly, I was flattered."

"Oh," I said, soprano-style. "Regardless, I should have never written it." *And could you please stop touching me?* The woozy feeling was back in full force.

"It's a shame you feel that way. Perhaps if you just owned it, then maybe we could be friends."

"You mean like be adult and healthy about it? You know, I don't know if I want to take that risk." I grinned.

He chuckled. "Think about it." He removed his hand from my knee.

"I will." Maybe. "Anyway, I have ice cream that's melting."

"Yes, and I promised Andi I would pack turkey roll ups in her lunch tomorrow."

That was attractive. Not thinking about it. Okay, I was totally thinking about it. Doting dads were sexy. "Sounds yummy."

"Do you want me to pack an extra one for you?"

Did he sound flirty, or was I an imbecile? I was going with the latter. "That's okay. Thanks, though."

"Just let me know anytime you want a good turkey roll. I'm

your man." He used that phrase again. I guess it was his thing, as he obviously didn't mean it literally.

I nodded, before my mouth could say something stupid like, *"I would love to try your turkey rolls."* Translation: be my man. I was over men, especially him.

He easily stood and held his hand out to me.

I stared at it, wondering how I could get out of taking it. My body liked his touch way too much.

"Josie," he delighted in saying.

I narrowed my eyes at him.

He wasn't deterred. "I think the first step on our road to friendship begins with using first names, don't you?"

"I don't remember agreeing to being friends."

"No time like the present," he challenged me.

"Still not convinced."

"That's okay. I've faced tougher opponents than you in the courtroom."

"Let me guess: you always win."

"Not all the time, but I always put up a good fight."

"Have you stopped to think that I might be a terrible friend?"

"I highly doubt that." He held his hand out farther to me. "Are you afraid I'll bite?"

I was definitely afraid he would leave a mark.

When I said nothing, he persisted. "I don't know about you, but I could always use another good friend. Especially now." No doubt he was talking about his current family situation.

Way to get me in the feels. I sighed and held out my hand. "This is not me acquiescing." My lips twitched.

He took ahold of my hand like a lifeline. "Yet." He was adorably cocky. This was not good news for me. Neither was the connection I felt when we clasped hands. All I could see was the scene in my book where the heroine learns the truth about her wicked family. She runs off to be alone in her favorite spot on the shores of Weymouth Bay, where she watches the waves crash and break, just like her heart. The pirate chases her there, afraid of what will happen to her if she's left alone. She refuses to be watched over by him, but he persists. It's that night he kidnaps her, knowing it's for her own good. Knowing he can't live without her.

Somehow Reece's touch made it feel as if he were kidnapping a piece of my heart. For a split second when his hand curled around mine, I wondered if, just like in the story, opening the door to Reece was exactly what I needed. If he would protect me if called upon. It was a ridiculous thought, yet I didn't pull away from him once I was upright. I couldn't help but peer into his eye, which almost seemed to be asking the same question—is it possible that we need each other? I couldn't imagine why that would be true, but there was something between us, that I knew.

I eventually pulled away. "Thank you," I barely managed to say.

"You're welcome." He sounded as bewildered as I felt.

"Have fun shopping." I waved, half-desperate to get away from him, half wishing to stay, which made me more compelled to flee.

"So, I guess I'll see you tomorrow morning and we'll discuss my Royal Highness duties."

I ran a hand through my damp hair. "I give up. I'll see you tomorrow morning, but don't expect me to call you *Your Royal Highness.*"

"Hey, that was part of the deal. I have it in writing."

I rolled my eyes. "See you tomorrow, *Reece.*"

His eye widened, a smile growing on his face. "I'll take Reece. Good night, Josie. I think this is the start to a beautiful friendship."

We shall see. I grabbed my basket and walked off.

"Hey," he called out, "just so you know, you don't have to hide from me anymore when you see me around town."

I stilled, my back to him, feeling as if I were on fire.

"I wouldn't want you to hurt yourself. That banana display

64

dive looked a little painful," he took a little too much pleasure in saying.

Holy. Freaking. Shiz. I was calling off our possible friendship.

"Don't be embarrassed. I've always been nervous to talk to you too."

I highly doubted that. I mean, why would he be nervous to talk to me? Regardless, I stalked off while considering moving across the country.

Reece chased after me and gently grabbed my arm. "Hey there."

"Please, just go," I pleaded, not able to face him.

"Josie," he said my name so beautifully, I couldn't help but turn toward him. "I'm sorry. I've gotten used to using humor to deal with awkward situations." He pointed at his eye patch. "I forget sometimes that's not how everyone copes."

I stared at his patch, and for the first time it dawned on me that perhaps he didn't always deal well with his loss. He just seemed so confident, and everyone in high school fawned over him, so I'd assumed he just took it all in stride. Unlike me, who was used to diving behind things as her coping mechanism of choice, which I'm pretty sure didn't really count as coping. At least not of the healthy variety.

He leaned in with a thoughtful expression as if he were mesmerized by something. "You have beautiful eyes," he whispered.

I was not expecting that to come out of his mouth. I bit my lip, not sure how to respond. You know, other than returning the compliment, which was so inappropriate given our past and the fact that he was my student's parent.

He dropped my arm, shook his head, and stepped back. "How was that for awkward?"

"Yeah, totally awkward." I blinked like a million times.

"I mean, I meant it." He smiled.

"Okay, thanks." I made it even more awkward. Why did I always sound like a dolt?

"You don't like compliments?" He was spot on, like he could see right into my head.

"I don't trust them," I openly admitted. For someone who wasn't an open person, this was a shock to my system. Reece Cavanaugh was breaching barriers, and I wasn't sure I liked it.

"I hope one day you'll trust me, Josie." He walked off without another word.

I watched him go, stunned. Why did he care if I trusted him? More importantly, why did I want to?

Eight

"GOOD MORNING, YOU CUTE THING you," Libby drawled as I walked past the front office toward my classroom, after arriving extra early to meet with you-know-who.

I wasn't sure how cute I felt this morning. FYI, I don't recommend mixing chocolate ice cream, chocolate syrup, and chocolate-covered pomegranates. The first few bites are divine, but it doesn't settle well. It didn't help that I was up half the night worrying about seeing Reece that morning. I ran the entire grocery store scene in my head about a million times. Which meant I pretty much withered in shame. Why couldn't I have just behaved normally?

My only saving grace came from my Turkish drama. Except I kept picturing Reece kissing my neck the way the male lead was always doing to his female love interest. Did I ever love to have my neck ravished. Obviously, I was giving that up along with men. Unfortunately, I have a fantastic imagination and some- how imagined kisses pressed to my neck, which led to other things, which led to other things, and I wasn't sure I would be able to look Reece in the face that morning without either blushing or congratulating him on becoming a father again. Yikes. I should probably ground myself.

I leaned against the door and smiled. "Good morning."

"You look as pretty as a picture this morning."

I looked down at my pink flutter-sleeved dress. Okay, so maybe I overdressed this morning. I told myself just to wear some khakis and a plain blouse, but this urge to look pretty and feminine overtook me. Was I proud of this fact? No.

"Pink was calling me this morning." And some other things I wouldn't mention. Except he had the worst timing ever and strolled in through the front doors, carrying two Starbucks cups with the most darling girl glued to his side.

"Good morning, Josie," he took pleasure in saying my name. "I didn't know what kind of coffee you like, so I went the safe route and got you hot chocolate. Judging by last night, I felt confident in my assumption." He held out a lidded cup for me.

Libby's brow popped like a corn kernel, fast and furious. "I see pink wasn't the only thing calling to you this morning."

I flashed Libby a look that begged her to not say another word. I was going to get fired at this rate.

She made a motion like she was zipping her lips, but her eyes said she wanted all the details. There were no details.

"He only means he ran into me at the grocery store last night," I practically shouted. "You should have seen *allll* the chocolate in my basket."

Two fellow teachers in the vicinity stopped and stared, specifically at Reece, who was probably wondering if he'd made the right choice to place his daughter in my class. His daughter, who giggled at me and suddenly made me not care that everyone was wondering if I was insane.

I knelt and let her infectious laugh drown out the world. "Good morning, Andi. How are you?"

"I'm good," she said barely above a whisper.

"I'm glad to hear that. Your hair looks very pretty today." It was done in a side-part French braid, letting her dark hair fall at her shoulders.

"My daddy did it."

I looked up at Reece, impressed.

His smug grin said he was amazed with himself. "I watch YouTube tutorials," he admitted.

I was still in awe but didn't mention it. I didn't need more reasons to be attracted to him. Or draw more attention to us. I only stood when I felt like my coworkers had gone about their business. Except Libby, who I noticed carefully studying us with a Cheshire grin. That was my cue to make my getaway.

"I can take Andi to class while you get a visitor pass," I offered.

"Am I missing something?" Reece asked. "Is Starbucks forbidden?"

I looked around me to see if anyone could hear. "Of course not, but some other things are."

"Paper cups? I plan on recycling."

"No. I mean, it's good you're into recycling, but it has nothing to do with drinks or cups."

"Then what?"

Did I really want to say it? Reece had zero romantic interest in me. And did I really need to embarrass myself further in front of him? "It's nothing. I'll meet you in my classroom."

Andi unexpectedly took my hand and looked up at me with her big green eyes, almost pleading with me to never let go. More than anything, I wanted to grant her request but knew there was a fine line I needed to walk as her teacher. There was just something about her that called to my heart. It was as if I was meant to hold her hand and protect her.

Reece stared at Andi's hand in mine, and a soft expression washed over his chiseled face.

"Is this okay?" I didn't want to overstep bounds. Though I felt as if so many had already been crossed, given our weird history.

"Yes," he was quick to answer. "I'll see you ladies soon." He gave Andi a wink.

Andi gripped my hand, and I held on tighter to her, somehow knowing she needed me to. This was all so strange.

Before we could make our way to the security door, I heard Libby say, "My, my, I think this is about to get delicious."

There was nothing tasty going on here. Ugh. I would have to talk to Libby ASAP. Right after I fired His Royal Pain in My Neck. No way now was Reece going to be the room-parent coordinator.

"Ms. Peterson," Andi spoke so quietly as we walked down the hall.

"Yes?" I smiled at her.

"Can you help me with my multiplication tables?"

"I would be happy to."

"My daddy doesn't do it as good as you."

I held in my snicker. "He does good hair."

She covered her mouth and giggled.

I could seriously get addicted to that sound.

"He's going to take me to the pumpkin patch this weekend." She sounded as excited as I had ever heard her, which wasn't saying much. But it gave me hope she might go back to the bubbly kid Reece said she was before. I was beyond nervous about her dad making an appearance at the farm. I would have to figure out a plan to keep Mom and Aunt D. away from him. Unfortunately, the gorgeous man was too dang recognizable.

"I can't wait to see you there." I truly meant that. Her dad, not so much.

"Do you really dress up like a pumpkin?" she asked with wide-eyed wonder.

"I sure do."

"My grandma is making my Halloween costume this year."

"That's nice. What are you going to be?"

She shrugged. "I don't know."

It broke my heart how downtrodden she sounded. I wanted to fix whatever was broken inside her. I squeezed her hand. "Maybe when you come to the pumpkin patch this weekend, you'll get an idea."

Her eyes brightened with a spark of hope. It did my heart good.

When we arrived at the classroom, she let go of my hand and rushed to the reading nook. I admit to feeling the loss.

By the time I made it to my desk, Reece arrived wearing a wicked smile I was sure didn't spell anything good for me.

He sauntered my way. I grabbed my chair, feeling a little off-kilter. Fifteen-year-old me was all aflutter. She and I were going to have a talk later about how when fantasies came to life they were usually a disappointment, so there was nothing to be excited about. Besides, thirty-year-old us was swearing off men for our own good. And we were totally firing this man.

"Daddy." Andi held up *The Mouse and the Motorcycle.* "You read this to me last night."

Of course he did. Why did he have to be an adorable dad? I mean, for Andi's sake I was glad.

"We'll read more tonight," he promised. "Is it okay if I talk to Ms. Peterson now?" Every syllable spoke of how much he revered her opinion and wished to make her happy.

She nodded. Little did she know she was betraying me.

Reece finished his descent upon me and went to hand me the cup, but stalled when it was just out of reach. "Tell me what I was missing back there?"

"You can keep your hot chocolate."

His brow raised. "You know how to keep a man on his toes, don't you?"

"What does that mean?"

"I never know what you're going to do or say. I have to admit, it's wildly attractive."

I cleared my throat and patted my chest, sure that my stomach had come up my esophagus. This couldn't be real. "Um, I'm sorry, you aren't allowed to be attracted to me."

He gave me a blank stare. "Why not?"

I looked over at Andi to make sure she was preoccupied with a book, even though I was pretty sure arrythmia was setting in. She was snuggled into a beanbag chair, wearing headphones, and listening to one of the read-along books. She was perfection, bouncing her legs while she turned pages. I smiled at the scene before facing her father, who was eagerly awaiting my reply.

Reece came around the desk and was now in my space, and every sense I owned, including my sixth sense, said I was in trouble. Lots of it.

"Listen," I whispered, even though I was sure Andi probably couldn't hear us. "I don't know if this is some kind of joke to you, but it's not funny. Besides, this school has rules. Parents aren't allowed to be attracted to teachers and vice versa."

Reece stepped closer, an impassioned look in his eye. "First of all, I would never joke about being attracted to you."

This was not good news. I went from arrythmia to cardiac arrest.

"Second, I read the handbook. I didn't see any rules about attraction."

"It's an unwritten r-rule," I stuttered.

"Here's the problem with unwritten rules: they are always unfairly applied, which is why the rules of law must be written. If the law is not written, it can't be broken."

Wowzer, was he intelligent. Too intelligent.

I took a step back. "Regardless, it's the law here and . . . well . . . you can't be attracted to me."

He chuckled. "You can't exactly help who you're attracted to."

Did I ever know. The biggest attraction of my life stood in front of me as living proof. "True, but nothing can ever come of it, so moving on." I fell into my seat and did some deep breathing.

He set the drinks down and leaned an arm on the desk, taking a moment to study me as he would a defendant. "When you say nothing can ever come of it, is that because of a nonexistent rule?"

"And my own." I grabbed the hot chocolate that had cooled considerably and downed a bunch of it, hoping it would put me into a sugar coma. I seriously couldn't believe we were having this conversation.

He hopped up on my desk as if he owned the place. "I have to hear these rules."

I took one more large gulp before setting down the cup and letting out a huge sigh. "I don't think we need to discuss them." Like ever. "And you know, honestly, I don't think it's a good idea if you're the room-parent coordinator. I mean, you have a busy career, and what do you even know about fall carnivals and class parties?"

His lips ticked up. "So, what I'm hearing is you don't think a man can do this job."

"I didn't say that." But that's exactly what I meant.

"Are you sexist?"

"No," I spluttered.

"Are we back to you don't like me?"

"Not exactly," I barely breathed out.

He inched closer, filling the air around me with my favorite scent.

I held my breath, doing my best not to think of things I shouldn't. Things like a scene from my story where the rogue pirate is upon the heroine, gently pressing her against the wall of his private cabin aboard the ship, trying to prevent her from escaping to what would be her doom. For days as they sailed, they had been at odds. He'd whispered to her all the things he admired about her and wished for her. She was desperate to not give into him while eagerly wanting to do so. How could she trust him? Herself? She couldn't help but think about the heated kisses they'd shared in the garden. How kind he had been to her, making sure her every need was met, including her want for books and paper to write upon.

It wasn't real.

I didn't know the real Reece. Except for the fact that he'd made Trevor take responsibility for all the wedding expenses and he appeared to be a kind and loving father. And he brought me hot chocolate, my second-favorite drink. Not to mention, he still wanted his daughter in my class, despite my erratic behavior.

And he was the only parent to volunteer to be the room-parent coordinator. So fine, he was probably a good guy. But that didn't mean I should like him. How could I open that door? We all know how that turned out last time. Besides, once upon a time I thought Trevor and all the losers before him were good men, too.

"I think I know what's going on," he said, with an abundance of confidence.

"What's that?" I genuinely wanted to know, because I was as confused as I had ever been.

"I think you're attracted to me too."

"What?" I coughed out. Who did he think he was? Other than right. I mean, I did write a freaking manifesto spelling out exactly how attracted I was to him.

"Don't deny it."

Oh, I was going to, if he gave me a moment to let my brain work again.

"But I get why you're going to," he beat me to the punch. "You just got out of a bad relationship with a man who lied to you and obviously didn't deserve you. And for some reason, you're embarrassed by the story you wrote. And you think by not liking me, it will help you continue to run away from that piece of yourself that was exposed to the world. It's why you always hide from me, but really, you're just hiding from yourself."

My jaw dropped, and for the first time in a long time I felt my eyes sting with the threat of tears. How dare he speak the truth. I pushed my chair back, aching to get away from him. He saw me too clearly, and I felt raw and naked.

He shook his head. "I'm sorry. I don't know what came over me. It's just, for so long I've wanted to know the woman behind the words. That story—" He didn't finish his thought; instead, he jumped off the desk. "Again, I apologize. I'll come back after school to discuss how I can help you as room-parent coordinator." He strode off in the direction of his daughter, leaving me unable to say anything.

I watched as he tenderly kissed Andi's head, trying to comprehend the fact that he wanted to know me because of that stupid story. Even more mind boggling was that it seemed he *did* know me. How could that be?

Nine

"SHE'S DARLING." ALINE WAS REFERRING to Andi, swinging between Hazel and Penelope. She wasn't talking much, but she wasn't glued to my side, so I took that as progress. I watched how timidly she swung while her two classmates soared into the sky. It looked as if Andi wished to do the same, but something was holding her back. It was like watching a living metaphor for my life. I so badly wanted to shout for her to soar, but how could I when I was afraid to myself?

"She is," I said absentmindedly.

"Are you okay? You seem out of sorts."

I looked out over the earth-toned, nature-inspired playground and the backdrop of trees that were just starting to turn into the majestic colors of fall. It felt more like a park than a school, as dozens of children ran around. I appreciated that part of the curriculum included playing outside. It was important for children's development. And I needed the fresh air—especially today.

I soaked in the sun's rays while contemplating Aline's question. The honest answer was, I *was* out of sorts. Reece had caught me off guard in more ways than one.

"It wouldn't have anything to do with your new room-parent coordinator, would it?" Aline laughed.

Libby had spread that news around.

"Maybe," I sighed.

She pointed at Trager and Teagan near one of the slides. They were attempting to make farting sounds with their armpits, and then they would smell their fingers. "Just remember you could have those beasts, I mean sweet, sweet boys," she gritted out.

That was true. They would probably give me less heartburn, though. I rubbed my chest, still feeling the sting of Reece's words—that I was trying to run away from myself. More and more, I believed it was why I had been ready to marry Trevor. I hoped Josie Kensington would vanquish Josie Peterson. How sad was that?

"Eight more months, right?" I commiserated with her.

"Eight more months?" She pinched the bridge of her nose. "Let's think positive. Next month is fall break."

Oh, I was counting down the days already. A week free of Reece. You know, unless I ran into him somewhere. Which, knowing my luck, I would. I was still cringing thinking about how many times over the years he had seen me trying to avoid him. How many dives did he see?

"I can't wait." I exhaled loudly.

"This man has gotten under your skin, querida."

"You have no idea." And I wasn't going to tell her, or anyone at school, exactly how much he had infiltrated my skin. As much as I loved Aline and most of my coworkers, school gossip was at a premium. The teachers' lounge was like TMZ. I did not need to be the latest and greatest news. Especially since it was vital no one ever thought I was breaking the unwritten rules. I liked to pay my bills, thank you very much.

Aline gave me a once-over with her gorgeous brown eyes. "Do tell."

See? I would be a hot commodity in the teachers' lounge.

"There's nothing to tell. It's just weird having to actually be around him." I hoped that satiated her need for more info.

Her shoulders dropped as if my answer disappointed her.

"Sorry, no juicy details," I teased.

"Yet." She perked right back up. "Libby told me that the juices seemed to be flowing between the two of you."

Darn that Libby. She was like TMZ's star reporter. "Oh no, no. There will be nothing juicy between us." I kept my voice down, hoping to quell any rumors. "Besides, it's against the rules."

Aline snaked her arm through mine. "Querida, my mamãe used to say, to get what you want in life, first learn the rules, and then figure out which ones you're supposed to break."

"Your mother and my mother had very different attitudes." I laughed. "And for the record, I don't want Reece." At least, I was pretty sure I didn't. But even if I did, I wouldn't take him, because I was sticking to my no-man plan this time.

"Uh-huh. I read the story."

Who hadn't?

"It's just a story." A stupid story at that.

She gave my arm a squeeze. "Is it? I see a lot of heart in it."

Whoa. Did she just mic drop me? I didn't get to formulate a response.

"Trager and Teagan," she yelled, as she marched off. "How many times do I have to tell you we do *not* tackle people when they come off the slide."

I glanced at Andi swinging away. I wouldn't trade her for the twins any day. But what was I going to do about her father?

Reece showed up a little before school let out. That dang Libby gave him a visitor pass and even escorted him down to my classroom. If I wasn't mistaken, she was making googly eyes at him before she said, "Bye-bye, darlin'." She walked off fanning herself.

Reece strode in smiling, as if he knew exactly how he affected women.

I set the book I had been reading to the class on my lap. I always liked to end the day with something fun. I sat up straight on the stool I was sitting on in the front, trying not to let Reece have any effect on me. Or at least not to show it. Inside, my emotions were all over the place, everything from feeling woozy to upset and raw. His words would not leave me. I think what troubled me the most was that I knew I should do something about the running. But I was afraid of what would happen when I stopped. What if I couldn't accept myself? Or what if I truly was only the pirate girl? I could hear all the popular girls in high school telling me how stupid I was for thinking someone like Reece would want me. *"Who do you think you are?"* echoed in my mind.

I wish I knew.

"Are you a pirate?" Wesley called out.

I cringed, wishing I could ban the word in my class, but just because their teacher was a nutjob, it didn't mean that my students needed to suffer.

Reece laughed good naturedly. "Not today," he teased.

I guess he wasn't stealing anyone's rings today.

"Then how come you wear a patch?" Elise asked.

"That's a good question." Reece turned my way, still looking a bit disconcerted from our earlier encounter. "I'm sorry, Ms. Peterson, am I interrupting?"

He was. So much interruption. "Not at all," I half-growled.

He flashed a hint of a smile in my direction, before turning back to his captive audience. "You see"—he tapped his patch— "a long time ago, when I was around your age, I went on a safari."

All the eyes in the class widened, except for Andi's. I believe she rolled hers. I assumed this story was made up and she wasn't impressed, or she'd heard it one too many times.

I had to admit to being more than curious what really did happen to his eye. In my story, it was something the rogue pirate never spoke of. The tragic event from his past was too painful, and he wished to spare his love. So ridiculous. If they were really in love, she would have insisted on being able to share his pain. Again, I was fifteen and knew nothing of the world. I wasn't sure I knew that much more now.

Reece stepped in front of the class, too close to me. His stubble made a nice appearance in the afternoon, and his scent only got better throughout the day. I gripped my stool, telling myself I couldn't help but be attracted to him, but that didn't mean I had to act on it.

"One night," Reece spoke in hushed tones, setting the mood, "we were camping near the Chobe River in Namibia. As we sat around the fire, in the distance we could hear the roar of lions and the trumpeting of elephants, while the parrots cawed from the trees above."

Some of the children put their hands to their mouths, completely enthralled with Reece.

"Then," he said suddenly, making the children jump, minus Andi, who just shook her head. I liked her more and more. "We heard a terrible noise at the water's edge. I jumped up and ran to see what had happened. There ...," he paused for dramatic effect, "our tour guide was being dragged into the water by a giant crocodile."

"No way!" Wesley called.

"Yes way," Reece responded. "It was at least twenty feet long." He spread his hands apart, telling the biggest fish tale ever. "Our guide called for help, but everyone stood frozen, not sure what to do. So, I sprang into action, and with superhuman strength I grabbed the tail of the crocodile and pulled him back with all my might before he could get into the water. The crocodile was so angry that he dropped the guide and came after me, seeing I was a much worthier opponent."

Oh man, was this guy telling a tall tale, but the kids were soaking it up.

"The crocodile lunged for me, but I was able to narrowly

escape by climbing up a nearby tree. I climbed as high as I could, making the crocodile so furious, he began to headbutt the tree."

A few of the children gasped. Meanwhile, I had to stop myself from thinking how attractive he was being.

"I gripped the branch I was on as tight as I could, but the crocodile wouldn't give up. He kept ramming the tree harder and harder until he knocked it out of the ground."

"Oh no," Harper cried. "What did you do?"

"Don't worry," Reece assured her. "You see, the crocodile wasn't very smart. The tree came tumbling down on him and crushed him. Unfortunately, my eye got injured when I fell to the ground and landed on a rock. But it was okay because I saved our guide, and I got this cool patch." He tapped his finger to his patch.

The children cheered.

"They even built a monument for me."

It was my turn to roll my eyes.

The bell rang, exciting the children. They all rushed to grab their backpacks, but several kids made sure to stop and talk to Andi. I caught a few of them saying things like, "Your dad is so cool." "I wish my dad had a patch." "See you tomorrow, Andi."

Andi smiled, seemingly pleased with the attention. Apparently, Reece really was a superhero. At least in his daughter's eyes. Which, unfortunately, made him one in my eyes too. All good parents were superheroes in my book. Not the stupid book, that is. There was only one hero in that thing.

"Okay, everyone, line up." I stood, ready to lead them outside. "And don't forget tomorrow is music, so bring your recorders." Bless the music teacher. She was a braver woman than I was.

To prove what a chicken I am, I had to grab the stool to support myself as Reece approached me.

"I'm sorry for stealing your thunder there."

"It's fine. Your story was much more interesting than the one I was telling."

"Hey, that was autobiographical." He winked.

"I'm sure. I'm surprised you didn't ride off into the sunset on a giraffe."

"It was a zebra," he was snappy with his comeback.

I couldn't help but crack a smile. "Okay, *Dr. Livingstone*, I'll be right back."

"I see myself as more of a Mungo Park: daring, intrepid traveler and explorer."

"You know he died a very early death."

"Yes." Reece leaned in. "But he was fearless and determined."

I swallowed hard, feeling as if Reece were giving me fair warning. If he wanted something, he went for it. Surely he didn't want me. Right?

Ten

I RETURNED FROM CAR LINE duty and leaned against the doorframe to observe father and daughter in the reading nook. They were reading brainteasers back and forth to each other.

"What has a face and two hands but no arms or legs?" Andi asked.

Reece tapped his lips. "Hmm . . . a clock."

"Good job, Daddy," Andi squealed. It was the cutest thing ever. "Now ask me one." She handed him the book.

He flipped through a few pages. "Okay. This is a tough one. Are you ready?"

She nodded.

"What is at the end of *everything*? Think carefully," he encouraged.

I stood mesmerized at the way he looked at his daughter, as if she were his world. Reece was getting more attractive by the second. *Attraction does not have to lead to anything,* I reminded myself. *And please, for the love, do not write a story about the man this time.* No worries there: I would not be bleeding out my heart onto any pages. There would be no need, as I would not get to the point of longing for him. It sounded like a solid plan.

Andi pressed her lips together and tossed her head from side to side. "The end of everything," she said to herself. "Everything.

Everything." Her eyes lit up. "*G.* The end of everything is *G.*" She was so proud of herself. As was I.

Reece put his arm around her and gave her a good squeeze. "Very good, honey."

"I love you, Daddy." She snuggled into him.

He wrapped her up tighter and kissed her head. "I love you to the moon and back and back again."

My heart raced a bit. Reece was killing me softly. I cleared my throat before I had second thoughts about my no-man rule.

Andi and Reece looked my way.

"Sorry to interrupt." I walked in.

"It's your classroom." Reece grinned.

Andi jumped up and ran over to me with the book. "I stumped my daddy."

"You did?"

"Yes! I asked him what has to be broken before you can use it, and he didn't know it was an egg."

I shook my head, faux disappointed. "How could he miss that one?" I played along.

"I know." She was so animated.

I loved seeing it.

"I'm going to find some more good ones." She skipped back to her dad, who was now standing, gazing at me.

I rubbed my neck, feeling as if he could see right through me.

"Andi, I'm going to talk to Ms. Peterson for a minute." He kept his eye on me, like if he didn't, I might disappear. It was a good call on his part. I wanted to flee like always when he was near. His words haunted me, reminding me that in doing so I was only hiding from myself. He was right. It was me I was uncomfortable with, not him.

In all my uncomfortableness, I headed toward my desk. I refrained from diving behind it. Instead, I did the non-psycho thing and sat on my chair.

Reece grabbed one of the children's chairs and set it next to me. He was so tall that when he sat down in it, he was eye level with me. I felt as if he did it on purpose.

I scooted back some, clasping my hands together.

He sighed. "I am sorry about this morning."

"It's fine." I didn't want to talk about it.

"Josie," he said my name with such meaning. "It's not fine. I don't know how to explain it, but there's something about you that makes me say things I wouldn't normally say."

I could so relate to that, but didn't mention it.

"I'm usually more suave and debonair," he said half-teasingly. He knew he had it going on. "That said, I made you feel uncomfortable, and that was never my intention. I know what that's like. I spent most of my growing-up years, until we moved to Carson City, feeling so uncomfortable about my situation." He pointed to his patch. "I wished my life were different and I could run away every time someone made fun of me."

My jaw dropped before I could stop it. "People made fun of you?" For some reason I couldn't fathom the idea. He was practically worshipped back in the day. Even today.

"All the time. It's why I quit wearing the glass eye and got a patch. It's what I hid behind," he admitted.

"But everyone loved you in high school."

"In *this* high school. When we moved here my junior year, I was determined not to be the kid with the funny eye and tragic sob story. Honestly, when you wrote that story about me, it made me feel like a rock star. That I had arrived somehow."

"Really?" I could hardly believe it. I'd always just assumed he thought I was a crazy stalker chick like his friends had accused me of being, to the point that I'd believed it myself.

"I wish I would have been brave enough to let you know, but I was trying to navigate my own waters at the time. And I could tell even then I made you uncomfortable. I'd really like to change that."

"I don't know if that's possible." I wasn't sure the pirate girl and the pirate could coexist, because I had come to despise them both. But what about Josie and Reece? It kind of had a ring to it. No. No. No. Why would I even have such a thought? I was whacking all the moles.

"It's going to get awkward since I am the Royal Highness to the Educational Professional." He had a way of making me smile.

"You don't have to do this. I'll figure it out." That was my way of begging him to give up the position.

He inched closer and placed a hand over my own, which were clasped so tight that veins appeared. "I want to do this." He paused. "I want us to be friends."

His more-than-friendly touch had my entire body in a tizzy. "Reece," I could barely say, "you were right this morning. Confronting you means facing myself, and I'm adult enough to admit I'm not adult enough for this."

He chuckled. "I don't believe that. I don't think you do either."

Perhaps he had a point. It was more like I didn't really want to face that part of me. Too much pain was associated with it.

"What's the worst that could happen?" Reece asked. "That we find out we like each other."

Oh, that was more dangerous than he would ever know. Was he just begging for me to write a sequel and get fired?

"We can't. There are rules against it."

His thumb brushed against my skin, sending shivers throughout my entire nervous system. "The last thing I want to do is get you in trouble."

"We're on the same page, then." I pushed away from him.

"You didn't let me finish." He flashed me a crooked smile. "There are no rules against us being friends."

"Friends?"

"You sound disappointed."

"No, I don't." Oh my gosh, I totally did. "You're confusing me. This morning you told me you were attracted to me," I whispered, hoping Andi wouldn't hear, or anyone else for that matter.

"That has not changed."

I rubbed my forehead, half-flattered, half-flustered. "You just represented my ex-fiancé, and won, I might add. Which I'm still salty about, by the way. And let's not forget, if people ever saw us together, even as friends, do you know the kind of attention that would attract? Everyone in this town knows about that stupid story. Sorry." I folded my arms. "We can't be friends."

"You don't want to be friends with my daddy?" Andi about cried.

Way to pierce my heart, kid. I turned and met her doe eyes. "Oh, honey, it's not like that." I mean, it kind of was, but there was no way I could explain it to her. Especially when it made me sound like a crazy person.

Reece used this to his advantage and rushed over to comfort his daughter. He wore such a sneaky smile when he wrapped an arm around Andi. "Yeah, Josie, why don't you want to be friends with me?"

Believe me, I had a list.

"He's so nice, Ms. Peterson," Andi added.

"I really am," he flattered himself.

I refrained from grimacing since Andi was present. "I'm sure you are." Honestly, I was almost positive he was. But I had also thought Trevor was nice, and we all know how that turned out.

"Please, Ms. Peterson, be his friend," Andi begged.

Reece gave me a look that said, *Say no to* that.

Andi had the cute pouty mouth and batting eyes going. She was too adorable for my own good. I knew I would regret it, but what other choice did I have? I let out a heavy sigh. "Fine."

Eleven

"A FEW MONTHS AGO, I woke up to find my husband's wedding ring on the desk with a note that said he was leaving me to move in with some nineteen-year-old woman he'd met on a gaming site," Belinda sobbed at our Ex-Filers Halloween Bash planning meeting. She was a first-timer.

My heart broke for her, but this was the dose of reality I needed. Men were not to be trusted—not even ones with adorable daughters.

"The kicker," Belinda continued, "is yesterday after finally filing for divorce, he shows up out of nowhere at my office and begs me to take him back."

There was a collective gasp by the nine of us attending the meeting.

"Girl, he did not." Jackie shook her finger.

"He did." Belinda sniffled.

"What did you do?" Cami rubbed Belinda's arm. Cami, though happily married and cutely pregnant, was always so kind and empathetic. I mean, she could still throw some zingers out there, but she was most often the first one to offer a shoulder to cry on.

I was surprised she kept coming to these meetings, but she, more than anyone, knew the humiliation an ex could bring upon you. I guess it's something that never goes away. Maybe the key was learning how to cope from it and glean the lesson such experiences tend to teach. I should probably have taken that to heart. Though one could say giving up men entirely meant I had learned my lesson and had a great coping mechanism. Some out there—not my mother or even Jenna—but *some* would agree with me. Trevor wasn't the only person I needed to deal with. The biggest battle I faced was myself. Yikes.

Belinda perked up a bit and wiped her eyes. "I handed him a pen and gave him directions to my lawyer's office, where he could sign the divorce papers."

We all laughed—even Belinda, whose countenance lifted after telling her sad tale. I think we were all relieved she didn't give the louse a second chance.

I didn't say anything about my own recent encounter with my ex. Sometimes listening to others helped me more than anything. It gave me perspective and helped me not feel so alone. I was so very grateful I didn't marry the jerk and have kids with him like so many women in the group.

Once everyone had their say, Cami got down to business. "Okay, we are just over six weeks away from our annual Halloween Bash. I want this year to be epic. Well, not as epic as the Magic Mike action we had last year."

Several people chortled.

I'd heard about that. Apparently, some guy had jumped up on the stage and lost all inhibitions. He had to be tackled and dragged out.

"Annnddd." Cami ran a hand though her hair. "We will allow couples this year. Not like that stopped anyone last year," she grumbled. "Since I'll be bringing my husband, I don't want to be a hypocrite. But, I still want this to be an event where singles feel like they have a place and a voice."

"Hear! Hear!" Jackie shouted. She was a lot of fun.

"How are the decorations coming?" Cami asked me.

"Good. My committee is going with a vintage look. Think

Edgar Allan Poe–style. Ravens on branches for centerpieces. Black and white pumpkins. Lots of candles and lanterns. We're pretty excited about it." Well, I was mainly tired thinking about all I had to do, but this was for a great cause. The women and children's shelter offered an invaluable service. I could sleep after Halloween.

"That sounds amazing." Cami offered me a big smile before she moved on to the rest of the committee heads.

I listened and took notes, and while I was exhausted from the past crazy few days, a sense of wonder filled me. I loved this time of year. There was something so magical about one night where a little bit of your fantasies came to life, and not just to *your* life, but collectively as a community. Just thinking about it helped soothe my soul a bit. Reece had me wound up tighter than the apron strings my mom would like to keep around me.

Feeling a bit better, I stood after the meeting ended, ready to head to the farm. I needed to unwind a bit more, and kicking and punching the crap out of something was the ticket. The best thing my dad ever did for me was installing that punching bag.

Before I could even grab my purse, Cami walked over to me. "I'm looking forward to taking the photo booth pictures at the fall carnival."

Say what? Cami was an award-winning, highly sought-after lifestyle photographer for some pretty swanky people. Why would she be taking photos at a school's fall carnival?

"Reece called me this morning."

Of course he did.

"He's also asked Noah to help him build the photo booth."

What? That was so unnecessary. I told him all we needed was a backdrop, some bales of hay, and a few parents with a good camera phone to snap some shots that could be emailed or texted to people.

"Wow. That's so nice of you, but really, it's too much." As in way too much. What was Reece playing at? His Royal Highness was a Royal Pain in My Side.

"We'd love to. Noah and Reece go way back."

Noah Cullen had gone to the same high school as us, just a grade below Reece. He was every bit as beautiful as Reece too. Thankfully, I had not fallen victim to his charms and written about it.

"That's right. I forgot they were friends." At least I could say Noah never tortured me.

"Our nephews are so excited we're helping with the school fall carnival."

"Jaxon is such a cute kid." He was their oldest nephew and in second grade.

Cami rubbed her burgeoning belly. "He really is. I hope our son gets those Cullen eyes."

They were stunning.

I stared at her baby bump, longing for one of my own. The whole swearing-off-men thing was going to really put a damper on that wish. I swallowed down the lump in my throat, telling myself I loved lots of children. But, oh, did I want some kiddos to call me Mommy.

"Congratulations! You're having a boy?"

"We just found out." She beamed. "Noah is beside himself. He's already constructing a jungle gym in the nursery."

I would like to say I wasn't jealous, but that would be a lie. Not that I wasn't happy for my friend, but I longed to have a family of my own. If I was honest, even a husband. I just wasn't sure I had it in me to trust another man. And I couldn't marry Can Divit, considering he was a fictional character.

"That's so cute," I said as happily as I could.

"It really is. Speaking of cute. Reece is adorable. Look at him being the room parent. He can't say enough good things about you."

"Really?" I clasped my hands.

"Honestly, he went on and on about you. I mean, I already knew what a stellar teacher you were. My sister-in-law, Shanna, has already requested that Jaxon be in your class next year. But, if I'm not mistaken," she sang, while circling her finger in the air, "I think Reece has a little crush on you."

I cleared my throat. "I don't think so," I adamantly denied. "We're just friends. Not even that, really. I mean, I hardly know him."

"Uh-huh." Cami smiled, not buying it.

"I'm being honest. Besides, there are rules at the school, and you know . . ." Because everyone knew about that story.

"Oh, I know. I was in your shoes last year, when Noah and I were 'just friends.'" She did the whole air quote thing.

"This is different. Believe me." Please believe me. P.S. I was going to fire Reece before I got fired. I couldn't believe I was having this conversation.

"Okay." She shrugged, wearing a smile that was calling me a liar. "Believe me, I get it. You're just out of a bad relationship and you're hurt. By the way, I should have your cropped photos to you soon. They are turning out amazing. Anyway." She rested a hand on my arm. "There's nothing wrong with being single. In fact, it can be wonderful at times. But I have this feeling I should tell you that you shouldn't let your ex rule your life. He doesn't deserve the power. And . . . Reece is a great guy."

I appreciated her sentiment, and she was right until the end there, so I had to roll my eyes. Not to say Reece wasn't a great guy. Chances were good that he was, but it didn't mean he was supposed to be *my* guy. Because it was impossible. Besides, I doubted he had a crush on me. Attraction was one thing; crushes were entirely different. I had firsthand knowledge. Crushes led to craziness, like steamy rogue pirate stories.

She laughed. "I see Reece has his work cut out for him."

"No, he doesn't," I said, well above my normal pitch. There was nothing to work on.

She patted my arm. "You keep telling yourself that. Good luck." She walked off, laughing.

I watched her go, not sure what to make of it all. Why was Reece talking about me? Didn't he know the rumors that were bound to spread? My mom was going to flip if any of this got back to her. Let's not forget Mr. Nelson.

I pulled out my phone to email the maddening man. He was so fired.

My fingers were flying as I marched out of the room we met in at Aspen Lake Community Center. It was a forty-minute drive from my townhome. I basically planned on not sleeping through Halloween. It was pretty much a Peterson family tradition. If you got more than six hours of sleep a night during this time of year, you were considered soft.

I walked out into the cool evening; the sun had long since gone down. For a moment I lowered my phone and breathed in the lake air, listening to the rustle of the nearby aspen trees adorned in the perfect shade of gold. Such a loss washed over me. I thought I would be calling this place home. That finally I would be free of the pirate girl here. Instead, the pirate girl was smacking me right in the face.

My phone buzzed, bringing me out of my personal pity party.

Unknown Number: *This is Reece. I wasn't sure if you would recognize my number from the school paperwork. I just wanted to let you know that I'm calling you now. Talk to you soon.*

How did he get my number? There was no need for us to talk. Well, I guess I could fire him over the phone right after I asked him how he got my personal cell number.

My phone rang, startling me, despite Reece's warning. He had me so on edge. I pressed the green button and immediately said, "How did you get my number?"

"Well, hello to you too. I'm fine by the way. How are you?"

"To be honest, I'm annoyed with you."

"That's apparent." He chuckled. "But you gave me your number."

"No, I didn't. Besides, that's not the only reason I'm annoyed with you."

"We will come back to what I've done to deserve your wrath after I prove you wrong," he took way too much delight in saying. "Which I'm guessing will annoy you more."

He had no idea. I headed for my car.

"Your silence says it all." He was enjoying this way too much. "Josie," he said my name so beautifully. He needed to stop doing that. "The room-parent coordinator paperwork you bestowed upon yours truly, the Royal Highness to the Educational Professional—"

I smiled, more annoyed that he could make me smile.

"—says in paragraph two, and I quote, *Please feel free to call me if you ever have any questions or concerns. My personal number is—*"

Ugh. He was right. How did I forget that? "You better have a major question or concern," I snarled.

"It's of the utmost importance." He was not deterred by my snarkiness. "But first, why are you annoyed with me?"

I got into my car and shut the door before I responded. "Let's start with you're going to get me fired, and then we will move on to the photo booth you're building that we don't have the budget for."

"Why would I try to get you fired? Andi adores you."

I adored her too, even though she'd only been in my class for a few days. It was weird how it seemed longer, like I'd always known her.

"I think she's wonderful too, so you need to stop talking to people about me. I don't know what you said to the Cullens, but Cami and I just had a very interesting conversation where she said some pretty ridiculous things," I ranted. "Things that if Mr. Nelson heard, would have me polishing my résumé." I let out an exaggerated breath and leaned my head on the steering wheel.

"Wow. You're a passionate woman. I like that. It says you care."

"About your daughter," I made sure to make that clear.

"Come now, Josie, you said we were going to be friends. You can care about me, too."

94

Was this guy for real? I felt like I kept asking that, but he was throwing me for a major loop. Unfortunately, he was charming. That trait in a man was the worst, because it was the best until they weren't so charming. The other possibility was . . . "Is this a joke? Am I a joke to you?"

"Absolutely not." He sounded offended.

"Then what gives?"

"I'm not following you."

I leaned back against the seat. "Reece, Cami is under the impression that you like me."

"I do like you."

"Not to sound juvenile, but she thinks you *like* like me."

"Ah. I see."

I waited for him to invalidate Cami's assertion before I responded. Then I waited some more. "You need to tell her you don't," I finally said into the dead air.

"I'm not really sure I can do that."

"Of course you can."

"Josie, my life's work is about truth, justice, and the American way."

"So now you're Superman?"

"I mean, maybe. How long can a guy keep up the Clark Kent angle?" He asked it so seriously, I would have believed him if he weren't being so ridiculous and freaking charming. "Think about it: if you were a superhero and immortal, you'd have to switch professions every now and then to keep your secret."

I pressed my lips together, refusing to smile even though no one could see me.

"You're trying not to smile, aren't you?" he guessed.

My lips twitched. He was . . . he was . . . tempting. That was the perfect word for him. But resist him, I must. "Reece," I sighed. "Please just tell Cami she's wrong."

"Josie, I like you, and I'm reserving my right to *like* like you," he said unabashedly. "Before you say I can't—"

"You don't know me," I interrupted him.

95

"That's why I'm calling you. I want to get to know you better."

"That's what's so important?"

"Yes."

"Reece—"

"Josie, please listen. You won't always be Andi's teacher. So, let's say for the next eight months we get to know each other. All friendly, of course. Then come May twenty-fifth, we'll see where it goes from there."

I was at a loss for what to say. In my wildest dreams, and I'd had some very wild ones, I never thought Reece would pursue me. It's all my young heart ever wanted, but that heart had been ripped to shreds inadvertently because of Reece. I knew it wasn't his fault. "I don't even understand why you want to get to know me."

"Even more reason for us to get to know each other better, then."

"What does that mean?"

"It means you shouldn't even have to ask that question."

Oh. Wow. That was a sweet thing to say. I gripped the steering wheel. He was all too tempting. But, I could hold strong. Right? Please tell me I'm right.

When I said nothing while warring with myself, he added, "If you need to know exactly why I want to get to know you, here's my list: You're a little crazy," he chuckled. "You're passionate about everything you do, as far as I can tell. You're talented and gorgeous. I can't stop thinking about you," he admitted.

"That sounds more than friendly." I held on as tight as I could to the steering wheel while my heart pounded erratically. My teenage dreams were coming to life. But those dreams had turned into nightmares that still haunted me.

"I have no doubt you'll keep me in check. I won't jeopardize your job," he sounded as if he were pleading with me.

What about my heart?

"This is crazy" was all I could say.

"Is it?"

"Yes," I whispered, hardly able to speak. The rogue pirate was never supposed to really want me.

"Think about it," he offered. "By the way, I'm donating all the materials and labor for the photo booth."

"You don't have to do that."

"I want to. Maybe it's time you get used to a man who exceeds your expectations."

"They always do at first," I was quick to say. Trevor had pulled out all the stops.

"Well, think of this as a try-before-you-buy type of situation."

I couldn't help but laugh. "Good night, Reece."

"Think about it," he called out, before I could hang up.

I wasn't sure I would be able to think of anything else.

Twelve

"WHEN WILL HE BE HERE?" Jenna nudged me, looking all cute in her Peterson's Pumpkin Patch attire, which consisted of a pumpkin hat that kind of resembled a beret, except it had a green stem that stuck out of the middle. Add to that an orange shirt with the farm logo on it and either jeans or shorts depending on the weather. It was perfect, in the 70s, so Jenna was showing off her long, shapely legs. Meanwhile, I was in my pumpkin costume, looking orange and round around the middle, with striped, orange-and-black tights. It was super attractive.

"I don't know," I responded, while I made sure all my storyboards were in order. I was quite proud of the illustrations I had drawn myself. "I'm trying not to think about it." Except it was all I could think about.

She tugged on my orange beanie. "I'll try to keep the sisters away from him."

I fell onto one of the specially made pumpkin beanbags set up around the most darling room, with a mural of Priscilla Pumpkin and all her friends painted on the back wall. It was cozy and smelled like pumpkin spice. "Good luck with that. I fear my mom has ESP when it comes to these sorts of things. She was in here earlier asking about *the pirate*. I need her to quit calling him that. He's bringing his daughter and mother here for crying out loud." I was sure to be embarrassed. It might actually not be too bad now that I thought about it. It might convince Reece it wasn't a good idea for us to get to know each other.

Jenna took a seat next to me. "Wait until she discovers he wants to live out your teen fantasies."

"Shh," I begged. "He never said that. He wants to be friends." Friends who apparently call each other every day. Reece had called me again the night before and wanted to know all about the pumpkin business and what my role was, right down to my schedule. I think he was wanting to get together in person. Thankfully, I could nip that in the bud. Saturdays and Sundays I was at the farm pretty much all day. I read stories from ten to six, every hour on the hour, and then sometimes I stayed and helped during the evenings. From seven to eleven the farm was crawling with teenagers, and even adults, who loved a spookier atmosphere when walking through the corn maze. The hayrides after dark were accompanied by ghost stories.

"Rigghhht," she trilled. "I see that lasting all of two seconds. Men don't choose to be friends with women. It's the door they knock on, seeing if you'll let them in. You open that baby even a crack, and before you know it, he'll be pushing you up against that cave wall you wrote about in grand detail." She fanned herself.

It was getting toasty in here. I had to blow down the long-sleeved orange shirt I had on. Visions of the rogue pirate backing me up against the cave wall, while I wrapped my legs around him and he ravished my neck in kisses before my dress . . . you know, never mind. That scene was inspired by *Road House.* Yep, I saw it on HBO during the free trial month. Some of the best two hours of my life.

I shook my head. "Please, stop. There will be no cave scenes, or any scenes for that matter."

"Okay, pumpkin," she sing-songed. "If you say so."

"Go sell some tickets or something," I playfully snapped.

"Everyone, gather round," the sisters called out.

Jenna and I gave each other a knowing look. It was time for the Peterson opening-day tradition. We took our time emerging from the "patch," as this ritual, I mean tradition, was a little on the weird side. I feared if our guests ever saw us, they might think we were in a cult or something and never return.

We walked out to find our entire family, including Olivia's brood, who were dressed like they were headed for a fall photo shoot. They were all matchy matchy in mustard yellow, navy, and designer jeans. I wasn't even sure why they showed up anymore. They basically walked around and told the rest of us how to do our jobs. Olivia had suggested earlier this morning that I be sure to use my best inflections when reading today. I almost told her where she could shove her advice, but Aunt D. was nearby.

The sisters were in all their glory, decked out in orange shirts and mom jeans. I always loved that, even though the farm came through the Peterson family line, they had embraced it as if they themselves had tilled the land over a hundred years ago. It's why Dad and Uncle Craig stood in their overalls, in awe of their wives, with eyes full of love and adoration.

All my life I wanted that kind of love. The kind where you come together as a couple and work toward something of lasting value and support each other. I wanted someone to love me for who I was, the way my dad loved my mom. Part of me felt like I had screwed up that possibility when I was fifteen. Somehow Josie got lost and was replaced by the pirate girl. And who could love her?

"Everyone hold hands." Mom grabbed Dad's hand. The love in Dad's eyes was replaced by a momentary look of *I might have married a psycho. A psycho I love, but a bit insane, nonetheless.*

My esteem for my dad always grew when I realized he was not blind to my mother's craziness, yet he embraced it anyway. That was true love right there.

Reluctantly, we all gathered round and held hands, though Jenna and I could hardly contain our snickering. Seriously, this was bizarre. The seasonal employees all stopped and stared, probably wondering if they had made a grave mistake in coming to work here.

"Okay," Aunt D. whispered conspiratorially, adding to the weirdness of it all. "Here we go. Pumpkin, pumpkin, pumpkin," she chanted, while looking around the circle, making sure we were all joining in.

"Pumpkin, pumpkin, pumpkin," we got louder and louder with each iteration. Literally it was all we said. Like somehow the Great Pumpkin from Charlie Brown would appear. The louder we got, the closer our circle came together, like we were about to sacrifice something. After exactly thirty "pumpkin" chants, because it had to be thirty, we threw our hands up in the air in one loud shout of "PUMPKIN!"

The sisters took in deep cleansing breaths as if they had just performed a miracle. There was no doubt this was where I had inherited my crazy. Along with it came passion, but it was a steep price to pay.

"Let's make this the best year ever!" Mom yelled.

"Remember the guest-first rule. Make sure everyone leaves with the pumpkin spirit," Aunt D. added.

"We'll be extra pumpkiny," my kiss-up brother, Oliver, said in his deep, manly voice, which only added to the ridiculousness of him saying *pumpkiny*. Add that to the fact that he was a well-established estate planner. But he knew how to work the system, which was why when my parents had grounded him for his entire junior year after he passed out my story, he only served a three-month sentence. Was I still irked about it? Maybe.

After that, Jenna and I walked away as fast as we could, before either one of our siblings said anything else that made us question whether we all came from the same gene pool. More like beg that we hadn't. Don't get me wrong: I would totally give my brother a kidney if I had to, but I didn't think it was fair he ruined my life and then got to live the life I always wanted— happily married with beautiful children.

Jenna was manning the ticket booth in the little orange house near the entrance where the donation jar was on full display. I reached under my pumpkin costume and into the hidden pocket where I was keeping a crisp hundred-dollar bill. I had this thought that I wanted to be the first one to donate. As much as my family drove me crazy, I loved them and this place. More than that, I knew how much my parents and aunt and uncle loved this place. For them it was a legacy.

I dropped my small donation in the large pumpkin-shaped jar. Next to it was a picture of the old beloved barn.

Jenna grinned at me. "You're a good person."

I shrugged. I hoped I was, but sometimes I wondered.

"Take my word for it." She smiled. "And don't forget to be extra pumpkiny," she mocked my brother.

"Oh, I'll do my best," I said, in the same mocking attitude.

"I'll keep an eye out for you-know-who and run interference if I can."

I swallowed hard, fearing his appearance. Reece was throwing off my equilibrium. I couldn't believe he was even slightly interested in me. He'd told me during the previous night's phone conversation he'd wanted to talk to me for a long time now. It was implausible to me. I shouldn't worry too much about it. All he needed to do today was run into my mom and come Monday he would be pulling Andi out of my class and would thank his lucky stars he didn't *like* like me yet. I should probably say something more grown up than *like* like.

"Thanks," I sighed, knowing the odds weren't in my favor. There was bound to be a major embarrassment in the coming hours. Mom would make sure of it. "I guess it's showtime."

"Good luck," Jenna shouted, as I walked away, down the path to the pumpkin patch playhouse.

Just as I was about to enter the beloved place, Mom appeared and threw her arms around me. "I hope you know you're the heart of this place."

I squeezed her back. For as nutty as she was, she was endearing, and I knew she loved me. "Thanks, Mom."

"Okay, my gorgeous pumpkin girl, get ready to unleash your magic." She kissed my cheek and flitted off to join forces with Aunt D. They tried to greet every guest and make sure everyone was happy. This would not be working in my favor today.

I walked into my sanctuary, feeling a bit magical. Regardless of my adolescent mishap with the written word, I believed in the magic of stories.

I took a seat on the big pumpkin pouf surrounded by the large stuffed animals made to look like the characters in my story. My mom had made them. Another reason to love her. There was Priscilla Pumpkin wearing her signature green tutu full of magical fairy dust, Sadie Scarecrow in her plaid patchwork shirt, Tate Tabby Cat sporting his collar from which hangs a bell with special powers, and the twins, Benny and Bobby Bunny. The twins were always getting into trouble in my stories, and their friends had to help them out. But they were the funniest bunnies around.

In no time, children's laughter rang through the air. It was my favorite sound. It was time for the farm to come alive, just like it did in my story.

Within minutes, children and parents began filling up the patch. I recognized many faces from years gone by. It meant the world to me that people came year after year. There were even older kids filing in, trying to grasp the last bit of childhood magic they could, even though they had no conscious knowledge it was slipping from their grasp. There was new magic in store for the tweens, but there was nothing like the power of childhood magic.

In the commotion, Reece, Andi, and Molly appeared. I held my breath as they entered. Their presence caught me off guard. I don't know why I didn't think they'd be here at opening—I'd figured it would be later in the day.

Reece caught me in his gaze. Oh. My. He was wearing tight jeans and a tee, defining all his physical assets—and believe me, there were a lot of them. He completed his look with a pair of boots. Don't ask me why, but a man in boots and jeans did me in.

I was grateful Andi shyly waved at me. It kept me from licking my lips and going against all my recent proclamations of remaining man-free for the rest of my life unless I met Can Yaman. I motioned with my finger for Andi to join me at the front. Her little soul called to my own.

Maybe it wasn't a good idea, as her dad came with her, followed by Molly, who wore a look like she knew something about me. Maybe even something I didn't know about myself. Whatever it was, I liked it. I had a feeling she and I would get along famously.

I reached out for Andi when she neared. She placed her little hand in mine, and something just clicked inside of me. Almost like something that was broken instantly repaired itself. So weird.

"How are you?"

"Good," she whispered, while swaying back and forth in all her shyness.

"Good morning," Reece said in his gravelly *I'll own you* voice.

"Good morning." I felt awfully flushed.

"You look darling," Molly complimented me.

"Thank you." I smiled at her before focusing back on Andi, who looked so cute in a pintucked dress and boots. She wore her hair in a ponytail. "Would you like to help me this morning?"

She nibbled on her lip and looked to her dad.

Reece knelt in front of her and tapped her nose. "I think you would do such a good job, and Ms. Peterson obviously needs help," he teased, before throwing me a wink. I mean, he wasn't wrong. I could use all the help I could get. How many adult women did you know who dressed up like pumpkins and made diving behind displays a sport?

"Do you think you could hold Priscilla Pumpkin for me?" I asked Andi, hoping to help her come out of her shell a bit.

She bravely nodded.

"Thank you." I scooted over a bit on the pouf. "You can sit by me."

She grinned and joined me, nestling in close to my side.

"Thank you," Reece mouthed.

"You're welcome," I mouthed back, though he didn't need to thank me. I was quite fond of his kiddo.

Molly and Reece stood to the side to watch me do my thing. It made me nervous, but for Andi's sake I didn't let it show.

I handed Andi the stuffed Priscilla Pumpkin. "Hold her tight. She's full of magic."

Andi's eyes went wide. "Really?"

"Uh-huh." I nodded. "She helps all the boys and girls feel the wonder of Halloween."

Andi's grin said she wanted to feel it. I would do my best to make sure she did.

I grabbed my storyboards and heard a little boy say to Reece, "I have a pirate costume too."

I watched as Reece gave him a crooked grin and whispered, "I'll tell you a secret. I'm a real pirate."

The little boy put his hands to his mouth, astonished.

I had to give it to Reece—he handled his disability with grace. But . . . perhaps he was telling the truth. He had, after all, stolen the largest jewel I had ever owned. It still irritated me a bit, but I couldn't think about it. I had to stay in my happy place.

"Welcome, boys and girls," I sang, in my best lyrical alto voice. "I'm so very happy you came to the patch today. I have a little helper I would like to introduce to you. This is Andi." I gave her a squeeze.

Andi hugged Priscilla Pumpkin tight.

I held up my first storyboard, ready to begin. "Priscilla Pumpkin opened her eyes and stretched and yawned. She looked up to the night sky, and to her surprise, the harvest moon appeared. 'It's here! It's here!' she shouted. 'September has arrived.'" When it was October, I would change the story up a bit.

Several children clapped, even Andi, as I showed the next storyboard. "Priscilla rose high in the air to look over the patch to find her friends. 'Sadie Scarecrow! Tate Tabby Cat! Benny and Bobby Bunny! Where are you?' she called. 'It's time for an adventure. A Halloween adventure,'" I whispered.

While I grabbed the next storyboard, I caught Reece's eye and that stubbled jawline. Yowzer. It called to me like Priscilla to her friends. But what got to me the most was the impassioned look he wore that said, *How about an adventure? You and me?*

My fifteen-year-old self was shouting *Yes, let's sail the seven seas together.* My thirty-year-old self was yelling at me that I would only be left alone and shipwrecked. Sometimes I really missed that Josie Peterson girl.

Thirteen

"THAT WAS THE BEST STORY ever," Andi gushed. It was the most animated she had ever been around me.

"I'm so glad you loved it." I gave her a side hug.

Several people rushed to the front, including Reece and Molly, though they lingered back, allowing me to talk to the children first. Andi stayed by my side the entire time, holding my hand. I loved every second of it. Once the crowd was off to enjoy the rest of the farm, Molly and Reece approached.

Andi left my side and threw her arms around her dad. "I know what I want to be for Halloween," she exclaimed. "I want to be Priscilla Pumpkin!"

Oh. Wow. I rubbed my heart, right where Andi had pricked it in the most wonderful way.

"Grandma, can you make me a Priscilla Pumpkin costume?" Andi asked Molly.

"I'll try my best," Molly promised.

I wanted to tell her my mom had made the original Priscilla and could help, but thought the better of it. I was only grateful my mother hadn't appeared yet. Her sensors must be broken. Hallelujah.

"Yay!" Andi shouted. I didn't know she could shout.

Reece's face shone; he was obviously thrilled to see his little girl so happy.

"Ms. Peterson, can I stay here and help you?"

"Sure, if it's okay with your dad."

"How about we go get some doughnuts and cider first," Molly interceded before Reece could answer. "I think your daddy would like to talk to Ms. Peterson for a minute."

Reece flashed his mother a grateful smile.

I wasn't all that grateful. I liked Andi's plan better. She could stay and her sexy dad could go. Alas, I was thwarted. Molly took Andi's hand and whisked her off like this was some well-coordinated plan. That left Reece and me alone. I reached down and grabbed Priscilla, hugging her to me like a security blanket. I had no shame about it. It was the least embarrassing thing I had done around him. Like always, I had a need to hide from him—because hiding from him let me hide from myself.

"You are amazing," he said in awe. "That story is brilliant."

"Thanks." I squeezed the heck out of my pumpkin.

He suavely slid closer, giving me an up-close view of his toned arms. Not to mention a front-row seat to his scent, which mixed well with pumpkin spice. Like they were meant to mingle with one another. "No, thank *you*. You are exactly what Andi needs."

"She's great. I think she'll be back to her bubbly self in no time."

"With you around, I have no doubt."

"I don't know that I can take any credit. She obviously loves you."

"Well, I am pretty lovable," he said, with no shame.

I tittered before I could stop myself.

"I like your laugh, Josie." There he went saying my name again like he was meant to.

I blushed big-time.

"I make you nervous." He glanced at the pumpkin I was squeezing to death.

"Yeah," I admitted.

"Let's work on that. How about dinner at my house tonight with Andi?"

I dropped Priscilla. "Uh . . ."

He picked up the stuffed pumpkin and held her like he was keeping her hostage. "As friends, of course."

I still had no idea what to say. I wasn't sure I could say anything.

He stepped even closer, paralyzing me. "I'm going to take this to mean you're so excited, I've left you speechless. So, let's say seven. I'll text you my address. Are you allergic to anything?"

Yes, him. I was starting to feel itchy all over. "Um . . . no. But wait—"

"Great. See you at seven." He handed me Priscilla and turned to go, as if he knew I was working on all the reasons why having dinner together wasn't a good idea.

I was just about to have a coherent thought, when none other than the sisters appeared. Oh shiz. Their faces were a brighter orange than the shirts they were wearing, like they had run here.

Mom even had sweat dripping down her wrinkled brow. "Are you okay, Josie?"

"Yes, Mom," I gritted.

"Mom?" Reece got excited. He reached out his hand and walked toward the woman who was ferociously scowling at him. "It's a pleasure—"

"Are you in here looking at Josie's panties again?" Mom blurted, before Reece could finish his sentence.

I rubbed my hands over my face. "Mom," I complained loudly.

Reece dropped his hand and gave her a blank stare. "I'm sorry, you must have mistaken me for someone else."

"Oh no." Mom pointed her finger at his patch. "You're the pirate."

"Mother! Please, stop," I pleaded.

"I am indeed the pirate," Reece chuckled, totally owning it.

Mom and Aunt D. blinked, as if they weren't sure how to proceed after his admission.

Reece, however, continued to use his charm. "It's such a pleasure to meet you. You have raised an amazing woman. My daughter is absolutely enthralled with her. And what she just did in here with the kids was pure magic. My daughter is already begging to be Priscilla Pumpkin for Halloween."

"Well." My mother cleared her throat and adjusted her pumpkin beret, at a loss for words. Praise the pumpkin gods.

Reece reached his hand out again. "Honestly, it's an honor to meet you."

Mom had no choice but to reach out her hand.

Reece took it and shook it heartily. "I'm Reece Cavanaugh, by the way. I play a pirate sometimes."

My mom and Aunt D. cracked a smile. He was too dang charming. Though I did enjoy watching someone render the sisters speechless.

Once Reece was done shaking Mom's hand, he reached for Aunt D.'s. "Let me guess, sisters? The beauty gene is apparent."

Oh, brother, was he good. Too good.

Aunt D. actually blushed. "I'm Dana," she giggled. "Josie's aunt—really more like a second mother," she bragged.

"Bravo to you as well." Reece shook her hand.

Mom came to her senses a bit, for better or for worse. She pointed between Reece and me. "So, you're not in here looking at her panties."

Please, someone just let a house fall on me or something. I guess at least Reece would see that crazy ran in our family and would stay away.

Reece tugged on his collar. "No, ma'am. I swear, I have never seen your daughter's underwear."

"Hmm." Mom was reserving judgment.

Before any more award-winning awkward questions could be asked, Jenna rushed in carrying a box. "Doughnuts, anyone?"

I appreciated her trying to rescue me.

"Don't mind if I do." Reece went with the flow and plucked a doughnut out of the box. The fact he hadn't left running and screaming was impressive.

Behind Jenna came Andi and Molly, holding cups of apple cider.

"Daddy, we brought you and Ms. Peterson cider," she whispered, in the group of unfamiliar people.

Mom set her sights on the most darling girl of all time. A softness washed over her wide eyes.

"Thank you, honey," Reece responded.

Andi did not share her extra cup with him. Instead, she headed straight for me.

Mom couldn't take her eyes off the girl who was continually working her way into my heart.

"Mom, I would like you to meet Josie's mom and aunt," Reece made introductions.

Molly approached the sisters. "Wonderful. Josie is becoming our favorite."

Jenna raised her brows, intrigued with the Twilight Zone thing we had happening. She wasn't the only one wondering which dimension we had just entered.

I knelt, waiting for Andi, ignoring the grown-ups the best I could.

She handed me the cup with a toothy grin.

I set down Priscilla. "Thank you."

"You're welcome." She was a ray of sunshine in all this crazy.

"Can I help with story time again?"

"I would love that." I tapped her nose.

"Are you going to have dinner with me and Daddy?"

Oh, dear pumpkins, we had a situation.

Every woman I was related to in the room gasped—well, Jenna's was more of a snort-gasp.

"Please," Andi pleaded, her cute button nose all squinched. Try saying no to that.

I bit my lip, desperately attempting not to look at anyone else in the room despite feeling the heat of everyone's stares.

"Daddy said we can make s'mores," she sweetened the deal.

I did love a good s'more. I mistakenly looked up and caught a glimpse of Reece daring me with his eye to turn down his daughter.

Jenna also caught my attention. "Do it. Do it," she mouthed on repeat. She was zero help.

Andi batted her long dark eyelashes. She was good, like her dad.

"Okay," I squeaked.

My mother clutched her heart. I was going to have to hold on to mine too.

Fourteen

JENNA PEEKED HER HEAD INTO the pumpkin patch, deviously smiling. "How was your day, darling?"

I rolled my eyes at her. She knew the kind of day I'd had. The entire town may very well have known what kind of day I had. It wasn't every day that the pirate and pirate girl were seen together. I saw the looks and the pointing between Reece and me. Add in the sisters, who kept checking in on us for the few hours that Reece, Andi, and Molly were here. Not sure what they thought was going to happen.

Reece had taken it all in stride, making sure to always engage the sisters in conversation. I kept Andi near me the entire time. Not only did I adore her, but she was a great deterrent. Apparently, Mom had some decorum in her and wasn't into frightening other people's children with her crazy ways.

I dramatically fell into one of the orange beanbags. "What even happened today?"

Jenna walked in and shimmied her way onto the beanbag with me. "I like Reece."

I rested my head on her shoulder. "Ugh," I groaned.

"I think you like him too."

"I can't like him."

"Why?"

"You know why."

"Because maybe he's everything your story made him out to be? How awful for you." She laughed.

"We hardly know each other. I can't possibly know how he really is."

"I almost believe you, except I see the way you look at him and his daughter. And you have to be impressed that he owned the sisters today. Come on. That was classic."

"That was pretty good." I smiled. "But, Jen, I'm his daughter's teacher, and you should have seen the way some people looked at us today. I felt like I was back in high school and everyone was making fun of me. And I did promise not to be with anyone but Can Divit," I teased.

"I hate to tell you this, but in real life he cheated on his girlfriend," she groaned.

I sat up and held my stomach. "Nooo. Ugh. How can I watch the show now?"

"Just compartmentalize it. I have to find out how it ends, and you have to watch it with me."

"I'll try, but what a pig. His girlfriend is stunning. Do any men stay true? You know, besides our dads, and I guess my brother." I had a hard time giving Oliver any credit, except for fathering two of the cutest kids ever, who adored me. But I mostly gave Kitty props for that.

Jenna sat up. "There are good men out there. I think Reece might be one of them. He, uh," she lowered her voice, "he put two thousand dollars in the donation jar today."

I whipped my head in her direction. "How do you know? Are you sure? Why would he do that?" I rapidly fired off questions.

"Calm down." She patted my head. "Yes, I'm sure. He was trying to be sneaky about it, which I give him extra props for, but it was him. As soon as he left, I counted the wad he'd thrown in. It smelled yummy too, like spring rain."

"That's him." There was no denying it. "But why? That's so much money."

Jenna pushed herself up and stood. She pointed at me. "Look in the mirror and I think you'll find your answer to why."

"It makes no sense. He hardly knows me."

"Jo Jo, things between men and women hardly ever make sense. Sometimes you just meet someone and you know that you need to explore the possibility with them. They call to you, and you have to answer. You obviously felt that way about Reece."

"In high school."

"Are you sure that call ever went away?" she asked poignantly. "Or did you just bury it because your stupid brother gave the world access to your hopes and dreams? How would you feel about Reece now had that story never come to the light of day?"

My mouth fell open and I began spluttering. I didn't particularly care for the existential crisis she was giving me. She hadn't just given me food for thought—it was more like a feast I couldn't consume, because deep down, I knew she spoke a lot of truth. If the pirate girl never existed, Josie would have jumped at the chance to explore her dreams. You know, after Andi moved on to fourth grade.

"That's what I thought." She smirked. "Go have dinner with the man and his daughter. Be friends like he's offering for the next eight months. But don't look back and regret that you had the chance to fulfill your fantasy and you didn't even try. How many people get that opportunity?"

"Reece and I won't be sailing the seven seas together or, you know, doing things in caves," I poorly defended my position while inside, I was squirming. I'd been running from all my dreams for so long, I never even stopped to think any of them could come true. Even the secret one I had of being a published author someday.

"You never know, but I bet he's good at rolling around in the hot, sticky sand and ravishing you." She wagged her brows. "And at the very least, maybe you can stop diving behind displays."

115

"Oh, ha ha." I grinned, while in my head I couldn't help but picture rolling around in the sand with Reece. Yikes. I wasn't sure this was good. It meant confronting the pirate girl and my dreams. Scary.

"Have fun tonight, Jo Jo."

I twirled a strand of hair. "I'll try. Did you tell the sisters about the donation?"

"Nah. That money was because of you. I don't think Reece would want anyone else to know."

"I can't believe he did that."

"Maybe it's time you believed in something again. Maybe start with yourself." She walked off.

I hugged myself, thinking this might be the scariest Halloween season I had ever experienced. Wicked witches, vampires, zombies, and hobgoblins had nothing on the monster living inside of me. Her name was self-doubt, and she was terrifying.

I emerged from the patch to find the last few families leaving for the day. The evening sun illuminated the farm poetically, as if bestowing a kiss of thanks for bringing such happiness and light into the world today.

I hustled down the well-worn path lined with wildflowers for about a quarter of a mile, to the place I would always call home. A little red farmhouse with a wraparound porch stood like an oasis surrounded by acres and acres of farmland. Mom and Dad kept the front yard tidy and as colorful as they could with a well-kept lawn, and this time of year, pansies and mums were on full display. Mom always decorated the porch for every season. Currently it was bursting with pumpkins, hay bales, and scarecrows. I smiled at the fall scene.

I wished I had time to head to my townhome, but if I had any hope of looking halfway decent for dinner, I would have to settle for getting ready in my old bedroom. I was grateful I had brought a change of clothes and a few cosmetics. Not that I wore a lot of makeup, but you could never go wrong with some mascara and a swipe of lip gloss. I was more concerned about my

116

hair that had been tucked under a beanie all day. To be honest, my hair was the least of my worries. Jenna's words kept assaulting me. I feared Reece was every bit as charming as he seemed to be. I was flabbergasted by his generosity, especially since my mother had been nothing short of rude to him. Sure, she warmed up a bit. But the fact he still wanted me to have dinner with him and his daughter, after my mother called him a pirate and asked if he was looking at my panties, either said he did indeed like me or he was going to seek his revenge. I wouldn't blame him.

I walked up the paved path to the front porch, skipping up the steps to the double front doors proudly displaying matching sunflower wreaths. I turned the knob to find the door unlocked. My parents were too trusting, especially considering the number of people who flocked to the farm this time of year.

I made my way back to my old room in the far corner of the house. The wood floors creaked as I went. It added to the charm of the place. My grandfather had built the house many years ago and raised his six kids here, including my dad and uncle Craig, the only kids interested in carrying on the Peterson farm legacy. Family pictures covered almost every inch of the hallway walls. Mom may be crazy, but to her, family was everything. I put my hand up to block the view like I always did, lest I see a picture of me back in junior high or high school. Those were not good years for me. I wished I didn't despise that girl so much.

Without any accidental peeks at my pictures, I turned the brass knob and entered my room that now served mostly as Mom's craft room. My twin bed was still there, covered in a peach quilt, but the room was full of card tables stacked with fabric and scrapbook paper. Mom was still old school and preferred printed photos over digital ones. She and Dana were probably the only people in Nevada who still had photos developed. I had offered to buy her a digital photo printer and show her how easy it was to take and print pictures right from her phone, but she wasn't having it.

I grabbed the bag I had left earlier this morning off the bed and looked inside. I had brought a pair of cutoffs and a brown sweater that fell off one shoulder. It wasn't exactly classy, but it would have to do. I began stripping out of my costume, making sure to carefully drape it across the bed so it would be ready to go the next day. I would wear clean tights and an undershirt tomorrow.

While I changed, I thought about how Andi wanted to be Priscilla Pumpkin and how I had gotten her to giggle as I read my story. She had even been brave enough after the third go-around to hold up the stuffed characters as I read about them. She was so sad when they had to go home. I was too. You know, because of Andi. Not because of her daddy, who clapped the loudest during every performance and told me I was brilliant and the most gorgeous pumpkin he had ever seen. I mean, how many women did he know who dressed up like pumpkins?

What was I getting myself into? Whatever it was, there was no backing out now. I promised Andi I would come, and I never broke my promises to my students.

I quickly finished dressing and walked across the hall to the tiny bathroom Oliver and I shared once upon a time. I shuddered to think of how disgusting he was back then. Poor Kitty. I hoped he had learned how to put the toilet seat down and improved his aim. I wondered if he still preened for hours like he used to. Granted, I would own up to him being a nice-looking man, but he was so in love with himself back in the day. I never understood why girls always wanted older brothers. The movies make them out to be these loving protectors. Wrong. Either that or I got a raw deal.

Walking into the bathroom was like visiting a time machine. The floral wallpaper hurt my eyes, and the mauve countertop made me chuckle. Honestly, how was this motif ever popular?

I looked at my reflection in the small mirror that hid a medicine cabinet. My chocolate-red curly hair had seen better days. I guess messy bun it was. I pulled it up and thought it was kind of sexy. Holy shiz. I shouldn't be thinking sexy. I was having dinner with my student and her father. But the way some tendrils fell around my face reminded me of how much the pirate in my story loved to play with those same strands of hair. How he longed to tangle his fingers in my hair until it fell around us. I pictured it so vividly.

I closed my eyes, trying to shake the heated visions of Reece and me out of my head. I couldn't jeopardize my sanity or my job. I would go and have a nice, friendly dinner with him and Andi, and that would be that. However, I did long to thank him for his donation. I knew I couldn't. He'd given it anonymously, which spoke to his character. I had a hard time not liking him and thinking about living out some of my fantasies.

Get it together, Josie.

I opened my eyes to find they were brighter and greener. They spelled out how excited I was, even though I would never admit it. I tried to tamp down the emotions while I did my hair and applied mascara and soft-pink lip gloss.

When I was ready, I gazed at myself. I had the whole come-hither vibe going with the bare shoulder sweater. Maybe I should change, but I knew my mom wouldn't have anything I would want to wear, and Jenna would tell me just to wear what I had on. She would probably encourage me to pull the sweater down a smidge more.

I took a deep breath. I could do this.

"Josie, are you here?" Mom called out.

Dang it. I was hoping to escape without seeing anyone.

"Back here, Mom."

"Oh good. I brought your brother. He has something he wants to tell you."

I peeked out the door to see Oliver and Mom headed my way. Oliver was walking very stately as if he were on an important mission. Mom was wearing her pensive, *I'm so ready to overreact* look. This couldn't be good news for me.

I opened the door all the way and stepped out into the hall.

Mom zeroed in on my bare legs and then my exposed shoulder; she didn't say anything, but, boy, was it written all over her face.

Oliver gave me a smug smile, showing off his capped teeth. "Hey, sis; Mom said you're having dinner with Reece."

"Yep."

"I don't think it's a good idea."

I narrowed my eyes at him. "Why?"

"I don't like the guy. In high school, he told me I was a douchebag and threatened to beat the crap out of me."

I pressed my lips together, trying not to smile. I would have loved to see that scene, but . . . "I don't believe it. Why would he do that?"

Oliver cleared his throat and looked down at his dirty work boots. "He . . . um . . . he was upset about the story."

"You mean he defended me," I guessed.

Oliver rubbed his neck. "Maybe, but he was a real prick about it."

"Good. You deserved it."

Oliver's head snapped up.

"You heard me right. I wish he would have beaten the crap out of you. Maybe then you would know just an inkling of how I felt back then."

"Josie Marie," Mom scolded me. "That's your brother."

"Yes, he's my brother. And a brother should have never done the things he did to me. Do you know the kind of humiliation I have lived through over the last fifteen years?" My voice cracked, yet the tears would still not form. "I'm glad to know someone besides Jenna stuck up for me."

Mom slapped a hand across her chest. "I've always been on your side."

"I know you tried, but you seemed more worried about whether I had done something wrong than you were about protecting me." My hand flew to my mouth. I'd always wanted to say that, but my mother's quivering lips and the tears in her eyes made it feel like a hollow victory.

For a moment, time stood still while we all stared at each other, not sure what just happened. I think it was something akin to me growing a backbone. I was kind of trying it on for size. It felt a little weird and a tad uncomfortable. I didn't like upsetting my mother.

"Mom." I stepped closer to her.

She held up her hand to stop me. "Go to your dinner."

Oliver reached for her, but she waved him away and rushed down the hall to the other side of the house to her bedroom.

I watched her go, feeling a mix of emotions. Obviously, I felt terrible for hurting my mother, but I felt as if I could breathe easier. I had gotten something off my chest that had been bearing down on me for years. The truth.

"Way to go, Josie," Oliver berated me. "Look what you did to Mom."

"You know what, Oliver, Reece was right about you. You are douchebag. Not once did you ever apologize for what you did to me. Not once did you care that you embarrassed Reece and me. You were too busy with your buddies having a laugh at my expense. Even now, all you care about is yourself. I know why you don't want me to hang out with Reece. Because heaven forbid I bring someone around who sees you for who you truly are. Now excuse me, I'm late for dinner."

I marched right past him, my heart beating out of control. Never, ever had I stood up for myself like that. You know what? It wasn't half-bad.

Fifteen

I SAT IN MY PARKED CAR in front of Reece's, staring at his chic urban-style three-story home with a gorgeous view of the Sierra and the sun setting for the day. I couldn't stop shaking as I contemplated how I'd told off my brother and hurt my mother's feelings. I tried to call her on the way over, but she wouldn't answer. I called Dad instead. He was never one to take sides, and I wasn't asking him to; I just wanted him to understand why I'd said the things I said. Without saying too much, he asked if I felt like he hadn't protected me. The anguish in his voice about did me in. It was as if there were no worse thought in his mind than that he might have failed to protect me.

How could I have dinner with Reece and Andi now? I'd basically blown up my family. But I'd made a promise to Andi. I leaned my head against the steering wheel, wishing I could cry, but that part of me was still broken.

My phone buzzed. I thought it might be Mom so I reached in my bag.

Reece: *Someone in here is excited to see you. Andi is too. P.S. I don't bite on the first visit.*

I smiled at his message, though he might be the death of me. And maybe I also envisioned him nibbling on me. Holy schnikeys, I had to quit thinking like that. Reece was upending my life in more ways than one. He had given me the courage to tell off my brother and even my mom. Knowing that he had stood up for me in high school meant more to me than he would ever know.

With that thought, I grabbed my bag and hauled myself out of the car. I surveyed his quiet neighborhood that wasn't overly posh, but rather cozy. It fit him. It was comfortable, but classy. Perfect for an up-and-coming lawyer and single dad. Perfect for me. *Oh. My. Gosh. Stop thinking things like that, Josie.*

I tiptoed up the sidewalk to his front porch. Before I could even get to the door, it flew open, and Andi ran out to greet me by throwing her arms around me. I could get used to that. I gave her a tight squeeze while fixing my sights on Reece, who was leaning against his door, looking too good for my own good. The jeans and tee thing really did me in.

Reece was giving me the same once-over. His smile said he was pleased with my casual outfit. "Hi," he breathed out sexily.

"Hello." I bit my lip.

"You have to come in. We're going to make bread on a stick and roast marshmallows." Andi could hardly contain her excitement.

"That sounds like fun. I've never made bread on a stick."

"I'll show you how." She grabbed my hand—really my heart.

My fingers curled around hers. "I can't wait." That wasn't a lie.

As I walked past Reece, he tugged on my sleeve. "Are you okay? You seem shaken." How did this man read me so well?

"I am a little," I admitted. No sense in lying to the human emotion detector.

"Do you want to talk about it?"

I looked down at Andi, who was bursting with happiness. I didn't want to ruin that. "Maybe later."

"Okay." Reece shut the door behind us.

His house was, in a word, handsome. The dark furniture in his living room had clean lines, and the black-and-white wall art depicting wild horses was stunning. Something about those horses reminded me of Reece. Perhaps it was their free spirits or maybe how utterly gorgeous they were.

"Come on up. The kitchen and access to the balcony are on the second level," Reece informed me.

"We're making dinner using the firepit." Andi pulled me along.

That sounded perfect.

We all walked up the wooden steps; Reece and I were goofily smiling at each other. It seemed more than friendly, but I reminded myself it wasn't an option. There were school rules, and I was utterly confused at the moment. It seemed I'd entered a new reality and was attempting to figure it all out.

When we arrived on the second level, I had to take a moment. I was in love. Not with Reece, but his home. The open kitchen with all the bells and whistles and family room with the coziest modern stone fireplace were perfection. My favorite thing was all the framed photos of Andi he had on the mantel. She was the cutest baby and toddler, with her dark hair and emerald eyes. I wanted to eat her up. Not in a Hansel and Gretel sort of way.

"Your home is beautiful." I stood in awe.

"It feels good to have a place of my own." His tone said I was missing something. I wondered what. He didn't elaborate— instead he pointed to the patio door. "Why don't you ladies go get settled on the balcony, and I'll bring the food out."

"Are you sure I can't help?"

"You are." He nodded toward Andi.

I loved that he thought so.

"Come on, Ms. Peterson. I know how to turn on the firepit. Daddy said I can if I have an adult with me. You're an adult." She tugged me toward the door.

I tried to be one on occasion. You know, when I wasn't dressed up like a pumpkin and playing with stuffed animals. Or running from myself.

"Let's get this party started, then." I let her lead me.

Reece's balcony had a perfect view of the mountains, which were just a mere outline now in the early-night sky. Antique bistro lights lined the railing. The soft hue added to the ambience of the place. In the center of the balcony was a gas-lit stone firepit filled with white stones. Andi flipped a switch, and it came to life, adding warmth to the cool evening. Autumn nights were my favorite. You could smell the cozy change of air. It made me feel snug and secure, as if the season were wrapping me up in a blanket, begging me to drink hot cocoa or warm apple cider.

"Can you sit next to me?" Andi asked.

"Of course." I would love nothing better.

We took a seat on the built-in stone bench. She immediately snuggled into my side. I naturally held her close to me. I was walking a fine line here between teacher and friend of her father. Several teachers at the school taught their own children or children of close family friends, where an outside relationship existed. I never wanted any impropriety to sneak in. But this felt different somehow. Andi was different. I didn't know how, but she was. She needed this. And I think maybe I needed her and Reece. That thought scared me in ways I couldn't articulate.

"Did you have fun today at the pumpkin patch?"

"Yes. We played with the bunnies, and I picked out the biggest pumpkin. Daddy and Grandma got one too."

"That is fun. I love the bunnies."

"Me too. Daddy said I can go back next week and play with them and help you with story time."

"I would love that." Though I wasn't sure how my family would feel about it. Especially now that they were upset with me. Oliver had just spluttered at me before he'd stomped off, muttering to himself. It wouldn't take long for the word to spread among all my relations that I'd upset the equilibrium of the family. The Petersons had an unspoken tradition of pretending everything was perfectly pumpkiny all the time. Well, I hadn't been pumpkiny in forever.

In no time, Reece joined us carrying a wooden tray full of meat and vegetable kebabs, dough-wrapped skewers, and all the things for s'mores. It was beautiful. He was too. That was a problem. I seriously wanted to kiss him for making that donation and sticking up for me. I had to stop thinking like that. I loved my job, and I wasn't sure I could handle the scrutiny of being with "the pirate."

"I hope you're hungry." Reece set the tray down on the edge of the firepit.

"I'm starved." I hadn't eaten anything since Jenna had brought in those pumpkin doughnuts.

Reece sat on the other side of Andi. "Let's dig in, then."

"Show me what to do. I've never made bread over a fire."

"I'll show you," Andi volunteered.

Reece proudly handed her a dough skewer while flashing me a grin. That smile was going to be the death of me.

Andi took the long skewer and kept it just above the flames. "You have to be very patient and not get too close to the fire, so it doesn't burn."

Man, was that good life advice. Why did I feel as if I were jumping straight into the flames being here?

"You have to turn it all the time," she instructed.

"I'll do my best," I promised her.

Reece handed me my own skewer, and with it came a compliment. "You were amazing today. I can't get over your story."

I took the skewer, kind of uncomfortable with his praise. "Thanks."

"You really should think about publishing it."

I had thought about it, but decided I couldn't because it might mean my name getting out there, and then people would connect me to my stupid other story, and my life would be ruined forever. That was dramatic, but the fear was real.

"I have some contacts in New York."

"Of course you do." I smiled.

"What does that mean?" He was curious.

"I don't know. I'm just beginning to think that you are, in a word, magical."

He popped a brow. "You think I'm magical? This is good."

"Not that magical." I laughed. "I just meant you seem to know how to solve all life's problems. How do you do that?"

He gazed at Andi and then me. "I wish that were true."

I gave him a thoughtful glance. "What do you wish you could solve?"

He reached over and tugged on a tendril of my hair. "Can we talk about that one later?"

I nodded, trying not to hyperventilate over the fact that he'd tugged on my hair just like I had written.

"Look, look!" Andi shouted, "my bread is turning golden brown."

"Yay." I squeezed her, appreciating her interruption.

"Now you try," she cutely commanded.

"Yes, ma'am." I mimicked her and held my skewer just above the flames.

"Do you want me to contact my friend in New York?" Reece wasn't going to let me off the hook.

"I don't know." I carefully kept watch of my bread. I needed carbs ASAP.

"Why not?" Reece turned his own skewer of bread.

"I don't know if it's good enough for the children's market right now." That sounded like an excellent excuse.

"There's only one way to find out." He was persistent.

I shrugged, hoping he would drop it.

No such luck. "Let me talk to Cari—I met her in law school. She's fantastic. She works for one of the big five . . . publishers, that is."

I stopped twirling my bread, paralyzed by the thought.

"Your bread's going to burn." Andi nudged me.

Some other things were going to burn if this conversation kept up.

I turned the bread, trying to think of a good excuse for why I couldn't pursue this dream of mine. "I'll think about it," was the best I could come up with.

"Promise." Reece meant business.

"Make her pinkie promise, Daddy." Andi was not helping my situation.

"Good idea, honey." He kissed Andi's head before holding out his hooked little finger. "Pinkie promise."

I stared at his finger, gripping my skewer with both hands now. "I'm kind of busy with my bread."

"You have to do it!" Andi exclaimed. "Because it's the best story ever."

"There you go. Eight-year-old wisdom is unbeatable." Reece inched his pinkie closer, daring me. Always daring me.

I bit my lip. "Reece, it's complicated." I mean, not really. But that sounded better than that I was a nutjob.

"I'm good at complicated."

"I'm not," I admitted.

"I'll help you."

Those were beautiful words.

"Me too." Andi grinned.

I was running out of sane excuses. And something about the way Reece and Andi were smiling at me filled me with a sense of hope and gave me a shot of bravery. "Okay." I gave in and interlocked my pinkie with Reece's.

He locked them up tight together, and some of his magic went through me, making me shiver despite the warm flames. We sat motionless, peering at one another as our tangible connection became intangible. As unexplainable as it was, I knew one thing: it was more than friendly.

"Your bread is burning!" Andi yelled.

I dropped my pinkie and the skewer. More than my bread was on fire. My heart was, and I wasn't sure if I could put those flames out.

Sixteen

WITH NO SHAME, I FINISHED off my fourth s'more, making sure to stretch the melted marshmallow out as far as I could before I demolished it. "Mmm." I savored every last morsel.

Reece chuckled, holding Andi tighter to him. She'd fallen asleep leaning against him, two s'mores ago.

I'd been trying not to stare at the beautiful sight. I didn't need to be attracted to Reece any more than I already was. But the way he held Andi so tenderly was making me feel oh so zingy. I had to stop myself from accosting him.

"Thanks for an amazing dinner and dessert," I said, after properly chewing and swallowing.

"It was my pleasure."

I stared at Andi so peacefully sleeping. I loved all her giggles throughout the night as we ate, and she'd told me a silly story about a moose and a duck both named Sam. "I should probably go and let you put her to bed."

"Don't go," Reece was quick to say. "I mean, I would love for you to stay if you can. I'll put her to bed, and then I can pop a bottle of wine, if you're interested."

Oh, I was interested. "Um, sure." What was I doing?

"Perfect." He stood, careful not to jostle his daughter. "I'll be right back. If it's more comfortable for you, we can sit on the couch in the family room."

I looked up at the night sky, a million stars twinkling. "I love it out here."

"I'm glad to hear you say that." He said not another word before carrying Andi inside.

Oh, holy pumpkins, what was I doing? I panicked and grabbed my phone. I needed to text Jenna.

Uh . . . I've agreed to drink wine with Reece under the stars by the light of fire. Please tell me this is a bad idea.

Jenna: *Heck no, girl. Get your freak on with him.*

Me: *You are not helping. I'm going to get fired at this rate.*

Jenna: *Totally worth it.*

Me: *I'll have to cancel the Turkish channel subscription.*

Jenna: *Bummer. Well, let's finish bingeing the show, and then you can get all freaky.*

Me: *I won't be getting freaky with anyone.*

Jenna: *There is a first time for everything, and Reece is an excellent candidate. By the way, the sisters have been locked up in your mom's room all night. Do you know why?*

That could not be good.

Me: *I kind of told my mom and brother off for ruining my teenage years.*

Jenna: *Whoa. Good for you. It's about time. But you may want to think about moving. I'll come with.*

That wasn't a bad plan.

I saw Reece come down the stairs into his kitchen.

Me: *I have to go. He's coming back. Pray for me.*

Jenna: *I'm praying you get your freak on.*

She was not helpful. I tossed the phone in my bag. I gripped the bench, reminding myself I loved to eat and pay my mortgage.

Reece was back in no time, carrying a bottle of red wine, two glasses, and a blanket.

I stared wide-eyed at the blanket. What did he want to do with that thing?

My deer-in-the-headlights look didn't faze him. He set the wine and glasses down before approaching me and draping the blanket over my shoulders. "It's getting a little nippy out here."

Wow. He was the best. Like, if I weren't a psycho, I would be falling head over heels now.

"Thanks." I wrapped the blanket tighter around me.

"You're welcome." He grabbed the wine and glasses. "I hope you like red."

"Love it."

He sat next to me and handed me an empty glass before filling it halfway with the sweet-smelling liquid. It went perfectly with the night air, with him.

"Thanks for tonight. I had a great time. Andi is perfect."

"She is." He set the bottle of wine down after filling his own glass. "She's been through a lot lately."

"Can I ask about her mom?" I took a sip of the fruity concoction. It was yummy.

Reece fixed his gaze on the fire, holding his glass steady. "Nicolette," he sighed.

"You don't have to say anything. I'm sorry to bring it up."

Reece turned my way. "Don't be. I'm glad you asked. It means you care about Andi."

"I do." That earned me a smile.

Reece took a sip of his wine. "It's just I never saw our lives turning out this way. I met Nicolette while I was attending UNLV. She was a few years younger than me. We had this whirlwind love affair, and the next thing I know, I'm popping the question and she's following me to law school in Louisiana. And then we get pregnant with Andi, and we're getting married." He blinked like he was caught in a daze. "It all happened so fast, I don't know that we ever really stopped to think if it was the right thing. I mean, don't misconstrue that—I wouldn't trade Andi for anything, but Nicolette and I were so different. But I checked most of her boxes."

"Most of them?" I questioned.

Reece leaned forward. "Mainly one. I was going to be a successful lawyer and give her the kind of life she had growing up in Aspen Lake."

"Oh."

"Yeah," Reece groaned. "But that takes time. Even with all the scholarships I earned, money was tight. I didn't grow up with money, so for me it wasn't a big deal. I thought there was something romantic about us working together toward a common goal, but she didn't exactly see it that way. And being a mom so young was hard for her. I felt guilty about it. I should have been more careful."

I don't know what I was thinking, but I reached out and lightly grazed his back with my fingers. "Did she not want Andi?"

He smiled at the touch. "It wasn't like that. At first, she was thrilled. But reality didn't meet her expectations. It's not all cute pictures for Instagram. Babies and toddlers are hard work, and my studies didn't allow me to be as helpful as I wished I could have been." He took another drink before setting his glass down and sitting up straight.

"So, what happened?"

"We tried to make it work, and she became more and more miserable. She started partying with friends. Nothing crazy, but when we moved back here and I started making a little money, it wasn't enough for her. She wanted what her parents had, even though it had taken them years to get there. But she felt as if she'd paid her dues and I was purposely holding us back." He ran a hand through his hair. "Do you really want to hear all this?" He seemed uncomfortable.

"I do, actually. I feel as if we always talk about me. And for as tangled up as I've made our lives, I feel like I hardly know anything about you—other than you have the cutest daughter in existence, and you're maddening."

He chuckled. "I suppose we should change that."

"The maddening part?" I teased.

"No. I plan to stay maddening. I think it's one of my finer qualities. But I want you to know me. And I want to know all about you," he said so seriously, I felt it in my toes.

"First finish your story," I barely managed to say, for having to catch the breath he had stolen from me.

"There's not much left to tell. The resentment built up between us. I didn't want to ruin our future by making bad financial decisions, and she wanted a different future without me in it."

"I'm sorry, Reece."

"It's fine, except Andi was caught in the middle of it all. She knew she could use our daughter to hurt me. And so she did."

That pricked my heart.

"Thankfully, her parents and sister are great. They watched out for Andi when I couldn't be with her. They even testified in court on my behalf."

"They sound like good people."

"The best. They're having a tough time now watching their daughter go to rehab. I forgot to mention Nicolette's partying and doing drugs caught up to her."

"Did she do drugs around Andi?" I hesitated to ask.

A shiver seemed to go through him as his body shook. "Andi has nightmares about finding her mom unconscious."

I gasped, my hand flying to my mouth.

Reece clenched his fists. "Sometimes the law is unfair, but that was the last straw for me. I took her back to court and got a better outcome this time."

"Reece . . ." I didn't know what to say.

He reached over and took my hand, tenderly gripping it. "It's okay. You don't have to say anything."

That was good, because his touch had rendered me speechless. I stared blankly at our clasped hands, reveling in the feel of our inexplicable connection. I knew I should pull away, but I couldn't remember why.

Reece gave my hand a squeeze. "Is this okay? Friends can hold hands, right?"

"Um . . . I'm not sure. I've never held a friend's hand before."

"I'm glad I'm the first."

"You are maddening." And charming. So freaking charming.

"Listen, I've behaved myself quite well tonight, considering you came here looking more than sexy. I've been doing my best to keep it friendly. It is you who are to blame here."

"Excuse me . . . wait . . . you think I'm sexy?"

"Why does that surprise you? I don't think there is a man alive who wouldn't."

"I don't know about that. But you can't think I'm sexy because I'm Andi's teacher, and well, you know, that's not friendly at all."

"Like I said, you can't fault me here. I didn't tell you to wear those incredible shorts that show off your legs or that sweater that makes me want to kiss your shoulder." He leaned in, as if thinking about it.

I wasn't sure if I would stop him. Holy, holy shiz. "Now you want to kiss me?"

"Kissing would probably cross the friendly line." He leaned away, thank goodness. "But if you ever want to try it out, I wouldn't say no."

"Reece, this is . . ." I was so flustered for thinking of kissing him, I lost my ability to speak.

"Hey there." He brushed his thumb across my skin. "We aren't crossing any lines. I was just stating the obvious."

"And what's that?"

"That this is going to be difficult, but worth it."

"Oh," I squeaked. "Maybe this isn't a good idea."

"I don't think you believe that."

"Why?"

"Because your grip speaks to you wanting, maybe even needing, this as much as I do."

I went to let go of his hand, but I couldn't. He was right. Whatever this was, I needed it. More than that, I wanted it. For the first time in a long time, I felt like Josie, not the pirate girl, which was weird considering Reece was the pirate.

"Fine," I conceded. "But don't make me want to kiss you." You know, more than I already wanted to.

"I can't promise that," he crooned.

I was in so much trouble. "Keep talking," I was quick to say, before we did something stupid. Glorious, but stupid.

"There's not much more to say about the situation, other than I hope Nicolette gets well and can have a good relationship with our daughter someday. In the meantime, I'll do my best to undo the damage she's done to Andi."

"You're a good person. I don't know if I would be so generous to my ex."

"She's Andi's mom, and once upon a time I loved her."

"You don't love her anymore?"

"I'll always love her for giving me Andi, but I'm long past being in love with her."

That was good news. I mean, for his sake, not mine.

"What about you?" he asked. "Are you in love with Trevor?" he grumbled his name.

"No," I said emphatically.

Reece grinned. "Good. He's a loser."

"Says the man who helped him steal my ring."

"Are you ever going to forgive me for that?"

"Maybe."

"What can I do to make it up to you?"

I think he already had. I so badly wanted to thank him for his donation, but felt it would be in poor taste. I had something else in mind, though. "Tell me more about you."

"What do you want to know?" He seemed pleased with my request.

I pointed at his patch. "How did you lose your eye? You know, other than being knocked over in a tree by a giant crocodile. Or my favorite today was when you told that little boy about your grand sword fight with the Duke of Cornish Hen." I chortled. "I've never heard of him. He sounds delicious, though."

Reece gave me wry smile, but he shifted a bit in his seat.

"Oh, I'm sorry. I'm asking all the uncomfortable questions tonight."

"I'm glad you feel like you can. It's just I joke so much about my injury that sometimes I forget how painful it really was. That one moment shaped my life more than any other, besides becoming a father."

I sat still, gripping his hand, so curious to know what pain he hid behind the laughter. But I felt bad for intruding.

"You know, your story was eerily close to the truth."

I inadvertently let go of his hand. I didn't want to talk about my story with him. With anyone.

He reached right back for it, firmly keeping it in his grasp. "Don't be embarrassed. Please."

I stared into the flames, wishing so badly I had thrown my journal into the fire before Oliver ever had the chance to invade my most private hopes and dreams.

"Josie." Reece directed my face back toward him with the slightest touch of his finger on my chin. "What is it that makes you hate that story so much?"

"You have to ask?" He'd read the thing.

"I do, because after I read that story, I was like, hell yeah, I should be a pirate. And today your story made my little girl want to be a pumpkin. That's magic, Josie. You make magic with your words. How can you hate that?"

I didn't hate that. I hated me, but I couldn't say that. "No one should have ever read those words. Especially you. It's mortifying. Did you hear our old classmate, Clarissa, when she visited the patch today? She whispered to her husband that I was the pirate girl. He laughed. He was laughing at me."

"They're immature idiots who never grew up. To hell with them."

"Easy for you to say; my entire life, that's all I've been known for."

"Then own it."

"People tell me that all the time, but what does that even mean?" Own how stupid I am?

136

"Josie, when I lost my eye at nine years old, that's all I was known for. That, and how it happened." He didn't elaborate on how it happened, and I didn't ask again. "For years, I hated it. I was tired of the stares and questions. Kids at school teased me all the time. Then my mom got a job here the summer before my junior year. I knew then I had a choice. I could change the narrative and own my difference, or I could continue to let people tell me how to feel about myself. I was tired of the other way, so I owned it. When people saw I was okay with myself, it gave them permission to be comfortable with who I am."

"My situation is different," I whined more than I meant to.

"No, it's not. Own the story. Own yourself. Don't let anyone else tell you how to feel about yourself, except maybe me." He nudged me with his shoulder.

"What if I don't want to be the pirate girl?"

"That would be a shame. That girl . . ." He pulled my hand up, and close enough to his mouth that I could feel his breath dance across my skin. "That girl makes me dream of sailing around the world and hot, sticky sand glistening on smooth, creamy skin."

Every inch of my skin raised as he seduced me with his words. I could see us clearly on that beach. One hand tangled in my hair as the other glided down the bare skin of my arm. Warm sand engulfing us, providing the perfect bed.

He drew my hand closer to his mouth.

I longed to have his lips brush my skin. Then I came to my senses. "Reece," I breathed out. "I'm Andi's teacher," I blurted, while pulling my hand out of his grasp. "I better go." I stood, hot and bothered. Mostly hot. Reece was going to set me ablaze.

"Okay," he didn't argue, looking about as dazed as me. "Can I see you tomorrow?"

"I'll be at the farm most of the day."

"Andi will be spending the day with Nicolette's parents, so I'll come by after I drop her off."

"Sure," I said without thinking. I handed him the blanket and my glass. "Thank you for the lovely evening."

137

He took them and set them aside before standing. "Thanks for coming. It's the best night I've had in a long time."

"Me too," I admitted.

"So, how do friends say good night?"

I stuck out my hand to shake his, not knowing what else to do.

Without a thought, he grabbed it and pulled me to him, wrapping me against his hard, warm body. "I find hugging is highly underrated," he whispered in my ear.

I naturally sank into him, my head landing on his chest as if I belonged in his arms. I breathed in his spring-rain scent mixed in with the smell of chocolate and marshmallows. It was, in a word, divine. "I like hugging." Boy, did I ever.

Seventeen

I LET OUT A LONG sigh as I snuggled into my pillows.

"You've got it bad." Jenna settled in next to me on my queen-sized bed. She didn't want to drive back to Aspen Lake so late at night, only to have to come back to the farm early the next day, so she was crashing at my place.

It was like old times. Inevitably, every weekend when we were growing up, we'd slumber partied. We'd switched off whose house we stayed at, depending on what our moms were making for dinner. Tonight's menu included a big ol' slice of what-in-the-shiz-have-I-done with a side of what-in-the-shiz-am-I-going-to-do. For dessert I would be wallowing in sweet misery.

I gripped my comforter. "Jen, what am I going to do? I was supposed to be over all men, and now here I am getting awfully friendly with one of my student's fathers. And let's not forget I wrote a torrid story about him. A story I don't think he would mind living out." I could hardly believe it.

"Ooh. Do it."

I tossed a throw pillow at her. "Where is this 'get your freak on' and 'do it' attitude coming from?"

"Have you seen Reece? I mean, I'm not even thinking about going after your man, but honey, let's get real. He's a prime piece of real estate."

I couldn't help but laugh. "First of all, he's not my man. Secondly, prime piece of real estate? Who talks like that?"

"I'm just saying: put down an offer and take that man off the market."

"I can't. I'll get fired. Besides, we're just getting to know each other; and, you know, he's the *pirate*."

"Which makes this even hotter."

"Oh my gosh, you're insane. Speaking of insane, do you know if the sisters ever emerged from my mother's room?" Mom had never returned my calls.

"They did, but they aren't talking to anyone. Oliver started taking a poll, asking everyone in the family and at the farm if he's a douchebag or not. So far, it's a tie. Kitty is the only holdout. Which we all know means she thinks he is, but she shares a bed and children with him, so she's probably trying to keep the peace."

"I always liked her. Not sure what she saw in my brother."

"He does make a lot of money," Jenna surmised.

"But she married him when they were in college."

"Well, I got nothing, then." Jenna laughed.

"I feel like I disturbed the Force today. I'm kind of scared to show up to the farm tomorrow."

"It's a good thing. I mean, how long can one family pretend to be perfect? Maybe I'll tell my mom off tomorrow." Jenna hugged the life out of a throw pillow. "Just once I would like her to not grit her teeth when she tells people I'm an aesthetician. You know, right after she goes on and on about Olivia and how she does it all. Perfect mother of three who runs her own successful business organizing other people's lives. It's the perfect job for her—she loves to tell people what to do."

I wrapped an arm around Jenna. I knew how hard it was for her to live in Olivia's shadow. I felt like that myself on occasion with Oliver. I decided then not to tell her about Reece's friend in the publishing business. I didn't want her to feel any worse. Even though I knew she would be thrilled for me. And I wasn't sure I would talk to Cari. It was a long shot anything would come of it.

Although, my biggest worry was that they would be interested and I would be exposed. "Sorry, Jen. You should be proud of what you do. You're amazing at your job."

She rested her head on my shoulder. "I do love my job, but I'm living paycheck to paycheck with nothing to show for it. If it weren't for Cami having mercy on me and renting me her condo for below market value, I don't know what I would do."

"You know, you could always move in here with me." My townhome had three bedrooms. Small bedrooms, but it would work.

"I love you for that, but the commute to Aspen Lake every day would get old, especially in the winter."

"That would be tough. What can I do?"

"Keep bringing Reece around—that should keep the pressure off me," she teased.

"Well . . . he's coming tomorrow."

"Oh, really? Spill your guts."

"He just wants to talk."

"Uh-huh."

"It's true. Though I can't believe he wants to come back after my mom asked him if he was looking at my panties. Our family is crazy. But I have a feeling he has some weirdness in his past. He's very reluctant to tell me how he lost his eye."

"Just like in your story. How odd."

"Right?"

"You know what you should do? Take him up to the hayloft tomorrow, roll around a bit, and I bet he'll tell you anything you want."

"You are a nut." I nudged her off me. "I'm not taking him up to the loft. Go to sleep."

She snuggled into her pillow, giggling. "Think about it. It could be fun."

I nestled under the covers, not sure I would be able to think of anything but Reece. The drama I had created among my family might be the exception.

"Do you think my parents will disown me?" I whispered.

141

"Nah." Jenna yawned. "It's pumpkin season, and they need their pumpkin. Besides, that would tell people the Petersons aren't actually perfect. No way are the sisters letting that get out. Night, Jo Jo." She turned off the lamp on the nightstand next to her, plunging us into the dark.

"Good night." I lay still, thinking about Reece. How he saw the pirate girl much differently than I did. More importantly, he saw Josie. I curled into myself, reliving every minute of our time together. Never had someone's touch affected me in such a way. It was better than I had ever imagined all those years ago. So much so, I longed to be back in Reece's arms. They felt like a safe landing place. It was a ludicrous thought because I was smart enough to know that if we kept this up, we would be more than friends and I would be more than unemployed. Yet, it was tempting, so tempting. No. No. No. I liked being responsible and paying my bills.

Tomorrow I would keep a friendly distance. There would be no hand holding or hugging. What a disappointing thought. But it had to be. Yep, there was no other way around it. Bummer.

When I arrived at my parents' place the next morning to change into my costume, there was no one to be found. Normally, Mom was in the kitchen with muffins or some other baked goods. Instead, the house felt eerily silent, as if a thief in the night had come and stolen the heart and soul of the home. I held my stomach. Perhaps I was the thief. All I'd done was tell the truth. Was that so bad?

I fell onto the old lumpy couch in the living room, not sure what to do. I'd never been at odds with my mother before. I had always just acquiesced. But this time I felt as if I couldn't back down. I'd thought a lot lately about how different my life would have been if I'd felt shielded from the storm instead of having to trudge through it, constantly getting pummeled by the daily hail of verbal assaults throughout my high school years. Or, if like Reece said, I had just owned it. But I felt like I couldn't own it because my parents made me feel ashamed of what I had written.

That's not to say my parents are horrible people. They're good people who provided for all my needs and, when they could, my wants. They worked hard to put me through school, and they serve our community. I love them.

Amid my contemplation, the screen door opened, creaking and cracking as it went. I jumped up, expecting to see my mom. Instead, my dad stood there in his dusty overalls.

"Hi." I ran a hand through my hair. "Is everything okay?" Normally, Dad would be out on his tractor, making sure it was running well and that the trailer was hitched properly. This time of year, he and Uncle Craig spent their days hauling kiddos and their families out to the patches to pick the perfect pumpkins. Our farm was large enough to have two considerable fields full of pumpkins, so Dad and Uncle Craig were both needed. Our corn and hayfields had already been harvested. That allowed us to have one of the largest corn mazes in the western states.

Dad took off his straw cowboy hat. He wore a look of discontent.

"Dad?" He was making me nervous. The thought struck me that maybe something had happened to Mom. That's why she wasn't home. It wasn't because of me—it was a tragic accident. I clenched my fists, waiting for the blow to my heart.

"I'm sorry, sweetheart."

Oh my gosh. My mother was dead. I killed her. She couldn't come to terms with not being perfect, so she gave up the ghost.

"I thought a lot about what you said yesterday. You're right. I should have done a better job of protecting you," Dad added.

Phew. I grabbed my heart.

Dad stepped closer. "I said as much to your mother."

Oh . . . that could not have gone well. My entire body tensed for knowing how much that was going to be an issue. Yet I still asked, "How did she take it?"

Dad scrubbed a hand over his clean-shaven face, staring at the couch. I imagined that's where he'd slept last night. "We'll work through it." He didn't sound too sure.

"I'm sorry, Dad. I didn't mean to cause problems between you and Mom."

Dad came around the couch and wrapped me up in his strong arms. "Honey, don't you apologize. Things needed to be said. You struggled more than necessary. I knew that, and I should have done more. You were right; we worried more about what we thought you'd done instead of worrying about you. But despite all our mistakes, you grew up to be an intelligent, capable, and beautiful young woman. For that, I'm grateful."

I took comfort in his arms and breathed in the earthy scent of the farm mixed in with his Old Spice aftershave. It was the smell that said I was at home and safe. "I take it Mom isn't so grateful for me this morning."

Dad chuckled. "I don't think she's happy with anyone this morning, especially herself. But don't worry; she'll come around once she comes to terms with it and forgives herself."

"How long do you think that will take?"

"Well, kiddo, I've found we are the hardest on ourselves, so it could be a while. Probably best to give her some space."

"I take it you're giving her some too?"

He cleared his throat. "She requested it."

"Uh-huh." I bet it was more like demanded it. "I hope you work things out soon."

"We always do. Your mom loves you, and so do I."

"I love you, Dad."

"I love you, honey." He gave me a big squeeze. "I hope you can forgive your old man."

"I'll think about it," I teased. The fact he acknowledged it meant more to me than he would ever know.

"Glad to hear it. I best get going. I have a new helper for the day I need to show the ropes to."

I leaned away from him. "Who?"

Dad gave me a crooked grin. "You might know him. Reece Cavanaugh."

My mouth fell open. "What?" Was this a joke?

Dad put his hat back on. "He was looking for you at the front gate. Said he wanted to help out for the day. Something about a ring and the barn and trying to make up for it."

Was Reece determined to get me fired? I wanted to kiss his face so bad. My heart was pitter-pattering. "You know who he is, right?"

"Yes." Dad grinned.

"What about Mom?" She wasn't going to like Reece helping out.

"This will be good for her." Dad kissed my forehead. "See you soon."

I watched him go, stunned. Reece Cavanaugh was indeed a pirate. He was pillaging and plundering my heart. I couldn't say I didn't like it.

Eighteen

"ARE YOU SURE ABOUT THIS?" I leaned against the barn door, making sure to keep a few feet between Reece and me. This was no easy feat, seeing as he was wearing faded jeans that fit all his assets and a tight T-shirt and boots. The sun's rays were kissing his olive skin, and his hair was tousled to perfection. Plus, he was here to help my family. A family that had humiliated him on some level, and chances were great they probably would again today. It all made me want to accost his pretty face with my lips.

It was so sad I couldn't even keep to my no-man rule for two weeks. Granted, I hadn't dated anyone since Trevor and I had broken up. I still wasn't going to be dating anyone, because Reece and I couldn't.

"I'm sure." He inched closer, making me back up against the door.

"I have to warn you: my mother," I whispered, in case she was sneaking around nearby, "is kind of having a mini crisis, and if you haven't figured it out yet, she's a wee bit cuckoo. And my brother doesn't exactly like you. Which reminds me, I need to thank you for sticking up for me in high school. I had no idea. Also, I'm sorry my brother humiliated you back in the day."

"Are you trying to get rid of me?" He swept the hair off my shoulder, making me hold my breath for fear of breathing him

146

in and doing something I would quite enjoy, but would later regret as I applied for unemployment benefits.

"No," I managed to respond. "It's just I need you to understand this isn't exactly friendly territory for you right now." Even for me. "My mom thinks we, you know, did some things in high school."

Reece flashed me a wicked grin. "Things spelled out in your story?"

"Uh-huh." I blushed.

He pressed a hand against the door above me, leaning in, making all my senses go haywire.

I placed a hand on his chest, which was fantastic, but not a great idea. "This isn't exactly friendly behavior."

"Does the school enumerate what constitutes friendly versus nonfriendly behavior?" he grumbled.

"Not exactly."

"Let me talk to Ken about this unwritten rule."

"Please don't. I have a feeling he's already questioning whether he should renew my contract next year. He shakes his head every time he sees me now, thanks to you."

"Thanks to me?" Reece pointed at his chest.

"Yes. I was perfectly sane at work until you walked in the door." In other areas of my life, not so much.

"Are you saying I drive you crazy?" He was more than delighted.

"Something like that," I stuttered, hardly able to breathe with him so close.

"I suppose it's only fair since you drive me crazy. In the best ways," he added.

I bit my lip.

Reece stared at it. "Did you know in some cultures a simple peck on the lips is considered a friendly greeting?"

"Is that so?" I smiled, longing to be kissed by him. Wondering if he tasted like pineapple and rum as I imagined. "Which cultures?"

147

"Colombia, Argentina, Peru, Chile, Spain, Italy, Greece," he rattled off, like he was Google or something.

"Sure." I didn't believe a word he said.

"It's true. Look it up," he dared me.

"We don't live in those countries." I did want to, though.

"I'm part Greek," he boasted.

Why didn't that surprise me? I pressed my fingers deeper against his chest in a feeble attempt to keep him at bay, all while mentally trying to justify kissing him. But I knew exactly what kissing led to. It wasn't friendly, I'll tell you that. "If ever we wind up in Greece together, you can kiss me hello."

"What are you doing for fall break?" He was quick on the draw.

"Helping out on the farm."

"That's too bad. I have some frequent flyer miles we could use."

I swallowed hard, not believing this man wanted to fly to Greece with me just so he could kiss me. "Reece, we hardly know each other. I don't think we should be traipsing across the world together yet."

"Yet?" His brow quirked.

"I'm Andi's teacher," I reminded him.

"And a fine one at that. But don't you feel this thing between us?" he whispered intimately, his breath brushing across my cheek.

Did I ever. From the first moment I laid eyes on him my freshman year in high school, I was drawn to him. "I do, but it's complicated. For the last fifteen years of my life, I've felt nothing but awkward whenever I see you." I had the bruises from diving to prove it. "I don't want to make things more awkward between us this school year by doing something now that in the moment seems like a fantastic idea but ends up being a mistake. I can't exactly hide from you, for Andi's sake. Besides, there's a good chance after you spend the day with my family, you're going to leave here running and screaming."

"Hmm." He took a slight step back. "The last thing I want to do is complicate your life or make things awkward between us. I hate that you've felt so uncomfortable around me in the past."

"That's my fault, not yours."

"No. I should have spoken to you in high school and told you how much I enjoyed the story."

"I'm glad you didn't."

"Why?"

"Because that story was meant to be private. You were never supposed to know my adolescent feelings for you." I was still embarrassed to admit them. "And we both know you would have never returned them."

"Josie, our age difference at the time made that impossible. I could have been arrested for dating a minor."

"I know, but that's not the only reason. You were beautiful, and I was praying one day I would morph from being the ugly duckling into the swan."

He ran a finger down my cheek. "You've never been ugly. And just for the record, I'm attracted to you for more than your looks."

"I still have a hard time believing you're attracted to me at all."

"That's a shame, but I'll make a believer out of you yet." He grinned.

"Can we just take it slow and friendly?"

"Yes," he reluctantly agreed. "Of course," he said more confidently. "I said we would, but every time I get near you, I'm . . ."

"Tempted," I finished for him, knowing exactly how he felt.

"Very," he said sexily.

I cleared my throat before I was tempted to pull him to me and pretend like we lived in Greece. "Like I said, you may be thanking your lucky stars you never got involved with me after today."

"Everyone has a crazy family."

"Not Peterson-brand crazy."

"Some even crazier," he said with meaning.

I wanted to ask him about his own, but I needed to attend to my pumpkin duties. "I better go. Thank you for helping today. You don't have to do that. It wasn't your fault the barn burned down or that I got engaged to a jerk."

"Well, I helped that jerk, and you're here."

It was one of the sweetest things anyone had ever said to me. I threw my arms around him before I thought twice about it.

Reece wasted no time wrapping me up. "I'm glad we're keeping the friendly hugs."

"Me too," I sighed, while sinking more into him. I wished I could stay there all day breathing him in and daydreaming about how it would feel to be more than friendly. I closed my eyes and imagined running my hands up his strong back and into his hair, which was begging to be more tousled. My imagination told me it was oh so yummy.

"Eight more months," he bemoaned.

"Yeah. But it's good," I half lied. "This way we can really get to know each other."

"You know, you can tell a lot about a person by kissing them."

"Oh, really?"

"It's scientifically proven you can tell if a person is worthy of a long-term relationship just by kissing them."

"I think I can prove that wrong. Every one of my long-term relationships has ended badly." Not that I'd had many of them. Yet, I had enjoyed kissing each one of those losers.

Reece ran a slow hand down my back, giving me shivers despite the warm sun blanketing me. "You haven't been properly kissed yet, then."

There was no doubt in my mind he would do a thorough job and more than likely ruin me for life. The question was, would he be the one to stay forever? I feared the answer, not knowing if there would ever be a man in my life who would stay true. "I suppose you subscribe to Sylvia Plath's way of thinking: 'Kiss me, and you will see how important I am.'"

"No. I was thinking more along the lines of, kiss me, and see how important you are."

Stick a fork in me. I was done. He completely undid me. I stilled against him, listening to the pounding of his heart.

"Josie," he spoke my name in reverent tones when I didn't respond.

"I need to go." Yet I clung to him. It reminded me of a scene from my story, after the uncle was defeated and the heroine was given the choice to return to her genteel life and live as a proper lady or stay with the rogue pirate and live a life she never expected. One filled with adventure and probably even some danger. She held fast to the man who had shown her how much she meant to him. Who had helped her find her voice and then given her a choice. She was free to choose her own destiny. She chose him.

I feared I was mixing my fantasy world with reality. Trevor had wooed me, once upon a time. I mean, he wasn't as good as Reece. He never said things like, "Kiss me, and see how important you are." Dang, was that good. Definitely a rogue pirate line. Except my fifteen-year-old brain wasn't eloquent enough to script out a line like that. I wasn't even sure I could now.

"If you must," he acquiesced.

I must.

Nineteen

"YOU HAVE GOT TO CHECK this out." Kitty motioned with her finger for me to step outside the pumpkin patch. I had finished the last story time and was cleaning up. I'd tried to be as pumpkiny as possible throughout the day, but I had been a bit distracted knowing Reece was out there alone with my family. I hadn't seen him at all, which made me worry he had either left running and screaming, thanking his lucky stars we never pursued a romantic relationship, or he was buried somewhere on the property. We had a lot of dirt and excavation equipment on the farm, and the sisters knew how to use it all. And as I hadn't seen the sisters all day either, this was a major concern for me.

I rushed to the door, fearing Reece's dead body had been discovered already. The sisters had probably felt guilty and called 911 on themselves.

Kitty grabbed my hand and pulled me through the last straggling guests, over to where the burned-down barn had once stood. There I found Jenna drooling. It didn't take a genius to see why.

Oh. My. I gripped Kitty to keep myself upright. Reece was not dead. Reece was a god—with a little *g*, but a god all the same. Until this moment, I'd never thought of a tractor as sexy, like all the country songs make them out to be, but that was before I saw Reece at the helm of one, his muscled arms glistening in the evening sun.

My dad stood far off in the distance, calling out instructions to Reece.

I couldn't believe my dad was teaching him how to drive a tractor. I would have to thank him later.

Jenna sidled up to me. "If you don't date him, I'm checking you into the psych ward for a mental evaluation."

"You know I can't."

"Can't schmant. Keep it secret if you have to. Seriously, look at the man."

I couldn't take my eyes off him. My custom-made green felt shoes were melting into the dirt along with my heart. A secret relationship was sounding quite yummy. But I'd tried to hide my feelings for him before and it hadn't worked out so well. And sadly, I kept thinking about how wonderful Trevor was in the beginning. Was I so naive to think this time it would be different? I so badly wanted to, but how could I trust myself? Or Reece?

Reece noticed me and waved. His big smile spoke of how happy he was.

I waved back, resisting the urge to run and take a ride with him. I could feel his arms around me as we shared the small seat. I knew it would be nothing like when I was a little girl and Dad would drive me around in the tractor, telling me stories of when he was a boy. No, it would be more like I would want to see how limber I truly was and flip around on that seat until I was sitting on his lap, facing him. His T-shirt was coming off, too. I shivered in the warm evening air. Dang my vivid imagination.

Kitty blew down her shirt. "Honey, take one for the team and make out with him, then report back. By the way, the sisters saw you two this morning in the barn getting all cozy."

"What?" Jenna spat. "You didn't tell me this. How cozy were you?"

Not cozy enough. I shouldn't think like that. "Shh," I begged. I knew the sisters were nearby. I could feel it, even though I couldn't see them. I should have known they would be spying on us in the barn earlier, but Reece had rendered all my senses helpless. "We only hugged."

"Sure." Kitty laughed. "That's not what I heard."

"What did you hear?" I was now panicking.

"According to Oliver, it was pretty handsy."

"Was he spying on me too?" I was disgusted by the thought.

"He better not have been." Kitty contorted her face.

"You still need to vote whether he's a douchebag or not," Jenna reminded her.

"You know I can't." Kitty shook her head.

"Sure you can. It could be fun," Jenna sang.

"It's all fun and games until you go home with the man," Kitty responded.

"Why did you marry him?" I couldn't help but ask, all while keeping an eye on Reece. He looked to be enjoying himself, riding around in circles, kicking up the dust around him. Man, would I like to get dirty with him right now. You know, like actually dirty, not *dirty* dirty. Well, maybe a tad *dirty.*

Kitty flashed both Jenna and me a look of annoyance. "Look, I know Oliver is not the warmest or most emotionally intelligent of men. But he believed in me when no one else did. When I told my family I wanted to be a lawyer, they all laughed in my face. Oliver wiped my tears and told me I could do it and that he would do everything in his power to make sure I reached my goal. And he did. We're still paying off my student loans, and he happily writes the checks for them every month. Not only that, he's a stellar dad," she put us in our places.

Jenna and I stood speechless for a moment. I admit to feeling a bit shameful. And a little proud of my douchey brother.

"Sorry, Kitty," I offered.

"Don't be. He is a douchebag on occasion. But he's my douchebag and I love him. Heaven help me," she prayed.

Jenna and I tried not to snigger.

"And," Kitty added, "I think he's starting to see what he did to you was pretty terrible."

"You mean, you're helping him to see that?" I guessed.

"Well, yes," she admitted. "But he's coming around."

I would believe it when I actually saw it, but for now, I only wanted to stare at Reece, who was headed our way wearing a wicked grin that went well with his chiseled jawline.

"That patch is a turn-on." Kitty patted her chest. "I should probably go find my husband and children," she said half-heartedly. She did not move an inch.

We all stood mesmerized, waiting for Reece who was driving the tractor like a pro. Almost like he was meant to. It was odd how easily I saw him fitting in here. Even Dad seemed to stand in awe of him. My dad, who had never let Trevor drive his tractor. I was sure Mom stood somewhere nearby scrutinizing him. Wondering what he was doing here and what evil plans he had for me. As far as I could tell, he only wanted to get to know me, all of me. Meaning, the pirate girl too. The girl I so desperately wanted to forget.

Reece pulled up and threw the tractor in neutral, pressing evenly on the brake and the clutch.

I can't tell you how impressed I was.

He dipped the straw cowboy hat he was wearing. I assumed my father had gifted it to him. "Ladies," he drawled loud enough so we could hear him over the roar of the old tractor. He did a great impression of a southern man. Libby would be so proud.

Jenna and Kitty tittered like schoolgirls.

I bit my lip, so desperately trying not to fall for him. I was pretty sure it was a hopeless cause. I fell for Reece fifteen years ago. I'm not sure I ever got over him. I had done a great job suppressing those feelings, but they had never died. That, I was sure of.

"Take a spin with me." Reece held out his hand.

I stared at it, not able to breathe. Taking a spin with him

would mean sitting on his lap. And if I sat on his lap, I would want to be more than friends. And if we were more than friends, I would have to come to terms with the pirate girl. And if I came to terms with her, I would probably write another torrid story full of carnal knowledge. And if I wrote another story, it would more than likely get shared. Then I would be exposed and fired.

Kitty and Jenna pushed me forward when I didn't move an inch.

"Please." Reece reached for me.

"Do it," Jenna demanded.

Kitty grabbed my hand and put it in Reece's. I was about to give her a dirty look, but the touch of Reece's hand on mine made me feel all warm and fuzzy. I'm pretty sure I sighed dreamily.

Reece didn't waste a second and pulled me up toward him in the open cab.

"This is going to be a tight squeeze," I stated the obvious.

"I'm looking forward to it." He wagged his brows.

"I really need to go find my husband." Kitty left red-faced, fanning herself.

"Have fun." Jenna waved, before walking off.

That left me and Reece to stare at each other.

"Don't be shy." Reece patted his lap.

I wasn't exactly shy; I was more worried I wouldn't be able to control myself. I had imagined us in some very sticky—and steamy—situations. Also, sitting on a man's lap is kind of intimate. I'd never sat on someone's lap unless we were dating. And never in front of my dad—and let's be real, my mom. Oh, I knew she was out there, grasping for Aunt D., just waiting for me to succumb to the temptation. Believe me, I was going to. I was just working up to it, to see if by some small miracle my rational side would kick in, reminding me that my job was on the line. Nope. My insides were chanting for me to get cozy with Reece, and it would be worth living on ramen noodles. I at least had the wherewithal to look around and make sure there were no guests left. When I was sure the coast was clear, I took off my beanie and ran my fingers through my hair, knowing the hat would obstruct his view.

"Dang." Reece whistled.

"What?"

"You doing that with the evening sunlight behind you is a vision." He blinked in awe.

I wanted to believe him, but my nerves got the better of me. "I'm sure it's so attractive with me in my pumpkin costume."

"It is." He tugged on my costume. "Now let's get out of here. I have to pick up Andi soon, and I want to show off my new skills."

"All right." I carefully turned around, maneuvering myself between him and the steering wheel, my pulse rising—knowing soon I would be up close and more than personal with Reece. I knew I was crossing the friendly line.

Reece wasn't messing around; as he wrapped his arms around my middle, I let out a tiny squeal while landing squarely in his lap. He was warm and comfortable. He smelled of spring rain and dirt, mixed with a hint of gasoline fumes. It worked for him. Or was that me?

Reece tightened his arms around me and whispered in my ear, "Much better."

"You are incorrigible."

He chuckled in my ear, making me shiver while I settled against him like my favorite comfy chair. I resisted the urge to curl into him.

"Hold on." Reece grabbed the steering wheel with one hand and the stick shift with the other. It was a tight squeeze, but that made it all the more fun.

I realized it had been a long time since I'd had fun with a man. After Trevor and I got engaged last year, fun went out the window. It all became about his image. We fought constantly over his expensive image, which was out of my price range. I took out a loan to keep the peace. How sick and wrong was that?

I was so desperate to shed the pirate girl, I was willing to do anything. I didn't want to be that woman. But how did I own the girl I'd tried to forget and come to terms with her?

Reece commanded the tractor with ease, as we headed toward the back pumpkin field.

Dad stood off in the distance, watching us go. As far as I could tell, he was smiling. It wasn't as awkward as I thought it would be to have my dad see me up close and personal with Reece. I swore I could hear my mother gasping and clutching her chest. Was it evil of me to silently tee-hee about it?

Reece took the well-worn path out to the patch, slow and steady, kicking up very little dust. The sun was just starting to set, turning the sky pink and orange. A gentle evening breeze kissed my cheeks. In a word, it was perfect.

Reece didn't say anything, but his warm, minty breath played across my skin. I could feel how much he wished to give me a taste. I knew if I took one, I would devour him. Then where would we be? I tried not to think about it as we made our way to what I considered a little piece of heaven. There was something so magical about a field dotted with orange among green and browning vines, knowing that each pumpkin would end up in the arms of a child so excited to take it home and make it into their very own creation.

We stopped just on the outskirts of the expansive field. Reece parked and killed the engine. For a moment we soaked in the silence and the waning sun's rays. I found myself leaning back against Reece. He held on tight, his chin resting on my head.

"I picked the prettiest pumpkin in this patch."

I relished his words and touch. Why did it feel so familiar to me? "You're all sorts of trouble, you know that, right?"

"I'm just being friendly." I think he might have kissed my head, but I couldn't be sure.

"Very," I laughed.

"Thanks for today," his tone turned more serious.

"I didn't do anything. Honestly, I should be thanking you, though I'm not sure what you did all day. What did you do?"

"I spent the day with your dad, learning the ropes of farm life and helping people load pumpkins into their cars. Your dad is great," he said, wistfully.

"He is."

"You're lucky. He loves you. He wants you to know that."

"I do."

Reece held me tighter.

"Are you okay?" There was something in the way he was holding me that spoke to some need inside of him.

"You asked me last night how I lost my eye."

I squirmed a bit. "I know. It was rude of me."

"No. Not at all. It's just hard for me to talk about."

I entangled my arms with his, taking his hands into my own. I reveled in the feel of his muscular arms and heated skin. "If you want to talk about it, I'll listen."

He squeezed my hands. "Thank you, Josie. Days like today remind me of what I lost, but they are the greatest reminders that I get to wake up every day and choose to be the best father I can be for Andi." He spoke her name with such tenderness.

"Can I ask where your father is?"

"I don't know." He didn't sound angry—worse, he was heartbroken by it.

"I'm so sorry." I couldn't imagine not having Dad in my life.

Reece's stubble tickled my cheeks as he leaned in against me. "I haven't seen him since the day I lost my eye."

I held in my gasp, only stilling in his arms, waiting patiently for him to tell me his story. I closed my eyes as our breaths fell into sync. I'd never felt so at one with anyone so fast. Maybe ever. The thought both delighted and frightened me.

"My mom was at work," he said in hushed tones. "Dad had been fired again. He was a brilliant engineer, but he couldn't handle the pressures of life. He often drank and missed work. He promised me this time would be different. He was going to find

159

a good job and buy the video game system I had been begging for."

I gripped him tighter, feeling as if he needed it.

"I wanted to believe him. I think I did," he choked out. "So, when he told me to get in the car to run to the store, I ignored the beer on his breath."

I held my breath, guessing what was going to come next and aching for Reece.

"It happened so fast," Reece whispered. "I don't even remember the accident. All I know is I woke up in a hospital bed, my mother weeping by my side."

"Oh, Reece."

"She had to tell her son his eye was gone and so was his father. The coward couldn't live with what he had done to me, so he just left."

"No." I didn't want it to be true for him.

"For a long time, I was in denial. I knew he would come back, but all I got were a couple of phone calls with more empty promises. Meanwhile, my mom took on two jobs to keep a roof over our heads and pay for all my medical bills. Somehow, she managed to always help me with my homework and tuck me in at night." Such pride filled him.

"She sounds like a good mom."

"She's the best. Even now she's still taking care of me, helping me raise Andi."

"Andi's a lucky kid."

"I hope so. I don't want to screw her up. I hate that I didn't fight harder to get full custody of her from the start. To think of what she witnessed kills me. Especially given my own past."

"She'll be okay because, like you, she has a parent willing to fight for her."

"Thank you for saying that, Josie." He kissed my cheek. This time there was no doubt. His lips set fire to my skin. Oh. That was not so friendly. But he made no apologies nor drew any attention to it. I assumed he did so, hoping I wouldn't challenge him. I couldn't bring myself to oppose to the simple act. It would be a lie if I told him I didn't wish for such tender affection from him.

"Josie." He paused. "For a long time, I wanted to be someone else. I didn't want to be different. But my mother made me see there is strength in being different in a world where we crave to blend in. My mom used to say, "Why would you want to be thrown into the blender in order to mix in with the masses, only to get cut by the blades?"

Wow. That was a profound thought.

"For years, I let others cut me with their words and insults, but I realized it was because they so badly wanted to be in the mix. When I finally learned it was okay not to be, it changed my life. From then on, I didn't give a damn about what anyone thought of me."

I clung to him tighter, wishing so badly to be brave enough to jump out of the blender. "Are you trying to give me advice?"

"I'm just asking for a chance."

"Reece." I closed my eyes and breathed him in.

"I know, you're Andi's teacher and I'm the rogue pirate," he said, as if he were proud of the moniker. "But you can't tell me you don't feel this thing between us."

I felt it with every fiber of my being. "I feel it, but I just can't believe it."

He threw off his cowboy hat before leaning in, his lips skimming my neck. "Believe it," he whispered against my skin.

I swallowed hard, reaching out to grip the steering wheel. I needed to be steadied as my heart relentlessly pounded. A line was about to be crossed. One we couldn't come back from.

His lips brushed my neck. "Tell me to stop and I will."

It was the last thing I wanted. I leaned my head back, giving him more access to my neck, crossing that line.

He groaned and took advantage of the room I gave him to work his magic. And oh, was he good. He started low, blowing his hot breath across my skin, inducing shivers and goose bumps. Next, his warm lips pressed gentle, slow, and steady kisses up my neck. He took his time, which drove me so wild, I dug my fingers into his thighs. When I thought it couldn't get any more sensual, his tongue worked its magic against my skin, leaving a trail of heat, only for him to blow gently across his handiwork. Oh, mother of pumpkin, the shivers it produced made me gasp.

He must have watched a lot of HBO, and probably SHOWTIME.

He blissfully worked his way up to my ear, where he nibbled on my lobe before whispering, "Get ready to see how important you are."

"Show me." I got all sorts of limber and adjusted myself, with Reece's help, until I was on his lap, facing him. My hands immediately found their way into his tousled hair, matted down from wearing a cowboy hat all day. It was just as luxurious as I had imagined.

Reece employed his own hands to cup my face and caress my cheeks. "You are so beautiful."

His words infused my soul.

He drew my face closer to his until our breaths became as one. His lips teased my own until they gently landed upon mine. He took his time getting acquainted with my lips, brushing and tugging on them, even gliding his tongue across them as if he wanted to intimately know every part of me. He tasted like teen fantasies and mint.

When he knew every part of my lips, he moved on to my mouth, where his tongue subtly explored and twisted with my own in a sensuous dance where he carefully led me to an ecstasy I had only dreamed about. His hands moved down my back, drawing me closer to him, making the kiss deeper and more heated. I twisted my fingers in his hair, trembling under his touch. In that moment he owned me, yet I didn't feel as if he wanted to possess me. I felt wanted, and as if this meant the world to him. I was important to him—as implausible as it seemed, I knew it was true. Never had a kiss conveyed so much.

I came to the realization I never wanted to taste anything but him for the rest of my life. It was almost as if he knew he had accomplished his mission. He slowed the kiss, letting us both take a breath. When his lips glided off mine, I rested my forehead against his, deeply inhaling and exhaling, knowing my life would never be the same from that moment on.

"Things just got complicated." I didn't regret it, but there was no denying it.

"I'm good at complicated." He kissed my nose. "We'll make this work."

"I don't want to lose my job." But I didn't want to lose whatever this was either. I wasn't sure I could explain what just happened. Magical didn't seem to cover it. It was something more. It was like a homecoming to a place I had dreamed about, but thought I would never see in reality.

"You won't. We'll be discreet," he promised.

"Not even Andi can know. We can't expect her to keep such a secret." I wasn't even sure how we were going to.

"I would never place that burden on her."

"This is crazy, Reece." I couldn't believe this was happening. It was as if at any moment I would wake up and someone would tell me I was late for school or something.

He ran a hand down my hair. "No. This is right."

He wasn't wrong.

Twenty

JENNA COULD NOT STOP SNICKERING as we counted the money from the donation jar in the front office. Really the only office the farm had. The small orange building not only acted as the ticket booth but it's where we conducted the business side of things. Tonight, it served as a hideaway for Jenna and me as we took care of counting not only the donation money but the end-of-day receipts and transactions.

"I still can't believe you made out with him." She reached for a wad of crumpled cash in the jar.

I brushed my lips with my fingertips, still not believing it either. "I know." I could hardly form words. Reality was setting in a little. I wasn't normally a rule breaker, but with one glorious act I had jeopardized a job I loved and needed. Was it worth it? Absolutely. If I were still writing torrid stories, I would have a lot of new working material. But it still scared me.

"Was it as good as you imagined?" She wanted all the juicy details.

All I could do was nod for how good it was. So good we went a few rounds. Did I find out that he had washboard abs and a smooth, carved chest? Yes, I did. I wasn't normally so handsy, especially with someone I had never been on a real date with, but I knew him. I know that sounds so cheesy and cliché, but it was the truth.

"So good, you're speechless?"

I nodded again.

"Hurry and snap out of it. I need all the deets. Starting with: Is he your boyfriend now?"

I blinked a few times, trying to make my brain function properly, but all it wanted to do was relive Reece. "Um . . . no. We didn't talk titles. Actually, we didn't talk a whole lot." And what we did talk about, I didn't think I should share. I was honored Reece felt like he could open up to me about his father. What a heartbreaking story. And here I'd thought Reece had lived some charmed life. No, he had his own demons. But he had learned to slay his. I really needed a sharper figurative sword. Or perhaps I should learn how to climb out of the blender. Seriously, that was an amazing analogy. It made me want to get to know Molly even more.

Jenna rubbed her hands together. "You had a noncommittal make out. I am so proud of you."

"I wouldn't exactly say *noncommittal*." But now that I thought about it, maybe it was. It was a little early to define the relationship, and seeing as I technically wasn't supposed to be having one with him, maybe it was best to be noncommitted. Except if he was going around kissing other women like he kissed me this evening, I would have a big problem with that. As in an I-would-never-want-to-see-him-again kind of problem.

"So, what are you?"

"I don't know, Jen." I grabbed a wad of cash, feeling a tad unsettled. Had I just endangered my career for an hour of unadulterated bliss? I didn't think Reece was that kind of guy. I mean, he'd said he would call me later that night after he put Andi to bed and he would work out how we could see each other this week. And it wasn't like I was asking for a commitment. But since I was putting my job on the line, I should probably get some type of verbal agreement, other than that we'd be discreet. Honestly, I started hyperventilating a bit thinking about what I had just done. Sure, I would do it again in a nanosecond, but I was supposed to be on a permanent man hiatus. I mean, I joined the Ex-Filers for crying out loud and was helping with the Halloween Bash. That was commitment.

Jenna reached for me. "Breathe." She inhaled and exhaled slowly with me. "You're okay. This is good. Reece is good."

"How do you know?"

"Uh, hello, he helped the brothers all day long while the sisters, I'm told, spied on him. Our dads actually had to stop them from following you out into the field with him. My mother already had the other tractor fired up."

I did a major facepalm. "I wish I could say I didn't believe it, but that would be a lie. They can't be happy with the brothers."

"Oh no." Jenna laughed. "But it was hilarious to see my dad chase my mom on foot while she made a beeline for your mom. I have to say, I'm impressed with my dad. He jumped up on the tractor and wrangled her like a real cowboy. I captured it all on my phone for our viewing pleasure."

I would be checking that out later. "It's like the insane asylum over here. What did they think Reece and I were going to do?"

Jenna dipped her chin. "Uh, exactly what you did."

My cheeks pinked, while I cleared my throat. Boy, would they have gotten a show. I would have to find a way to thank the brothers later. I could never tell them what took place on the tractor, but what they didn't know wouldn't hurt them. Especially my dad. I was sure he hadn't taught Reece how to drive a tractor so he could take his baby girl out for a spin and show her what it meant to be properly kissed. Holy shiz, I don't know if Reece just had a lot of experience or if he watched some YouTube videos or something, but the man could kiss. My skin was still on fire.

"Yikes. I would have for sure been grounded." I grinned.

"A lot of carnal knowledge going on out there?"

"Maybe," I sang.

"Anyway, word out on the patch is the sisters are having a

crisis of faith. They can't find anything wrong with your boy Reece, and it's driving them nuts. Also, your mom is taken with that little Andi. Throw in the words of wisdom you spouted at your mom. They are having a hard time fathoming they were ever wrong."

I was taken with Andi, too. "That's what my dad said. He also said we should stay clear of them."

"That's solid advice."

"We better get to counting. My alarm is going to go off way too early tomorrow. Happy pumpkin season."

"I'm already tired." Jenna began stacking the bills.

I smiled for how kindhearted people had been, especially Reece. I wondered what my mom would think of him if she knew how generous he had been.

While we got into our groove counting, my phone buzzed. I picked it up to see a new text.

Reece: *Hey, when I left you looked a little dazed. I know we're moving faster than either one of us is used to, but I'm not doubting anything. I hope you aren't either. You amaze me, Josie Peterson. Talk to you soon.*

I smiled to myself, my doubts subsiding.

"This is weird." Jenna held up a fifty-dollar bill.

I gave her my attention, even though I was itching to text Reece. He had no idea what his words meant to me. "What's up?"

"There's a note on this bill. It looks like it's from someone's grandparents."

"I wonder why someone would donate that?"

"Maybe they didn't mean to."

"That would be so sad. Or maybe it belongs to some hot rich guy who was kidnapped. Of course, the kidnappers would be named Olivia and Oliver." I gave Jenna a knowing grin. Growing up we always made-up stories and all the bad guys were named after our siblings.

Jenna cackled and I ran rampant with some ridiculous story about extortion and the two bumbling idiots for kidnappers.

"Or it could just be some fifty-dollar bill with writing on it." I ended my masterpiece of a story very undramatically.

"How boring," she stared down at the money.

"Maybe you should do some investigating. See if it belongs to someone," I suggested.

"How would I go about doing that?"

"I don't know. You have some decent stalker skills," I teased her. "Or there's always the internet." I pointed to her phone on the desk.

"I suppose it wouldn't hurt to do a little digging."

"Maybe the kidnapped hot guy will be the man of your dreams." I wagged my brows.

"I won't hold my breath," she responded, but there was a look in her eye that said, *I must solve this mystery.*

I would leave her to solve it. I had a mystery of my own. His name was Reece Cavanaugh, and I had every intention of discovering everything about him.

"Hello," his smooth voice seduced me on the other end of the line.

I was snuggled up on my couch, with *Practical Magic* playing in the background. I'd been waiting for his call, even though I was exhausted from the long day.

"Hi. How's Andi?"

"Sleeping now. She had a good day with her grandparents, but as always, she wonders where her mother is. It's hard for her to understand what rehab is and why Nicolette has to be there, even though I know part of her fears seeing her mother again."

My heart broke for her. "I can't even imagine. That must be hard on you, too."

"Yeah." He sounded exhausted.

"You sound tired. We can talk later if you want."

"This is what I want. You're what I want, if I didn't make that abundantly clear earlier."

I curled into myself, overwhelmed, but thrilled. "I kind of got those vibes," I teased.

"I'll see what I can do to vanquish any lingering doubts you may have."

"And how will you accomplish that?" I said, in my best flirty voice.

"You'll see," he responded seductively. "But there will definitely be more of today in your near future."

That was excellent news.

"I learned a lot about you today during our time in the pumpkin field," he stated.

"You did?"

"I told you it's scientifically proven that you can learn a lot about a person from kissing. For instance, my observation that you are a passionate person was more than validated today."

My cheeks pinked. "I blame you." I still couldn't believe I had lifted his shirt right off him. I needed to see if I was right about his chest. It wasn't my finest moment, but I longed to be close to him. To rest my head against his bare chest and listen to the sound of his strong heart, beating for me. It was beautiful.

"I'll happily take the credit for that."

"I'm not usually so exuberant," I defended myself. I blamed the way he could use his tongue and blow across my skin. It was enough to drive anyone wild.

"I hope you're not embarrassed or regretting anything we did."

"I don't regret anything. I just surprised myself today. I was not expecting this—or you."

"I wasn't either, but your kiss told me something else."

"What's that?"

"That you will be an excellent long-term partner."

I bit my lip, hardly knowing what to say; you know, besides, *"Yes, yes!"* But, I showed some decorum and kept that to myself. Because it was crazy. Crazy that it felt right.

"Did I scare you there?"

"I am scared," I admitted. "I'm not used to my dreams coming true. And I just found out that my ex-fiancé was cheating on me and I had no idea. Worse, I realize now, I wanted to marry him because I thought he would rid me of the pirate girl. Now I'm with the pirate . . . I mean you. I don't mean any disrespect by saying that."

"Josie, I'm not offended in the least bit. I would be your pirate any day, if that's what you want. What do you want?"

I wasn't sure any man had ever asked me that before. At least not in the way Reece was asking me now. That should have said something to me. "I want to quit being afraid of myself. I don't want to have to worry about what people are going to say when they see us together."

"You know what they're going to say. They're going to think I'm the luckiest guy in the world."

"They're going to say the pirate girl and the pirate are together," I disagreed. You know, in eight months when I wouldn't lose my job over it.

"You know what I say to that? Hell, yeah. I would be down with that girl any day. You know why?"

"Why?" I half whimpered.

"Because a part of you *is* that girl. And I want to get to know all the parts of you. Let's start with, what is the most embarrassing song on your playlist?"

His abrupt change of subject threw me for a loop. I sat up, thrown off guard. He didn't even let me digest all the beautiful words he'd just said.

"I'm waiting." He began whistling the *Jeopardy!* theme song.

He had me smiling. "So, don't laugh, but probably 'Glamorous' by Fergie."

"That's not super embarrassing."

"What if I told you it's the Ludacris version?"

He chuckled. "Okay, that's embarrassing."

It really was, but don't think I wouldn't rock out to it the next time it played. I would proudly be spelling out *G-L-A-M-O-R-O-U-S* with Fergie. "Well, what about you?"

"First, you have to tell me how serious you are about me before I share. This is top-secret stuff here."

"Hey, you didn't tell me how serious you are before I shared," I fake grumbled. He was too charming for me to really grumble.

"That's because I know I'm more than serious about you."

I kicked my feet up in the air like a schoolgirl, grateful he couldn't see me. "I would think you'd understand my feelings by how I kissed you."

"That is serious," he said, low and sexy. "Then I can tell you, I own a ridiculous amount of Bee Gees songs."

I chortled uncontrollably. "Oh, wow. I don't think you should ever tell anyone that."

"You are the only person I've ever told."

Why did that make me feel so special? Perhaps disturbed on his behalf, but nonetheless honored. "I'll take it to the grave."

"Next question: UFOs, yes or no?"

"Ooh. Tough one. I don't know that we can discount alien life. I mean, are we so egotistical to think Earth is it?"

"I like that answer. I will agree with you. Okay. Best movie of all time?"

"Easy. *Roman Holiday.*"

"A classic. I like it. But you're wrong." He laughed.

"Excuse me? Enlighten me."

"Hands down, it's *The Godfather.*"

"That is such a guy answer."

"Well, I am a guy."

"I noticed." I was getting warm for how much I noticed him.

"I notice you too. I've noticed you for a while."

"You have?"

"I'm better at hiding behind things than you. Don't get embarrassed," he added quickly. "Because I'm not. I only wished I had talked to you sooner."

171

I couldn't believe he'd been checking me out.

"I confess to taking on your ex's case so that I could see you," he mumbled.

"What?"

"Please don't be mad. It was before I knew a spot would open at the school for Andi. I wanted to see you up close and personal to figure out this pull you've had on me ever since my divorce."

"I don't know if I should be flattered or angry."

"Let's go with flattered. With our history and your obvious attempts to avoid me, I didn't know how to approach you."

"So, you thought that was the best way?"

"I admit it wasn't my most brilliant move, but the day you walked into the office, I knew I didn't want to hide from you anymore."

Oh, he was good. Real good. "I don't want to hide anymore from you either." Or from myself.

"Will you forgive me?"

"You could have let me win," I complained.

"That wouldn't have been honest. But I did try to do what I could for you after I found out why he ended the engagement. Besides, you know I have to uphold truth, justice, and the American way."

"You are maddening."

"We have established that fact. Does this mean you will forgive me?"

"I'll think about it." I smiled.

"While you're contemplating that, I've come up with some ways we can see each other this week."

"I'm all ears."

"First, as Your Royal Highness, we should get together so you can see the booth I'm working on. I was thinking late at night after Andi goes to bed."

"I like that plan." I would do the same if he were any other room-parent coordinator. Maybe not so late at night, but it was plausible.

"You're going to love this one, then. I've joined the Ex-Filers, and guess who's on the decorating committee with you?"

"Are you serious? How did you work that out?"

"I talked to Noah, and he suggested it. He knows all about how to jump through hoops. Did you know that he used Cami's cropping services just so he could be around her?"

I didn't know that. That was cute. No wonder Cami had no choice but to fall for him after she'd sworn off men for good. I could feel her pain, but that wasn't the most important thing here. I was in a bit of a panic. "You told Noah about us?"

"Don't worry. We can trust him and Cami. In fact, they're happy to help us."

That didn't make me feel any better. "I am worried. I love my job."

"I know. I won't let anyone take that away from you, especially me. Besides, it would be against the law. It's not stated in your contract, and you didn't sign anything." He went all lawyer on me, which I kind of dug.

"Try telling that to your friend Ken."

"If had I to, I would," he said matter-of-factly.

"Please, let's not have to. I don't want to tempt fate."

"Will you settle for tempting me?" he sneakily, but sexily, switched gears.

Oh, baby, yes. I mean, "I'll see what I can do." I played coy.

"I look forward to it. I should probably let you get some sleep."

"Probably."

"Good night, Josie. Sweet dreams."

"Good night, Reece. Thank you for making my awake better than any dream I've ever had."

Twenty-One

I WALKED INTO THE TEACHERS' break room Monday morning, trying to act as nonchalantly as possible. Like I hadn't had a tryst with one of my student's dads. It wasn't as easy as I thought it would be. I felt like Hester Prynne from *The Scarlet Letter*, but instead of wearing a scarlet *A* exposing my supposed crime, I was wearing a big fat grin—that I couldn't for the life of me get rid of. My body was just so dang happy, which was kind of unusual, especially as of late. In general, I would consider myself a pleasant person to be around, but I was never giddy. And I'd come back from summer break a little jaded about life, considering my fiancé had called off our engagement and was suing me to get the ring back.

C'est la vie. I wished Trevor and emoji girl all the best. Okay, maybe I wasn't that giddy. I secretly hoped they crashed and burned, but I wasn't going to dwell on them. They deserved each other. And I got the better end of the deal. Trevor was of the "kiss me and see how important I am" crowd. He never made me feel the way Reece did.

"Good morning," I sang cheerfully when I walked in, not even needing any caffeine, though I'd hardly slept for thinking about Reece.

A few of my coworkers looked up from their coffees with faces that said, *It's Monday and too early for your chipper*

174

attitude. I totally got it, but none of them had made out with Reece over the weekend. It was enough to turn the crankiest person into a ray of sunshine.

Aline swished her way over to me and placed her hand on my forehead. "Are you feeling okay?"

"Right as rain," I couldn't help but say. I sucked at the nonchalant thing.

She tilted her head. "Wasn't it opening weekend?"

"It sure was." I headed toward the refrigerator to place my lunch inside.

Aline followed. "But aren't you exhausted?"

I opened the fridge and tossed my paper bag in, before turning around and grinning. "Nope."

She narrowed her eyes. "Okay. What's going on? Have you finally cracked?"

"I just had a great weekend." I laughed.

"Did you run over Trevor?" she guessed.

"No." Though that did sound kind of fun. "Like I said, it was a great opening weekend. The weather was beautiful." The kissing was fantastic, but no one needed to know that, except Jenna.

Aline pursed her perfectly pouty lips together. "Uh. If you say so."

"I do. How was your weekend?"

"Apparently, not as good as yours. It was mostly driving kids around and attending a million soccer games."

"How did they do?" I flitted toward the door covered in posters advertising the fall carnival. This year's theme was The Most Magical Time of Year. How apropos.

Aline didn't get a chance to answer because Marilyn, the PTA president, walked in looking like she'd just come from the salon, her wavy golden hair shimmering in the fluorescent lights. Normally, I would hustle right past the woman. She wasn't what I would call your typical wonderful PTA president, whom all the teachers worshipped. Marilyn was, let's say, special. She had five

175

children in the school, with three different dads. I'm not judging her choices, but it was apparent she married for money and moved on a lot. And there was a rumor going around that she became the PTA president using some sketchy tactics. Not sure why anyone would want to scheme their way into that position. There wasn't a lot of glory that came with it. Sure, the undying thanks of overworked teachers, but that was the only perk. Well, and we usually chipped in for a nice gift card at the end of the year.

"Josie, you are just the person I came to see," Marilyn said, in her hoity-toity I-go-to-the-spa-at-least-once-a-week voice.

"Godspeed," Aline whispered, before she hustled off. She had a major aversion to Marilyn. She taught her daughter last year, and she gave the Wittmore twins a run for their money. At least the Wittmores knew their boys were difficult. Marilyn thought her children could do no wrong. In fact, all the other teachers in the room rushed off, some of them leaving their coffee behind.

But not even Marilyn was going to ruin my mood. Reece was the best happy pill around. "What can I help you with?"

"You never sent me your room-parent coordinator's info. You did find one, didn't you?" she scolded. "You know how important it is for us to have at least one parent from every class for the PTA to run efficiently."

Okay, so maybe Marilyn was going to dampen my mood a bit. I didn't appreciate her condescending tone. It wasn't like I could magically make parents volunteer. Now that I thought about it, they probably didn't want to work with her. Poor Reece. "It took a while, but finally a parent volunteered last week. I'll email you his information."

"His?" she sounded too excited at the prospect.

Oh shiz. I forgot she was going through another divorce. "Um . . ." I hesitated to elaborate.

"Who is it?" She tapped her stiletto heels. Who needed to wear stilettos on a Monday morning, to a school no less?

"Reece Cavanaugh," I mumbled.

Her big brown eyes, full of fake eyelashes, widened in a scheming manner. Totally killing my mood. "Attorney Reece Cavanaugh, the most eligible bachelor in town?"

Is that what he was considered? How did I miss that one? "He's an attorney," I groaned.

She rubbed her hands together. "This is excellent news."

I grabbed my stomach, not at all liking her insinuations. I wanted to tell her that Reece was taken and didn't like to date older women. She had a good six to ten years on him. However, she was in excellent shape and obviously had a penchant for getting her man, based on the number of marriages she'd had. I was beginning to realize just what dating Reece meant. He was still the most popular boy in school.

Well . . . that boy wanted me. I stood tall. "I'll send you an email when I get a chance." Like never.

"Hurry, hurry." She pointed to the poster on the door. "The fall carnival is upon us, and your class is in charge of the photo booth. It's one of the most important booths."

"I am well aware. Mr. Cavanaugh"—I thought it best to be formal, for fear of saying his first name with too much affection—"has already secured a photographer and is working on building a booth."

"Is he handy . . . you know, with tools?"

I was sure that's what she meant. Insert eye roll. And yeah, he was handy. I had to stop from shivering just thinking about how handy his hands were. "I'm not sure about his power tool skills, but I do know he has limited time." All his extra time was going to be spent sneaking around with me, thank you very much.

What was it about sneaking around that made me so excited? Maybe it was the fact that I would get to keep Reece all to myself for a while. Or perhaps I just wanted to be sneaky for once. I only prayed I could get away with it.

"Well, we will just see how much time he has." She wasn't going to be deterred. At least that's what she thought.

"Good luck." I flashed her a snarky smile. I walked off and out the door, while pulling my phone out of my pocket. I got all warm and fuzzy reading Reece's flirty good-morning text. He may have mentioned some of his dreams from last night. They were along the lines of my torrid story, so I couldn't dwell on them too much. Wisely, I'd changed his name to *Superman* in my contacts, just in case anyone ever caught a glimpse of the screen.

Me: *Be on the lookout for an email from Marilyn Rogers. She's the PTA president. She's also a man-eater, and she's on the prowl for fresh new meat. She says you're the most eligible bachelor in town. How did I miss that memo? P.S. She wants to know if you're good with power tools.*

Superman: *Thanks for the heads-up. By the way, I am no longer eligible. Some gorgeous creature has captivated me and I'm at her mercy.*

P.S. Meet me at my place tonight at nine and I'll show you just how good I am with power tools.

Holy pumpkins.

Me: *It's a date.*

"Ms. Peterson," Mr. Nelson's deep voice reverberated down the hall.

Crap. I fumbled my phone, barely managing to prevent it dropping to the tile floor. I quickly turned it off and shoved it in my pocket before turning around to face my principal, praying he couldn't read the guilt flooding my face.

"Mr. Nelson," I stammered. Dang it. I was supposed to be acting nonchalant.

Mr. Nelson's face pinched. It was a common occurrence ever since that meeting with Reece. "Can I speak to you in my office?" he grumbled.

My heart stopped. He knew about Reece and me. I just knew it. I swallowed hard. "Sure," I eeked out, trying to think of any excuse I could for accosting Reece the day before. The only defense I could think of was: Look at the man. Who wouldn't accost him, given the chance? Pretty sure that wasn't going to fly. Unemployment, here I come.

Mr. Nelson darted back down the hall and turned, disappearing from my sight as I trudged slowly behind him, kissing my job goodbye and imagining the conversation with my mother over why I needed to move back home. The sisters were going to have a field day with this. It would be one big *"I told you so."* They would still be wrong. I mean, I was a most willing participant in all the carnal activities of the previous day. But they would never see it that way. Reece would be the pirate, once again.

With my heart in my throat, I rounded the corner and headed toward Mr. Nelson. His arms were folded as he waited impatiently for me by his door. He was likely anxious to fire me.

I hung my head in shame, walking past him to meet my doom. Maybe I could beg him not to put this on my record and let me go quietly so I could get hired somewhere else. Sadly, public schools paid less than private ones.

He didn't utter a word as I took a seat in one of the chairs I had moved earlier. I noticed Mr. Nelson hadn't placed them back in their original locations. Why that gave me an inkling of hope, I had no idea. I'd broken a huge school rule. I looked at the empty seat next to me, thinking it had only been a week since Reece had sat there. How did I go from loathing him to making out with him in a week's time? I wasn't sure if I should be proud of that or kicking myself. What I did know was, I never truly loathed him. From the moment I laid eyes on Reece fifteen years ago, I was smitten with him. I just hoped he was worth losing my job over.

Mr. Nelson took a seat behind his pristine desk and looked down his nose at me.

I braced myself for the worst.

"I wanted to . . ."

Fire me. I know. I squinted, waiting for the blow.

". . . see how things are going with Andi?"

My eyes popped open wide. Did I hear that right? I wasn't fired . . . yet. I sat a little taller. "Great," I breathed out, relieved. So, so relieved. "She has some work to do to catch up with the rest of the class, but I have no doubt she will. She's very bright, and I think as the year progresses, she'll find her footing."

"I'm glad to hear that. I've known Reece since our days at UNLV. He was a couple of years behind me, but we were roommates for a year. Best guy I know. He's been through a lot lately, so I want to make sure his daughter is doing well."

"I will do my best to make sure she's happy and adjusting well, academically as well as emotionally and socially. In fact, she helped me during story time this weekend at my parents' farm." I thought it best to be forthright about what I could. It's not like I could hide that, anyway.

Mr. Nelson nodded. "That's excellent. I'm glad to hear it. I assured Reece you were the right teacher for the job."

"I appreciate your vote of confidence." And for not firing me.

"Hmm," he harrumphed, as if remembering my crazy act in here last week. "I'm glad to see you got over your initial reluctance. I didn't realize you knew each other previously. Is there some issue I should be aware of?"

He hadn't heard of *Reece the Rogue Pirate*? That was a miracle. I thought everyone in this town knew of it.

"Um . . . no. No issues with him whatsoever." You know, other than that we're breaking the rules together.

"I hear he volunteered to be the room-parent coordinator." Mr. Nelson actually grinned. "Like I said, he's a great guy. In our college days he was always volunteering for something or other and making me go too. I met my wife at a voter registration drive he dragged me to."

"Really?" I sounded too enamored with Reece, but I couldn't help it. That was cute.

"Yes." Mr. Nelson cleared his throat, as if to remind himself not to get too personal. It was a shame. I wished he would be more personal. I found it was easier to work for people who didn't put up barriers, but I got it. I had my own. I was just grateful he wasn't firing me.

Mr. Nelson stood. "I'm sure you want to get to your classroom."

I jumped up, knowing I was being dismissed. "Yes. I have lots to do."

"Glad to hear it. Keep up the good work."

That was the plan. *Please don't let me lose my job.*

Twenty-Two

"I THOUGHT NINE O'CLOCK WOULD never get here." Reece grabbed my jacket and pulled me into his house.

I knew the feeling. I'd been counting down the seconds. So much so, I didn't even go home to change after helping on the farm and doing some kickboxing up in the barn loft. I figured this way it would raise the least suspicions among my family. Not to say they weren't already suspicious. Mom had finally said a few words to me. What were those words? "How was the tractor ride?" Uh, amazing. I did not say that. I went with a bland, "Nice." How nice, she would never know. She walked off after that, surely to confer with Aunt D.

Reece shut the door, before brushing my lips with his ready and waiting ones. "How was your day?"

"Long, but good." I snuggled into his chest, feeling right at home. "How was your day?"

"Same." He rested his chin on my head.

"Sorry, I'm a hot mess; I was anxious to see you."

"Don't apologize. Hot and mess work for you. Feel free to wear yoga pants anytime."

I lifted my head and smiled. "You're cute."

"How cute am I?" He leaned in, his lips teasing mine.

"Very," I whispered, before I bridged the gap between us.

Reece captured my mouth, inviting his tongue right in to do all the wondrous things he knew how to do. With every swirl of his tongue, I went a little weaker in the knees. I twisted my hands around his T-shirt to keep myself steady. Reece helped when he picked me up. What a guy. I wrapped my legs around him so fast, like that's what I was born to do. He groaned in pleasure and backed me right up against his entryway wall. It wasn't a cave, but it would do.

With his body securely pressed against mine, my hands found their way into his hair. For minutes, Reece devoured my neck and mouth. I reveled in every second of his stubble brushing against me while his breath tickled my skin.

"Josie," he whispered my name between kisses, as if I were all he had ever desired.

I couldn't speak, as he had stolen my breath. He could gladly have it. Who needed to breathe? In that moment, all I needed was him. All of him. That thought made me gasp. We weren't even close to that step. It was that story. It made me feel as if I knew him better than I truly did.

Reece stopped his glorious handiwork, lifted his head, and held my gaze. "Did I do something wrong?"

"You're doing all the right things." I could barely breathe. "I just don't want to go too fast, and you make me want to go at lightning speed."

"Mmm," he groaned. "The feeling is mutual. But you're right, we should be careful."

"Not too careful," I smiled.

For that, I was rewarded with a peck on the lips.

Regrettably, I loosened myself from him and slid down his tall frame, yet I still clung to him as he kept me pressed against the wall. I took a moment to allow our breathing to slow and fall into the same rhythm.

Reece wrapped me in his arms, encapsulating me in his yummy scent. I could seriously get used to this every day.

"Andi had a really good day today," I thought he should

know. She was more talkative and even raised her hand once to answer a question.

"That's what she said." There was a smile in his voice. "She went on and on about the marble leaves you made by mixing shaving cream and paint together. I would never think to do something like that."

"I can't exactly take credit for that. I read tons of teacher blogs and go to a lot of workshops."

"Yes, but you bring the magic. Andi knows you care about her and every student in your class. That's a gift."

"I love what I do."

"That is obvious." He kissed my head. "I'm just lucky Andi has you."

"I'm the lucky one. She's a great kid."

"She has an incredible dad," he teased.

I happily sighed into his chest, silently agreeing with him. "He's all right."

"Josie." He ran a hand down my back. "I don't want to screw this up. We will go as slow or as fast as you want."

"Thank you."

"Now let me show you what yours truly, Your Royal Highness, has been working on." He took my hand and led me toward his garage door.

"Did Marilyn contact you?" I asked on the way.

"She wants to meet for drinks to discuss my role and how she can best utilize me." He flashed me a devious grin.

Ugh. That woman. I tsked so loud it hurt my tongue.

Reece chuckled. "Do you really think I would agree to meet her?"

I shrugged. I had no plans to ever tell him what he could and couldn't do with his free time. He was an adult. And it's not like I was his girlfriend.

He tugged on my hand, drawing me to him. When I was close enough, he ran a finger down my cheek. "Josie, I'm a one-woman-at-a-time kind of man. And why would I waste my time when I plan to have secret liaisons with you in all my spare moments?"

I bit my lip, liking the sound of that. "I love secret liaisons." Not that I had ever had any—you know, except in my head and on paper. But there was no doubt I would be a big fan of them.

"I'm not a secretive guy, but I admit that the thought of having you only to myself for a while is quite appealing."

I stood on my tiptoes. "I promise to make sure each time you are more than appealed."

"Dang." He cleared his throat. "If you keep talking like that, we'll be heading for hypersonic speed."

It was so tempting. I fell back on my feet. "Sorry. You do things to me." Things I couldn't exactly explain, as I had never felt like this for any man.

"Don't apologize. I'm glad, because you are driving me wild, but I will control myself." He pressed his lips against mine for a sweet, stirring moment. No tongues, just a *Here we are, I want you and respect you* moment.

I could feel his goodness and his desire to show me how important I was to him. My eyes stung with tears. So much so, it scared me. It had been forever since I had felt such emotion. I pulled away from him, blinking back real tears.

"Josie?"

I wiped my eyes before any tears fell. "I haven't been able to cry in years," I admitted.

"I'm making you cry?"

"In a good way. A scary way." I realized I had been holding back my emotions for so long because I was afraid to let anyone make me feel anything, especially vulnerable. It was how I'd survived all the ridicule over the years. Reece was breaking down those barriers, and I wasn't sure how to feel about it.

His brow crinkled. "I scare you?"

"So much. You are making me face myself."

A tender look washed over his ridiculously handsome features. "Josie, I'm excited for you. I can't wait for you to see what I see when I look at you."

Could he have said anything better? I don't think so.

"Reece, don't make me go hypersonic all over you, especially before I truly confront myself."

He took my face in his capable hands. "As much as I would enjoy taking you up in my arms and kissing every inch of your skin, I won't until you are comfortable with all of you."

I fell against him and wrapped my arms around him. Never had a man been so careful with me. Trevor certainly hadn't cared how I felt about myself. All he cared about in the end was how others saw me.

Reece held on tight, making me feel safe and secure.

"Thank you."

"You don't have to thank me for being decent. That should be a given."

"That's not what I'm thanking you for. Thank you for seeing me."

"That's entirely my pleasure."

I took a few more moments to soak him in, before reluctantly leaving his arms. "I'm excited to see the booth."

Reece tucked a strand of hair behind my ear, then took my hand and led me to his garage.

I gladly walked by his side. "By the way, you never told me that you and Mr. Nelson were roommates. You only said you knew him in college."

"Did I forget to mention that?" he played innocent.

"Just a minor detail." I nudged him. "Why didn't you tell me?"

Reece opened the door leading to his attached garage. "I know what a precarious situation this is. I realize I'm basically asking you to lie to one of my best friends, in turn putting your job at risk. I didn't want you to feel any more pressure than I've already placed on you. Although, it's a ridiculous rule, written or unwritten. Ken and the school board have no right to tell you who you can and can't see." Reece sounded disgruntled with his friend.

We stepped out into his immaculate garage, where a shiny

black truck filled one side. On the other stood a darling photo booth made to look like an old-fashioned pumpkin stand. He had even begun to paint some pumpkins along the top.

I placed my hands to my mouth, forgetting about my principal for a moment. "Reece, this is amazing. When did you even have time to do this?"

Reece pulled me closer to his handiwork. "Noah came over one night last week, and last night he was here until almost midnight."

I was seriously going to go hypersonic on him. "You didn't have to do this." I ran my hands over the sanded and stained wood. "It's perfect."

"I wanted to do something your class would be proud of. Something you would be proud of."

"Mission accomplished." I kissed his cheek, wishing to kiss so much more. "Thank you." Those words seemed so inadequate.

"I thought we could place some bales of hay and real pumpkins in front of it." He sounded like an excited child sharing his vision.

"I love that idea. You are the best Royal Highness ever, but please don't feel like you need to overdo this. I know you have a heavy caseload right now, and more importantly, Andi."

"And you," he reminded me.

"I don't want to come between Andi and work either."

"You won't. I don't want you to feel like I'm just squeezing you in between. If ever you want me to, I will talk to Ken. For as much as I look forward to our secret liaisons, I am ready anytime for the world to see us together."

I swallowed hard, thinking about my stern administrator. Thinking about the pirate and pirate girl being seen together in the world. It was all daunting. "I don't see Mr. Nelson budging."

Reece ran a hand through his hair and groaned. "He doesn't have a leg to stand on."

"Yeah, well, I don't want to be the one to knock him off-balance. I like paying my bills."

"I understand that, but sometimes you have to stand up for what you want—for what's right. Not that I'm asking you to risk your job. I would never do that. I'm just saying it's okay to push sometimes."

"I'm not good at pushing. I mean, I just pushed my mother, and she's hardly said two words to me since."

"Was it something that needed to be said?"

I knew what he was getting at. My eyes hit my shoes. "Yes."

Reece tipped my chin with the touch of his finger. "Josie, you should always be the first person to stand up for yourself. I'm always happy to play backup for you, but the first step to getting out of the blender is to see your worth—and to realize you're worth fighting for."

Wow. He really knew how to get me right in the feels. But we were back to me trying not to feel for so long. It was a safe place. He was asking me to leave my place of security. "I'll try," I promised. It was all I could offer at the moment. "But, please don't talk to Mr. Nelson."

"All right," he said, with no qualms at all. "I will leave that to you if you ever want to."

The thought of marching into Mr. Nelson's office and giving him the-what-for made me tremble inside. I was sure I would never do such a thing, even if it meant being able to be out in the open with Reece before the end of the school year.

"I did talk to someone on your behalf." Reece gave me a crooked smile. "My friend Cari in New York."

I took a step back, in a daze.

Reece pulled me right back to him. "Don't worry. It was good."

That's what I was afraid of. "How good?"

"She wants to talk to you."

"Really?"

"Really." He paused. "The thing is—" He paused again. "She asked if you had ever been published. They prefer to sign those who have a track record."

"Oh. I understand." I couldn't hide my disappointment. As

much as it scared me, there was something about living my other dream that spoke to me and entreated me to listen. But I knew it was the longest of shots. Besides, the safe shot was never taking the shot.

"Josie, I mentioned your pirate story," he mumbled. "She read it."

"You're kidding me, right?" Please let him be kidding. "Why would you do that?" I complained loudly.

"Because it's incredible, and the following that story has online gives you traction. She loved it. She couldn't believe a fifteen-year-old wrote it."

That made two of us—well, four of us if you included my parents. I began pacing the garage. Reece had no right to tell her about that stupid story. He knew how much I hated it.

"I know you're upset with me."

"That's an understatement. I'm tired of being defined by that story," I choked out.

"Josie." He gently grabbed my arm, begging me to look at him. "I know you don't want to hear this, but you're the only person who is letting that story define you."

I opened my mouth to adamantly disagree, but I couldn't. I hated that he was right. He knew what he was talking about. He didn't let his patch or disability define him. Instead, he used it as a strength. I wished I could be like him.

"I'm sorry if what I'm saying hurts you. I only told Cari about the story because they aren't looking for children's book authors currently. Romance is where it's at right now. She's intrigued with a rogue pirate." His lips ticked up. "You are so incredibly talented. You deserve this chance."

"I can't," I whispered. "I can't be the pirate girl for the rest of my life."

"Okay," he sighed. "If you ever want her contact information, let me know. She would love to talk to you."

I knew I would never ask for her number. The pirate girl wasn't worth fighting for.

Twenty-Three

"ARE YOU SO EXCITED?" JENNA laughed into the phone.

I stared at the Aspen Lake Community Center, not at all excited that soon I would be seeing Reece at our Ex-Filers meeting. We were working on table centerpieces. I hadn't seen him since Monday night. That was three days ago. We'd texted some, but it felt awkward and strangled. We'd left things weird after he told me about his friend who worked for the big publisher. I hadn't mentioned any of this to Jenna, for several reasons. First and foremost, I didn't want to seem like a wishy-washy nutjob. Sure, I was one, but I didn't want to sound like one.

Monday night had made me realize that I liked being with Reece, in part because I knew for the next eight months it had to be secret. For me, it was the best of both worlds: be with the man of my dreams, literally, with no one pointing out that the rogue pirate and the pirate girl are together. I kept asking myself what was going to happen in eight months if we were still together. I knew Reece wasn't going to want to keep this secret going forever. And let's be honest, I was the aforementioned nutjob who constantly feared the pirate girl.

I also couldn't tell Jenna I was turning down the chance to be published. I kept telling myself it was a long shot anyway, so it didn't matter whether I called Cari or not. Who needed the heartbreak of rejection? But we all knew the real reason I wouldn't call.

"Yeah," I responded.

"That wasn't very enthusiastic. Are you okay?"

"Just tired." That was true. After teaching all day and grading fifteen essays about what it means to be a good friend, I had gone to the farm and helped in the office, tallying up the day's receipts. The farm took in a lot of cash on the weekdays from all the school kids who visited on field trips. Kids loved the souvenirs. Everything from Peterson's Pumpkin Patch T-shirts to novelty pumpkins they could use for trick-or-treating. My favorite were the pumpkin-shaped mugs. I owned several.

"'Tis the season," she quipped.

"Fall-a-la-la-la," I sang.

"I see what you did there. Clever."

"I try to be. How was your day?" I was stalling going in.

"Busy, but good."

"Are you still trying to solve the case of the fifty-dollar bill?"

"Maybe," she said mysteriously.

"Do you need some help?"

"No," she was quick to say, almost as if she were hiding something.

"Are you sure?"

"It's fine. It's all fine." She was acting weird.

"Okay. Well, let me know if you need some help. I'll get all sleuth-y with you. Pretty sure that's not a word." I laughed.

"Ha ha. I like it. I better go. Bye." She unceremoniously hung up.

I stared at my phone. That was odd, and so unlike her. It left me with no other choice but to face Reece. Maybe Mr. Nelson was right: you should never date a student's parent. But would I listen? No. The dang man had to go and take me on a tractor ride and properly kiss me. Although my mother would probably call what we did improper. Steamy kissing was my favorite. Still, I'd made it awkward. For Andi's sake, I would be an adult about it. I loved that kid. In her essay today she wrote, "To be a good friend is to be like Ms. Peterson. She's kind and always helps us. I want to be just like her." Oh, kiddo. I didn't wish that on anyone.

With a heavy sigh, I grabbed my bag and the box of realistic-looking ravens and heaved myself out of the car into the cool, dark evening. The birds were creepy, and I loved it. Totally what we were going for.

I admit to dressing on the nicer side. I was going for fall chic. Fit-me-right jeans, leather boots, the classic plaid blanket scarf, draped perfectly. I was Pinterest-ready. Not so ready to see Reece. Don't get me wrong, I missed him. I immensely enjoyed his company and the way he could make me laugh. He was attentive and intuitive. Maybe too intuitive. Perfect boyfriend material. Except, you know, the he-wanted-me-to-be-whole-and-healthy thing. It was annoying. As in, I was annoyed with myself that I couldn't see the woman he saw.

I trudged into the community center and said a friendly hello to the woman sitting behind the front desk, before heading back to our normal room. I took note of all the cute fall decorations on the wall made by local children. Misshapen pumpkins with crooked teeth and dozens of cutout leaves made me smile. It truly was the best time of year.

I tiptoed into the room, not sure if Reece was there. I didn't see his truck in the parking lot, but I didn't want to assume a thing. I was glad to find only Cami and a couple other women had arrived to begin setting up. Tonight, we were not only working on centerpieces but we would be shoring up those who wanted to donate gift baskets to raffle off. People were so generous. It gave me hope for the world.

"Hi, Josie," all the women said brightly.

"Hello." I headed toward the large round table already filled with painted black and gold branches. Jackie was in charge of those. I set my bag and decently heavy box down, anxious to see our vision come together.

Cami sashayed my way. She was the cutest pregnant lady ever. Her little bump was just starting to show. I really wanted one of those. A thought of Reece and me procreating popped into my head. It was a lovely thought until the words *pirate baby* came into my mind. I was ridiculous for even thinking about having a baby with Reece already. According to Mr. Nelson, we weren't even supposed to be dating.

Cami gave me a little squeeze. "How are you?"

"Good," I half-lied. Since Monday evening, I'd found myself having a major identity crisis, but other than that, I was dandy. Unless you counted the fact that the man who was giving me such heartburn would be in attendance tonight. And I was sneaking around with said man, putting my job on the line. But really, I was great.

"How's business at the patch this year?" she asked.

"Really good. Thank you for posting about it."

"Anytime. You know how much my family loves that place. Expect a big Jenkins family outing there next month."

"We look forward to it every year. By the way, thank you for cropping my engagement photos. It's weird how much better I feel knowing he isn't in them."

Cami nodded, as if she knew exactly how I felt. "I think it gives us permission to move on and let go."

"Yes." If only I could do that in other areas of my life. Crop something out. Maybe self-doubt? Or the weight of other people's opinions? Why were they both so hard to let go of?

"Speaking of moving on. I'm excited about your newest committee member," she sang deviously.

I rolled my eyes. This was all getting too weird. I mean, I appreciated the hoops Reece was willing to jump through to see me, but I worried this was all going to come back to bite me in the butt. We are talking a major chunk out of my rear end.

Cami laughed at me.

Amid her laughter, I heard a large group of women walk in. They were awfully loud and chipper. I turned to find out why. I shouldn't have been surprised to find Reece in the center of them. He was dressed to break hearts in his tailored-to-precision suit pants and dress shirt, buttoned down just enough to make you swoon. So much for these women being over men. You throw one hot-blooded male into the mix, and apparently they're all ready to give love another venture. Me included.

Cami snickered next to me.

"We have a new member," Rita loudly exclaimed.

All the women clapped. We are talking standing ovation. Cami and I refrained from the ridiculousness. No one had ever clapped before when introducing a new member.

Jackie rushed toward Reece. "Come in and tell us your story."

Oh brother. I couldn't wait to hear this. Not to say he didn't have a good one to tell. The ending of his marriage and recent events with Nicolette were certainly tragic. But I knew Reece would never try to crop Nicolette out of his life. He would always be connected to her because of Andi. As it should be. He was an honorable man, helping his ex the way he was.

Reece caught my eye. He was wearing quite the smirky smile.

I sat down at the table of decorations, thinking this was going to be a long night of watching women fawn all over my . . . well, I wasn't sure what to call him—other than the most gorgeous bane of my existence. Yes, that was a perfect title for him. Or world's best kisser. It was a toss-up.

The women all led Reece to the center of the room where there were some folding chairs set up. Before Reece took a seat, he held up his hands and said, "Ladies, I truly appreciate your concern, but it's just not something I can talk about right now."

A collective "Aww" went around the room.

"You know, that's okay." Jackie patted him on the back. "Sometimes you have to let the pain settle. We all know that in this group. Just know when you're ready to talk about it, we're here for you."

"You don't know how much I appreciate that." Reece sighed.

I could tell several hearts in the room were all aflutter. I couldn't blame them, but I still wanted to tell them all to back off.

Cami must have read my vibe. "Let's get started," she called out.

Bless her.

"Reece, do you want to help me call donors?" Lucy purred.

"Uh." Reece tugged on his collar. "I already told Cami I would help with decorations."

Lucy's loss was a lot of women's gain.

"Perfect." Jackie's dark eyes lit up like the Fourth of July.

All the women in the room gravitated toward my table. Yep, this was going to be a long night.

Reece settled in across from me. "Hello, Ms. Peterson. It's nice to see you."

"Hello, Mr. Cavanaugh," I returned, just as formally.

Jackie pointed between Reece and me. "You know each other?"

"Ms. Peterson is my daughter's teacher."

I supposed that was something we couldn't keep a secret. Not that I wanted to. I was proud to have Andi in my class.

"Oh," all the women said in unison. Jackie added, "Single dad," as if that were a huge turn-on to her.

"Yep," Reece said. "One perfect little girl."

All the women went doe-eyed. The night was getting longer and longer, and it had just started. It was almost hilarious to watch my supposed friends jockey for a position near Reece. Almost. Was this what I had to look forward to in dating him?

I held up my phone. "This is an example of the centerpiece. I made copies of the instructions for everyone."

No one but Reece paid attention to me. "I'll take a copy of those."

I reached into my box of creepy birds and placed the sheets

195

on the table, making sure to hand him one. It probably looked like I was fawning over him, but I had every right to. Except I hadn't exactly been warm the last few days. I wanted to get my act together. Really, I did. But Reece was asking me to confront things I had worked very hard to hide from. I had gotten great at shutting down whenever people mentioned the story, or anything related to it. It's what I had been doing all week. It wasn't a great start to our relationship.

Reece took the paper and offered me a smile. I was happy to return it. Glad he was still willing to smile at me.

Once he took one, there was a flurry of interest in the instructions. It didn't take long before everyone got to work and started chitchatting. By chitchatting, I mean that Reece was brought into every conversation. My favorite was the debate over which *Pride and Prejudice* was better. The Colin Firth version or the Keira Knightley one. The Team Colin ladies were hotly contesting anyone who dared make any argument for the shorter Keira version.

"What do you think?" Lucy asked, assuming Reece had even seen them. She was Team Colin all the way and had apparently forgotten she was supposed to be calling the donors.

I set down the bird I was ready to glue onto a black tree branch, eager to hear Reece's opinion. I'd tried not to pay too much attention to him throughout the evening in the name of discretion. I wasn't sure I could hide my feelings for him. But this, I had to hear.

Reece gave his signature let-me-own-you-with-all-my-words smile. "Personally, I don't think it has to be an either/or. Let's say my date needs a quick P&P fix: I'd happily watch the Keira version. Now, if she wants to spend an entire evening in my arms, Sir Colin it is."

The tongues in the group began to figuratively hang out of their mouths. Reece had just cemented himself as every woman in the room's desire. Minus Cami, who was already married to her own charming man. They all went from Ex-Filers to Reece

Cavanaugh Fan Club members. I had never seen so many eyes bat at once. Meanwhile, I was rolling mine.

"What do you think, Ms. Peterson?" Reece asked me, catching me off guard as always.

"Oh, she doesn't care about *Pride and Prejudice*." Jackie laughed, before I even had a chance to answer. "She's into Turkish dramas."

I had gladly spread the word in this group about my obsession. I felt duty bound to share the joys of Can Yaman with the world.

"Is that so?" Reece asked, obviously amused. "How did you get into those?"

"I saw a reel on Instagram." That sounded juvenile, but it was true.

Reece pressed his lips together, as if he, too, thought it was odd.

"Let me show you the reels." Jackie grabbed her phone. "Talk about chemistry," she swooned.

Reece eagerly anticipated the show he was about to get, while my cheeks burned with embarrassment. Sure, I could say I watched the show for educational purposes or that the humor was amazing, but it didn't take a genius to see why I was truly watching the show.

"Can Yaman," Jackie groaned his name, like she was going to have a private experience over there.

Yep. Can was the real reason for my obsession. I didn't need Reece to know this.

Reece's smile grew wider and wider with each reel Jackie showed him. He kept chuckling, too. "Erkenci Kuş, huh, Ms. Peterson?"

I bit my lip.

"I'll have to check this out." He gave me a meaningful look.

Hmm. Me, Reece, and Can. I suppose it could work. I couldn't tell Jenna, of course.

"Let's have a watch party at our next meeting," Lucy suggested.

I refrained from growling and giving her a scathing glare. That was *my* show, and Reece was my man. There, I said it. He was mine, all mine—so back off, ladies.

"Great idea," Jackie agreed. "I'll bring snacks."

"Tell us your favorite dessert, Reece."

This was getting out of hand.

I stood to get some more glue for the hot glue guns. At least that was my excuse. I couldn't take the women pawing over Reece. I headed for Cami, who was by herself near the boxes of supplies, laughing at all these women who were supposedly over men. Add myself to that list.

I leaned against the supply table, watching the scene.

"Charming men are the worst." Cami grinned.

"Definitely," I agreed.

"How goes it with Reece?" Cami asked in hushed tones.

I turned before I answered, hoping to keep our conversation private.

Cami followed suit.

"I'm not sure," I whispered honestly.

She gave me a look that said she knew exactly where I was coming from. "I should say, men who see you for who you really are and want you to see that woman, too, are the worst."

Yes. So much yes. "I take it Noah is one of them."

"He is the king of them."

"Well then, Reece is the prince."

"It's hard to be with someone who's so self-assured when you're not." She was preaching to the choir.

"Amen. So, how did you make it work?"

"I found me. All of me again."

I was afraid that was the answer. "What if you feel like you lost yourself at fifteen?"

"That's tough, but I think you owe it to that girl to find her. She turned out to be a fantastic woman."

"I don't know about that."

"I do. Being a good teacher alone makes you a hero in my

book. But look at Reece; do you think he would really choose to pursue someone who isn't amazing? He's not just thinking about himself. He has a daughter, and I know he wants the best for her."

I wanted the best for Andi, too. For all my students. "I appreciate your kind words." Truly, I did. I just wished I could know they were true.

"They're not just words." She patted my back. "But I know how hard it is to believe them when you don't feel them. You'll get there." She was much more confident in my abilities than I was.

"How did you find yourself?" I had to know.

She let out a heavy breath. "I had to do the toughest thing I've ever done. I had to face myself and stop hiding behind all the hurt and anger."

"Yikes." How was I going to face the pirate girl? She'd made my life a living hell.

"Yeah," she sighed. "But the good news is that men like Noah and Reece make for good companions on that scary road. You just have to be willing to let them walk beside you."

"That sounds so good in theory."

"I promise it's better in real life." She wrapped an arm around me. "Good luck."

We turned just in time—or was that at the worst time ever?

"Oh my gosh, I just made the connection," a woman named Sable announced loudly. "You are Reece the Rogue Pirate and"—she pointed at me—"you're the pirate girl. What a small world. How funny is that?"

It wasn't funny at all. I stood there paralyzed, unable to breathe. I didn't want this to be my life with Reece. I wanted to be Josie. All I could hear was the taunting and the jeers as I walked down the halls of high school. *She's such a loser. No way would Reece ever go for her. I hope those braces fix her buck teeth. No one would want to kiss that mouth. The only boyfriend she'll ever have is if she writes one. If I were her, I would never show my face again at school.*

That was my biggest wish. I wanted to run and hide. Eventually, I learned how to, but only emotionally. I guess, sometimes physically, diving behind things.

I could run now. That was a good idea.

Reece stood, his eye locking with my own, looking torn on what he should do. It was as if he knew I was about to bolt, and he was silently pleading with me not to.

I was grateful he acted discreetly and didn't rush toward me.

For a moment, I pleaded with myself not to go, to own this, but then several women asked, "Who's Reece the Rogue Pirate?"

"You have to read the story," Sable gushed.

Please. Please. Don't read the story.

"Excuse me," I stuttered to Cami, before walking briskly out the door. I didn't know where I was going to go. I didn't have my bag or phone with me, so driving was out of the question. Once in the hallway, I was able to take a breath.

The rogue pirate had captured me once again.

Twenty-Four

"JOSIE, WAIT UP," REECE CALLED out to me across the parking lot.

I was headed for the path around the small pond on the community center's property. In the summer, the large fountain in the middle spouted a spectacular amount of water. Now, all it boasted was the moon's reflection.

Great. Reece was apparently not going to be discreet.

On the path's edge, I turned to find him jogging my way with my bag. Why did he have to be so handsome and kind? And why did I have to have issues?

Reece stopped mere inches from me but said nothing, at least not verbally. The creases in his brow said it all. He was more than concerned.

"You should walk away now. You don't deserve this crazy," I warned him.

"What kind of person would I be if I left you hurting like this?"

"The thing is, I know I shouldn't be hurting like this. But I don't know how to make it go away. All I can hear in my head is people telling me how stupid I am and that someone like you would never want me. I've heard those voices for fifteen years now," my voice shook. "I've tried not to believe them, and sometimes I can even pretend I don't. Then nights like tonight happen, and all of a sudden I'm in high school again with out-of-control hair and teeth, and all I want to do is hide from the hurt. Hide from you, the boy I so desperately wanted, but knew would never feel the same." I wrapped my arms around myself, trying to stop the shaking.

Reece threw decorum out the window and took me into his arms.

"People are going to see us," I mildly protested.

"I couldn't care less who sees us."

I rested my head against his chest and breathed in his spring-rain scent, trying to soak in the comfort he was offering me. "I'm sorry, Reece."

"Why are you apologizing?"

"Because I thought I could do this. I thought we could be together, but I'm insane."

"You're not insane. You've been hurt."

"It's made me crazy."

"I like your brand of crazy." He stroked my hair.

"Reece, you have a daughter, and you're already dealing with your ex-wife's crazy issues; you don't need me on top of it. Let's just call it good. We can be friends." That thought hurt in ways I didn't want to admit. I was letting go of my dream. But it was for a noble cause—him.

Reece said nothing, but held on tighter.

I let him, because I knew it was our goodbye and I didn't want to let go.

"Let's go for a drive," Reece said, out of the blue.

"You should get home to Andi," I made excuses not to leave with him. My heart couldn't take the hope. A hope that I could get my act together and at least try to make my dreams a reality.

"She's at home with my mom, already tucked in and fast asleep. She won't even know I'm not there."

"You can't fix me." I needed him to understand he should just let this thing between us go.

"I don't want to. I learned a long time ago that you can't fix people; you can only help them."

"You think I need help?" I wasn't offended, because clearly, I did, but it was a little embarrassing that he noticed.

"We all need help from time to time, and that's okay."

I snuggled more into his chest.

"Come on. I want to show you one of my favorite spots."

"Okay," I acquiesced. "But just so you know, I'll still be crazy."

"I'm glad to hear that." He chuckled.

I followed him to his truck, keeping a friendly distance even though no one was in the parking lot. Which reminded me. "What did you tell everyone when you left?"

"I said, 'I should probably go check on Josie. She gets upset when I haven't kissed her in a few days.'"

"No, you didn't," I lightly laughed.

He opened the passenger door. "You're right. I guess I was just hoping you were as upset about that fact as I was."

I took a moment to gaze at the wonderful, maddening man. "I'm more upset about it than you will ever know." I meant every word. "But—"

He placed a finger on my lips. "You don't need to qualify that statement or give me a warning. I know what I'm getting into here."

"Do you really?" I murmured against his finger.

"Absolutely." He tapped my lip. "By the way, I told the women in there that I needed to check on my *friend*, Josie. And you know what they said?"

I shook my head.

"They said, 'We love Josie. She's always willing to help and offer a listening ear. She never judges anyone.' Never once did they mention the pirate girl."

"I do judge people sometimes in my head," I admitted.

Reece flashed me a sardonic smile. "I think you're missing the point. People see you for far more than your story. And after you left, Sable went on and on about how much she loved it. She's a fan."

I tried not to cringe. I knew I should be flattered, but I couldn't be. If only they knew the torture I'd endured because of that story. "Now all those women are going to read it."

"Probably," he surmised. "I'm sorry that will hurt you."

I was too. "I wish it didn't."

"You'll get there." He sounded so sure.

"I don't know."

"I do. Now get in this truck." He playfully waved me in.

"Wow. Bossy much?" I teased.

"I'm anxious to hold your hand." He was the sweetest.

My heart was melting all over the place. I stood on my tiptoes and kissed his stubbled cheek. "That's friendly, right?"

He touched his cheek where my lips had just been. "Do it again so I can gauge how friendly it was."

"You're trouble." I looked around to make sure we were still alone, before I pecked his cheek once more.

"Hmm," he debated. "On a scale from one to ten, I would rate that a six on the friendly scale."

I loved how he could make me smile, despite how stupid I felt. "Thank you, Reece." I hopped in the cab of his truck.

He leaned in and stole a kiss. "No. Thank you. You saved me from those women in there."

I laughed while he closed the door and ran around to the driver's side.

He hopped in, fired up his truck, and made a quick exit out of the parking lot.

"Where are we going?"

"My favorite lookout above the lake."

That sounded perfect.

"On the way there, you can tell me about this *Erkenci Kus*," he teased me. "That Can Yaman is some tough competition."

"There's no competition."

He raised his brow.

"I mean, you win—hands down."

"For that, you get ice cream too."

"Can we make it hot chocolate?" I just wanted to feel warm.

"Deal." He reached over and took my hand.

I held on to it like my life depended on it. "Do you want to fill me in on your love for *Pride and Prejudice?*"

"Hey, I'm a smart man. I learned very early in college if I said I loved that movie, I could always get a date. If I said I'd read the book, which I did, I had women throwing their numbers at me." He flipped on his turn signal.

"You know, I don't think that was because of *Pride and Prejudice.* Did you see all those women tonight? You're a hot ticket item." I tried not to sound jealous.

He squeezed my hand. "What other women? All I saw was you."

I cradled his hand in my lap, practically verklempt. "You take my breath away, Reece Cavanaugh."

"The feeling is mutual, *Josie* Peterson."

I stared out into the night sky, begging myself to get my act together so I could see if Reece and I had any hope for a future together.

The remainder of the drive was mostly silent, except for the sound of my beating heart and Smokey Robinson on the radio. Reece made good on his promise for hot chocolate, stopping at a little out-of-the-way place he knew, before we drove up the mountain to an overlook that I hadn't known existed.

Reece was pleased to see that no one else was atop his beloved spot. He backed in so that his tailgate almost kissed the edge of the cliff. "You grab the hot chocolates, and I'll grab the blanket."

I narrowed my suspicious eyes at him. "Blanket? Did you plan this?"

"Definitely." He wagged his brows.

I jumped out of the truck, careful not to spill the hot chocolates, and met Reece around the back.

He lowered his tailgate and set the blanket down. "Let me help you." He wrapped his hands around my waist, lifted me up, and set me on the tailgate. Before he took a seat next to me, he leaned in and brushed my cold lips with his warm ones. "Hi."

"Hi. I like this view." I could look at him all day, every day.

"Just wait." He sat next to me.

I handed him his hot chocolate and rested my head on his shoulder. I gazed out into the distance. The canvas of twinkling stars and a bright white moon illuminated the lake below. I could hear the gentle lapping of the lake hitting the rocky shoreline. Mixed in with the rustling of the golden aspen trees, it was the perfect music. For a moment, my heart felt at peace. I longed for it to last.

Reece set his drink down and draped the blanket around our shoulders, making sure I snuggled tight into his side. "I love this place," he said reverently. "I came up here a lot when Nicolette decided to divorce me."

"Why do you love it, then?"

"Because, in the quiet, I realized I would be okay. Perhaps even better than okay. I'd been trying so hard to make something work, that she clearly didn't want, simply because I thought it was expected. In this place, I learned that it was all right for me to let go."

"Is that why you brought me up here? So I can learn to let go?"

"No. I thought maybe this place might speak to you, like it did to me. What you hear is entirely yours to learn."

I took a sip of my hot chocolate and closed my eyes, trying to listen. One thing I knew for sure: I didn't want to lose the man next to me. The message I heard over and over was that I needed to let it all out, get it off my chest, lighten my load. I fought against the urge for several moments. But the relentless voice inside my head demanded it, until I finally gave in.

"Reece," I whispered. "I don't know how to feel about myself, or who I should be. Growing up, it was drilled into me to do the right thing and to be a good girl. At school, teachers loved me, but there I was labeled as a nerd and ugly. Then ...

then . . . ," my voice cracked, "the story came to light. And I went from being a good girl to a bad girl. But worse, I was a bad girl who didn't know her place. So, I was tortured daily because no one believed anyone would want to be with me." I cringed, thinking of the daily hell. "After all, I was unworthy of any attention from boys."

"Don't even get me going on my parents," the words kept vomiting out of my mouth. "They thought I had taken a terrible turn somewhere and had done the things I'd written about in the story. It made me feel so horrible about the stirrings I had inside of me. Like they were wrong, so I was wrong. Then I grew up and went to college and blossomed physically, or whatever you want to call it. Suddenly, men found me attractive. I finally felt I was worthy of someone's love. But I always ended up with the wrong guy because I was trying to prove I was the good and pretty girl, not the bad, ugly pirate girl. The girl I had come to hate. Now you're here and I just want to be Josie. Because Josie really likes Reece." I let out a huge sigh, feeling a little better for baring my soul.

Reece kissed the top of my head. "Reece really likes Josie." That's all he said for several moments, as we sat there listening to the sounds of nature in the chill of the autumn night.

I appreciated he didn't automatically try to *fix* me, or even think he could.

"Do you want to see what's under my patch?" he asked, after a few minutes.

I lifted my head, caught off guard by his question. "If that's something you want to show me, but I don't need you to. Honestly, I don't care what's under the patch, except for the pain it's caused you."

He grabbed my face, pressed his lips to mine, and murmured against them, "You're incredible."

I leaned away, confused. "Um . . . why?"

"Josie," he said, so carefully. "When you look at me, it's as if you don't see the patch. You just see me."

That was true. Sometimes I forgot it was there. "But I thought you didn't care about the patch, or what people thought of you."

"I don't, but you are the first woman I have ever been with who doesn't make a deal out of it, big or small. I think every first date I've had, the woman has asked what's behind the patch. You care more about what's inside of me."

"Well . . . if we're being honest, I do like the outside of you, too. A lot. Like, wow."

"I can't blame you there. I am a fine specimen," he teased through his laughter.

I could not disagree.

"But seriously, Josie." He touched his forehead to mine. "It speaks to who you are. Just like you don't see me for my wound, I don't see you for yours. And as amazing as I think you are, I can't tell you how to see yourself. No one but you can make that call. You choose who Josie is. And whoever she is, I'll like her."

I breathed in the sweetness of the hot chocolate on his breath—it wasn't half as sweet as him. I was indubitably falling for him. "What if I'm the bad girl?"

"I hate the good girl/bad girl culture. It's so unfair. But . . ." He nipped my lips. "If you want to be bad, then we'll be bad together."

Oh, holy pumpkin. I let out a tiny squeal, thinking of how *bad* we could be together.

"You okay there?" He knew he was getting to me.

"I want to be."

"Then you will be. You know, the fact that you admit you're crazy is quite refreshing."

"Hey." I grabbed his shirt, totally offended. "You really think I'm crazy?"

"Oh, yeah. I like it."

I could live with that. I mean, this way he could never blame me. He knew up front what he was getting into. "What do I do to own this, Reece?" I pleaded to know.

He took a deep breath in and let it out slowly between us. Our lips teased each other's, but I felt as if I couldn't let him consume me until I knew what to do.

"Josie, I hesitate to ask this, but when was the last time you read your story?"

Every part of me cringed thinking about it, making me twist my hands into his shirt. "Forever ago. But it's burned into my memory. Why do you ask?"

He ran his hands through my hair and held me steady against him. "Do you remember the part where we're on the cliff together?"

It was so weird for him to talk about it like it was us. Like how I thought of the story.

"Uh-huh," I squeaked. We were running for our lives. My uncle was chasing us, and there was nowhere left for us to go. Or so I thought.

"Take my hand and jump with me," he whispered, just like he had in my story. "I don't know how this day ends, but what I can promise you is that falling with you will be the thrill of a lifetime, and I will swim with you until you make it safely to the shore. Once there—"

"That's where our real story begins, if that's what you choose," I finished for him, tears brimming in my eyes, pleading with me to let them fall. To stop hiding my emotions.

"Take my hand, Josie."

"Are you saying you want to jump off the cliff with me?" I choked out, a single tear escaping. I flinched at the sensation. My cheeks hadn't felt the salty moisture in years.

Reece tenderly swiped the tear away with his thumb. "I do."

"I'm scared."

"I know, but I won't let go until you figure out who you are. After that, I'll let go if you want me to."

"What if I don't want you to?"

"Lucky me," he groaned.

I tugged on his shirt until our lips melded together and the tears fell, making it a sweet and salty kiss. While our tongues got more than friendly, my mind drifted toward the story. How I had agonized over whether or not to jump off the cliff, not knowing if I would survive. That seemed melodramatic for the current circumstances, but I knew if I wanted to own my life, I was going to have to leave part of myself on the cliff and bravely jump into unknown waters searching for Josie. I deepened the kiss, searching for my courage.

Reece was the one to pull away before the kiss took us to places I knew I wasn't ready for. "Josie," he whispered.

"What?"

"I want to show you what's under the patch."

"You don't have to."

"I want you to know all of me."

I wiped my cheeks and nodded. "I'd like that." So very much.

"Are you ready?" He reached for his patch.

"I am if you are."

He gave me a crooked grin, before lifting the patch off and setting it to the side.

I wasn't sure what to expect, but it wasn't shocking in the least bit. I brushed my fingers just below the desolate eye socket, admiring the luscious lashes on his droopy eyelid, masking what looked like a pink crater. "Does it hurt?"

"Not for a long time."

"I'm glad."

"I don't want you to hurt anymore, Josie. Take my hand." He offered it to me.

I dropped my gaze and stared down at it, waiting for me, *begging* me to jump off the cliff. "You know, the sticky-and-sandy beach scene came after they jumped off the cliff and swam."

"I'm well aware," he said, low and sexy.

I swallowed hard, feeling all sorts of warm.

"Let's vanquish the enemy together. Just like in your story." He inched his hand forward.

"I want to reach that shore." My hand crept toward his, feeling the same rush of adrenaline I had in the story, knowing there was no turning back. I focused on Reece's handsome face, all of it. His wound only made him more beautiful. That thought struck me. He was who he was because of the injury. Perhaps I could let my emotional injuries be a strength. I just had to jump off the proverbial cliff. This time, with someone who knew how to navigate the waters and was, for now, a stronger swimmer than me. I couldn't think of anyone better, so I placed my hand in his.

He smiled and securely cradled my hand in his own.

I let out the breath I had been holding. "It's time to jump."

Twenty-Five

"WHAT ARE YOU GOOGLING NOW?" Jenna peeked over my shoulder while I sat on my pumpkin pouf, waiting for the patch to open Saturday morning.

"How not to be a psycho girlfriend." I clicked enter, determined to own my life and be emotionally healthy and whole so I could live out all my fantasies with Reece. Google was the cheapest therapist around.

She snort-laughed while grabbing my phone. "You're not a psycho."

"Maybe psycho isn't an accurate diagnosis, but there could be some good tips in there."

Jenna scanned my phone. "Let's see: 'Have your own life.' You're good there. 'Encourage him to have one.' Check. 'Don't jump to conclusions and never accuse.' Yeah, I think you're good. Definitely not a psycho girlfriend. Why don't you type in this?" Her fingers went to work, before she flashed me the phone screen.

"'How to heal from childhood bullying,'" I read out loud. "Yeah, I guess that's better."

Jenna scooched in next to me. "I know you don't want to think of yourself as a victim of bullying, but that's the reality. It says right here, acknowledging it is the first step."

I took my phone from her and read a little bit more. "Oh man, this sounds like me: 'Many adults healing from childhood bullying often think about what they experienced and become obsessed with not feeling that pain again.'"

Jenna read along with me. "I like this one here." She pointed. "'Reject the lies the bully said to you or about you. Replace them with the truth about who you are. Focus on being you.'"

"That's all I've ever wanted to be—Josie."

"That's who you are to me." She leaned her head against mine.

"I know. Thank you for always being my best friend."

"Right back at ya. As your best friend, I think I have to insist you list all your positive characteristics like the article says. But you have to say them out loud to me, because I know there is no way you're going to write them out." She knew me too well.

"I think I'm going to pass."

"You can't. You're a girlfriend now," she sang. "And I know you want to do some sticky sand rolling."

Did I ever. I sighed. I could hardly believe I was Reece Cavanaugh's girlfriend. Yes, we'd had the define-the-relation-ship talk already. Don't judge. We were jumping off cliffs together. That was pretty serious stuff. It was also incentive to move on from the past. "Okay, fine, but this is ridiculous."

"I don't make the rules. This is science. Or so this health website says," she said, amused.

I let out a heavy breath and thought of some positive things about me. "I'm a good teacher. An excellent cousin." I laughed. "Except, your sister may not agree."

"Ugh. Olivia. What does she know, anyway? You know, except everything?" Jenna rolled her eyes. "Anyway, we're focusing on you. What else you got?"

I thought harder. I hated doing things like this. Which was probably why I was still dealing with these issues.

"Come on." Jenna nudged me when I hemmed and hawed too long. "You can do this."

She was right. I could do this. I wanted to get better. "Okay.

Let's see: I'm punctual. I draw well. My laundry is always folded, and it smells nice."

"There is nothing wrong with leaving clean, and maybe dirty, laundry on various chairs for days." Jenna was faux offended. "Though I have to say, that skill is impressive."

"Why, thank you very much," I did a horrible Elvis impression.

"Keep going," Jenna demanded. "You haven't even gotten to the really good stuff about you yet."

"I thought for sure that was the highlight reel."

"Oh please, you haven't even scratched the surface."

I thought some more. It was harder than one might think. "According to Reece, I'm an excellent kisser."

"Really? And how often are we kissing?"

"As often as possible," I said, all dreamily. "He actually ran five miles to my house, late last night after Andi went to bed and his mom came over, so no one would see his truck in front of my place, just so he could kiss me good night." I didn't have a garage like him where I could hide his vehicle.

"Jo Jo, if you don't marry this man, I will," she teased. At least, I thought she was teasing.

"It's way too early to discuss marriage. We aren't even supposed to be dating. But, yeah, most guys I dated wouldn't even run to the store for me in their car." I wouldn't mention how yummy hot-sweaty Reece was. Or the heat we managed to generate from all the kissing.

"When are you going to tell your mom?" she whispered, lest the sisters' bat radar went off.

I adjusted my pumpkin outfit. "I don't know. She's hardly said two words to me. And I'm pretty sure my dad is still sleeping on the couch. Apparently, she's having more of an identity crisis than I am. Either that, or she's just trying to figure out how we're all wrong and she's right."

"Who knows what is going through the sisters' heads," Jenna lamented. "Don't get me wrong—you know I love them, and they are good moms who did the best they could, but the more I think of it, it was pretty messed up how they reacted to that story. I have a feeling they're aware. Getting them to say that out loud is another story."

It was going to take a miracle.

"I think what bothers me most is that it added fuel to the fire. I was only tortured more for it. I could never get Mom to understand what I was dealing with at school. After a while, I just gave up and became the semi-psycho before you now." I laughed, though part of me wanted to cry.

"What I see before me now is someone who needs to finish telling me how amazing she is."

"I was hoping you would forget."

"I figured."

I closed my eyes and tried to listen to the voice I'd heard while looking out over the lake in Reece's arms. The one that had me spilling my guts. "I've got great hair."

"Definitely," Jenna agreed.

"I can kick the crap out of a punching bag. When I attend a party, I always stay until it's over to help clean up."

"That makes you golden. Keep going."

"I think that's good."

"I don't think so. You're forgetting some key things."

"Like what?"

"You know what. Say the things. Discount the lies you were told."

I coiled into myself, almost knocking her off the pouf. It shouldn't have been so hard.

Jenna grabbed my hand, trying to help.

I squeezed the life out of it, while I looked in the figurative mirror at myself. I did my best to see myself through a clear lens, unfiltered by others. "Jen," I whispered. "I think I'm beautiful."

"You are. What else?"

"I'm smart."

"Yep."

"And . . ." I held my breath, then slowly let it out. "I'm a dang good writer."

"Yeah, you are." She hugged me. "I'm proud of you. Please listen to your own voice from now on."

"I'll try my best," I said, muffled against her.

She patted my back. "Well, I better go sell some tickets."

"It's about that time. By the way, how goes the search for the owner of the money?"

She jumped up. "It's going. See you later." She waved.

I hardly had time to process the fact that she'd blown me off. What was going on with her and that fifty-dollar bill? I didn't have time to think about it, as I'd just had a great therapy session I really needed to process, and people were arriving. Some of my new favorites, even. I stood to greet them.

Molly walked in with Andi, Penelope, and Hazel. I was so happy Andi was making friends. She'd told them all about how she helped me out last weekend, and naturally the other girls wanted to help too. I should have thought about having my students help me in previous years. I would, moving forward.

Reece was working this morning. He had a big case he was presenting in court next week. On top of that, he and Noah were going to finish the photo booth. He truly was the best Royal Highness to the Educational Professional.

The three girls ran toward me with their matching pumpkin headbands. "Ms. Peterson," they shouted while hugging me.

I put my arms around them like a hen gathering her little chicks. "You all look so cute. Are you ready to help me tell stories?"

I got three enthusiastic head nods, before they rushed over to the stuffed characters.

Molly approached, smiling wide. I had a feeling it was she who'd bought the matching headbands. It was a total grandma move. One my own mother would have made.

"Good morning." Molly surprised me with a hug. Perhaps I shouldn't have been shocked, as her son was a big fan of hugging . . . and other things.

"It is a good morning." I hugged her back. I hadn't felt this light in a long time. Thursday night had been a game changer for me. There was something about confessing to Reece and asking for help. This seemed pretty significant, considering I had spent half my life running from Reece. Come to find out, if I would have stopped and faced him earlier, my life might have turned out differently. Not to say we would have gotten together—he had been married for quite some time. But I would have saved myself a lot of bruising and embarrassment from diving behind things. More importantly, I would have never agreed to get engaged to Trevor or hated myself for so long. And it's not that I was loving myself all of a sudden, but for the first time in a long time, I felt like I had permission to—if I so chose. I knew this would need to be my new reality if I wanted to progress in my relationship with Reece.

"I hope we will be good friends."

"Me too."

She leaned away from me. "How would you like to have dinner with me tonight before your late-night date." She gave me a knowing grin.

Reece and I had made plans for after Andi went to bed.

I was touched by her offer. "I would love to. Thank you."

"I can't wait. I'll be sure to give you my address before we leave today."

Before I could respond, people started pouring in. My mom included. She stood to the side of the doorway, her gaze ping-ponging between Molly and me. I swore she turned a little pale before she ran out.

I wasn't sure what to do about her. I didn't like the distance between us. But I wasn't sure she was ready to hear the whole truth. The truth was scary at times.

"Ms. Peterson," Andi called.

I turned around.

Andi was holding up Priscilla Pumpkin with a smile to steal my heart. "It's time."

She was right. It was about time for a lot of things. For now, it was time to be as pumpkiny as possible.

Twenty-Six

"HAVE A GOOD TIME TONIGHT, honey." Dad tapped my nose.

I had just informed him I wouldn't be staying to help tonight, and where I was headed.

"I will." At least I was almost certain I would. I was a little nervous about having dinner with Molly by myself. I had never had a meal alone with a boyfriend's mom. Trevor's mom and I had never done anything like this. She wasn't all that thrilled about me being a farmer's daughter. I wanted to kick myself for persisting in such a relationship. It spelled bad news, and it was like I had forgotten to read all the signs. All because I'd hoped it would point to a non-pirate world. I still wasn't sure about that world. About the pirate girl. She and I had a lot of work ahead of us. I knew one day soon she and I were going to have to make peace with one another. I ached for it yet feared it more than anything.

"Tell Reece he's welcome to come around here anytime."

I was wary about how Mom would feel about that. And I worried she wouldn't keep quiet about our relationship. However, I loved that Dad was open to this unexpected chapter in my life. "I know he would love that." As in, he would love to take me out on the tractor again. He'd spoken about it several times. I was all on board for another trip out to the field.

"Good night, Dad." I kissed his cheek and turned to go. I headed out of the barn, into the evening air that smelled of turned-up dirt and cinnamon apple cider, as it began to cool down with the setting sun. It was perfect. I inhaled deeply before hustling home to change. I wanted to look my best tonight, and I, admittedly, wanted to avoid Mom.

That was wishful thinking. She appeared out of nowhere just as I was rounding the empty face-painting booth.

I jumped back and grabbed my chest. Mom looked more than frazzled, with her pumpkin hat askew and her hazel eyes twitching.

"Hey, Mom." I tried to play it cool, though my heart was pumping a little harder than normal.

"How are you?" she asked stiffly.

"Good. How are you?"

She looked down at her feet. "I hear you're having dinner with Molly, is it?"

Of course she knew that.

"Yep." I offered no other details.

"She seems nice," Mom offered.

"She is."

"Andi is darling."

"Very." I smiled.

"So"—Mom's head snapped up—"you're doing things with Reece."

"Uh-huh."

"And you think that's wise?"

"Uh-huh," I repeated.

Mom pressed her lips together. "Hmm. I thought it was against your school rules." Everyone knew about poor Tad Fellows, who had gotten ousted for fraternizing with a parent.

"It is, but—"

"He doesn't care," Mom cut me off.

"Of course he does. He cares a lot about me."

Mom's face turned a shade of puce. She was holding back her words, but her head was about to blow for the effort.

I reached out and touched her arm. "He's a great guy. I think you would really like him."

"But he's, he's, he's the—"

I dropped my hand, knowing what she wanted to call him. "Please don't say it. He's much more than that. *I'm* much more than that," I added.

"What does that mean?" Her defenses were immediately up.

I closed my eyes, channeling the woman who jumped off cliffs. You know, the figurative ones. I might be crazy, but I had my limits. "Mom," I breathed out, while opening my eyes, begging for her to listen to me. "I love you. Truly, I do. But I need you to stop judging me by that story."

Her jaw dropped. "I've never judged you."

"Yes, you have. Maybe not on purpose, but you have. You made me feel as if I committed the ultimate sin. When all I did was express myself privately in my journal. What should have been something I could have gone back and read later in my life, and probably laughed about, turned into a nightmare for me. One I've had to live over and over for the last fifteen years. More than anything, I want to wake up from the nightmare and live my dreams." With Reece. I kept that to myself, but it was implied.

"What must you think of me?" she cried.

"Mom, I think you're a good mother. I just want you to see what this has done to me. That's all. I need your help to move on."

"You know, I always wanted you to have your dreams," she stammered, defending herself.

"What if my dream is Reece? Or what if I told you a big publisher is interested in that forsaken story and they want to talk to me about expanding on it?"

Mom reached for the booth to steady herself, as if her world might come crashing down. "Is that true? You're going to publish another pirate story?"

"How can I, when all that story has done is made me hate myself and disappoint you?"

"You hate yourself?" She blinked back tears.

"For a long time, I did," I choked out. I was working on it, though.

"I didn't know." Her lower lip trembled.

I wanted to ask her how she missed that. But I knew how. My walls were so good, I even kept her out. "I need to go." I knew it appeared I was running from my feelings again. But I didn't want to be late, and this conversation, as important as it was, wasn't what I wanted to be having before dinner with Molly.

"Go. Go." She waved me off, before covering her mouth and running toward the barn.

I stood paralyzed for a moment, wondering if she had gone searching for Dad. I hoped it was him she ran toward and not Aunt D. I loved Aunt D., but Dad had a better head on his shoulders about these things. Especially the whole publisher thing. I hadn't meant to mention that. Crap. Now I would have to tell Jenna. Which meant coming up with a better excuse for why I wouldn't be calling Cari from New York. That would have to be later. Right now, I had a date with the woman who had birthed the godlike creature who always seemed bound to get me into some type of trouble.

I stood in front of the quaint yellow door belonging to Molly's modest but well-kept brick rambler home. Reece had told me his mom had lived in the same house since his high school days. I had imagined Reece living in more of the type of neighborhood he lived in now. Not to say Molly's neighborhood was bad by any means. It was just in an older part of town. Not the part where most of the rich and popular kids had lived.

I smoothed my sage maxi dress, careful not to drop the bouquet of sunflowers I'd brought for Molly, before I knocked on the door. I still couldn't believe I was doing this. Reece was thrilled about it. He'd called on my drive over to tell me how happy he was I had accepted his mother's invitation. He also wanted to tell me how much he looked forward to seeing me later. I was pretty dang excited about it too.

Within a few seconds the door swung open, and there stood a beaming Molly. "Your timing is impeccable; I just threw away all the takeout containers and placed the food on my own dishes." She laughed.

She was my kind of woman—it made me like her even more. I held out the bouquet. "These are for you. I hope you like sunflowers."

"Darling, at this age I'll take all the bouquets I can get. Thank you." She took the flowers and breathed them in. "They're lovely."

I wondered if Molly dated. She was certainly an attractive woman. "You're welcome."

"Come in." She waved her hand, inviting me into her home.

I stepped in and was hit with the scent of Chinese food. I loved that aroma. What I loved more were the pictures of Reece and Andi resting on the old upright piano, directly in my line of sight. It was all I could do to hold myself back from rushing over to them and admiring each one.

"Do you play?" I pointed at the piano.

"I do . . . and so does Reece." She gave me the crooked grin she had gifted to her son.

"Why doesn't that surprise me?" I laughed. Reece was proving to be irresistible.

"Don't tell him I told you. I'm sure one day he'll want to try and sweep you off your feet with his talent."

"Consider me swept." I smiled.

She closed the door and took my hand. "Oh, darling, you are not the first, but perhaps you will be the last," she said mysteriously.

Her implications had my cheeks pinking.

"I'm sorry if that was too forward, but I see the way my son looks at you."

I could see where Reece got his blunt ways from. I liked it.

Molly pulled me along through the living room toward the small eat-in kitchen. "You know, I think he's had quite the crush on you for the last couple of years. It was nice to see him a little trepidatious. I wasn't sure he was ever going to work up the courage to talk to you."

When we entered the kitchen, I stood shocked. "It's so weird to me that Reece even noticed me."

She quirked a brow and gave me a good once-over. "Have you looked in the mirror lately? You are stunning." She was too kind.

"I think it might have been all the displays he saw me dive behind that caught his attention."

She laughed. "We all hide in our own way, don't we?"

I nodded.

"You make yourself at home." She pointed to the round, hand-painted antique white table filled with some of my favorites: orange chicken, fried rice, and egg rolls. "I'm going to put these gorgeous flowers in a vase with some water. What can I get you to drink? I have wine, water, soda?"

"Water is great." I scooted over to the table while taking in the view of the updated U-shaped kitchen. It was light and bright with white cupboards and new retro appliances. I was in love with the mint-green stove and refrigerator. Very cool. I dug Molly's style. "Your house is so cute," I commented.

She looked around serenely. "I love this old place. It was the first home I ever bought by myself. Reece keeps telling me I should sell it, but I can't. Here, I made my stand."

"It sounds like moving here was a big leap forward for both you and Reece."

She reached into a cupboard near the sink and grabbed a vase. "It was. I promised myself and Reece we would take our tragedies and make them triumphs here. I had just received my associate's degree and gotten what I considered my first real job as an assistant occupational therapist."

I hadn't known that's what she did. "What made you decide on that career path?"

She arranged the bouquet in the vase. "After watching all the therapy Reece went through after the accident," she said quietly but stoically, "I knew I wanted to help people like my son."

"It must have been so hard for you to watch him struggle."

She let out a meaningful sigh. "You have no idea. The guilt ate at me. I blamed myself for leaving him with his father," she grumbled out that last part. "He should have been safe at home." It obviously still pained her.

"From the sounds of it, you were doing your best to support your family. I know Reece doesn't blame you."

She walked over and joined me at the table, sitting across from me. "We have both learned who the blame belongs to, but we don't dwell on him anymore. He doesn't deserve the honor."

I liked her sassy spunk. "Good for you."

"Well, it took a lot of years and practice." She winked. "But I didn't bring you here to talk about tragedies; we are all about triumph tonight," she declared. "I want to know all about you, the enigmatic beauty who has captured my son's heart. We will start with your gorgeous chocolate-red hair. How is that possible?"

I smiled and twirled a tendril. "Believe it or not, it's naturally this color."

"That is amazing, just like you."

I bit my lip. "I'm not so sure about that."

"Did you see those little girls who worshipped you today? Andi talks about you nonstop. You've done, in a matter of days, what we couldn't do in weeks as her family. I was worried she would never string two words together again, much less ask to have friends over."

I was so happy to hear that. "I love the kids in my class. It's important to me that they feel safe at school."

"That is apparent. You turned your tragedy into a triumph,

not just for you, but for dozens of children and their parents. I hope you realize that."

I thought for a moment, letting what she said sink in. If what she was saying was true, that was all brought about because of the pirate girl. Perhaps I would come to like her yet. "Thank you, Molly."

"No. Thank you. Now let's eat. I have lots of stories to tell you about Reece." She flashed me a devious grin.

I liked her. A lot.

Twenty-Seven

"HOW MANY EMBARRASSING STORIES DID my mom tell you today?" Reece kissed my cheek.

I snuggled further into his arms with my back against his chest, sitting between his legs on his comfy couch. The mood was perfect, with the only light source being his TV. I wasn't sure what movie was playing, as Reece and I had been wrapped up in each other since I'd arrived half an hour ago.

"She told me all the stories," I teased. "I especially enjoyed the one where you were a ring bearer at your aunt's wedding and you thought the flower girl wasn't doing her job properly, so you took the basket of flowers and threw the petals yourself. The photographic evidence was adorable."

"In my defense, she was going to run out of petals at the rate she was going. She wasn't properly spacing them."

"Wow. I didn't know you were so passionate about the petal-to-aisle ratio." I giggled.

"I'm passionate, all right." He wrapped his arms tighter around me while nuzzling my neck.

I angled my head to the side, making sure he could be as passionate as he wanted to.

"You smell incredible." He brushed his lips against my skin, which begged for his touch. "Like pumpkin spice and cinnamon."

"They're the best," I stuttered out, for being so turned on by him. "You're the best."

"The feeling is mutual." His tongue came out to play, sending waves of shivers down my body.

"You keep doing that and we will be going past hypersonic speed."

He took one more taste before pulling away. "I am happy to place your desires above my own," he groaned.

Wow. He was going to have me falling so fast, I wouldn't know what hit me if he kept saying things like that and meaning them. "Part of me doesn't want you to," I admitted. "But I want to take my time with you. I want to love myself before I fall in love with you."

"You already think you're going to fall in love with me?" He sounded quite pleased, but not surprised. Of course he wasn't. I bet every woman he'd ever dated couldn't help but love him. I had to make a conscious effort not to. Honestly, I wasn't sure I really *could* love him until I loved myself.

"I mean, it's a possibility." I playfully shrugged.

"I can't wait to show you all the possibilities you have before you," he said low into my ear, turning my body into a goose bump garden.

"How was your day?" I said, well above my normal pitch. He was driving me wild, and I needed to change the subject.

"You okay there?" He laughed, knowing full well how he got to me.

"I'm working on it." I was talking about more than how much he affected me.

"I'm glad. What can I help with?"

"Let's talk about you first. I always feel like we talk about me more."

"I like talking about you."

"And I appreciate that, but tell me what's going on in your world. How's work and dad life?"

Reece swept back my hair and rested his chin on my shoulder. "You are incredible."

"No. I'm just really into you." I turned and pecked his cheek. "Now tell me about your day," I demanded in my faux-scary voice.

"A take-charge woman. I like it." He let out a meaningful breath. "If I'm being honest, work is taxing, and being a single dad is harder than I thought it would be. Don't get me wrong— I'm so happy to have Andi with me full-time, but I worry that I'm not giving her enough of my time. I try to get home at a decent hour, but sometimes work follows me here. I just want her to know she's my first priority."

"I'm sure she does. And, just so you know, I will never be hurt or offended if you can't spend time with me because of Andi or work."

"I appreciate you saying that. Here's the thing: I want to spend any time I can with you. This right here, this feels right."

It did. So right, it was scary. "What can I do to help you?"

"Just let me hold you and talk."

"That seems a little self-serving on my part, but you have yourself a deal."

He chuckled. "I love your sense of humor."

"I'm just a jolly pumpkin," I oozed sarcasm. No one had ever accused me of being jovial.

"I don't know about that."

See, no one.

"But"—he nipped my earlobe—"you are the most intoxicating and gorgeous pumpkin in the patch."

I could live with that. "Your mom mentioned that you're having troubles with Nicolette," I hesitated to bring it up or change the subject, but this was important. "You can talk to me about her. She's Andi's mom, and you were married to her. That's a big deal."

"Josie." He let out a long, heavy breath. "I'm not purposely keeping that part of my life from you. I'm just not sure what I'm dealing with at the moment. She keeps threatening to leave the treatment center and sue me for full custody."

I gasped at the thought.

"Don't worry, she won't. She says these things to hurt me. She's still angry because I didn't stop her from leaving me. And she thinks I humiliated her by taking Andi away."

I took his hand and kissed it. "I'm so sorry. I can't imagine how stressful that is for you."

"I'm just tired of her games. Deep down, she knows she's not best for Andi. But she's all about her image. If you look at her Instagram page, you would think we lived some fairy-tale life. It was anything but that, especially the last few years of our marriage."

That just goes to show that you should never compare your life to the one people portray, especially online. We all have our personal demons. Some are just better at hiding theirs.

"If it makes you feel better, I hate social media. I don't even have any personal accounts." For obvious reasons. I feared people would call me the pirate girl there, too. The farm had accounts I sometimes checked. I used them mostly to read Cami's posts.

"This is why I like you. You're real. I've wanted real for a long time now."

"I might be too real."

"No. You're perfect. I mean that."

He had no idea what those words meant to me. For someone who felt like she was never going to be anyone's perfect, it meant the world. I adjusted myself so I was sitting on his lap. I curled right into him. For a moment, I just listened to the sound of his heart through his soft cotton tee.

Reece cradled me and stroked my hair. "Tell me about your day. You sounded upset earlier on the phone about the conversation with your mom."

"My mom," I moaned. "I love her. I really do, but it's like she can't let go of what she thinks happened all those years ago. It makes it hard for me to let go. I get it, her generation has some weird hang-ups about sex that they inherited from their parents.

For them it was taboo, even sinful. Not to say our generation has it all right. We've gone from one extreme to another. I just want her to meet me in the middle. She freaks out if my nephew uses anatomically correct words to name all the body parts. I can't fathom why. It can be dangerous not to, and it makes it seem like we should be ashamed of our bodies," I ranted.

"You definitely shouldn't be ashamed of your body." He ran his hand up my dress but only skimmed my calf. I loved how he held back his own desires to honor mine. Not to say I didn't desire him.

"I don't want to be. Sure, did I write some pretty racy things no fifteen-year-old should be doing? Absolutely. But I wasn't actually doing those things. All I was trying to do at the time was figure myself out. You don't know how much I would have loved for her to just have sat me down and asked me if I wanted to talk about the stuff I had written. It would have been even more embarrassing than the situation already was, but at least I would have known I was normal. Instead, I grew up thinking there was something wrong with me because I fantasized about you in great detail." I cringed. Which just proved my point.

Although, I felt for my mom. I had overheard her and Aunt D. talking once about how neither one of them knew anything about sex on their wedding nights. My mom had been so nervous, my parents didn't have sex until three days after they were married. Mom gave me a science book about it when I turned fourteen after my period started. She'd said if I had any questions after I read it, I should come to talk to her, but her tone had indicated otherwise.

"You are very detailed. For that I compliment you."

I rolled my eyes. "You are such a guy."

"Guilty. But this is good. You're talking about it—with me, even. You're starting to own it." He tenderly kissed my brow. "I am sorry things are unsettled between you and your mother. I know how much that upsets you."

"I just want her to see my side for once." However, I was

beginning to wonder if my mother had never felt comfortable about herself as a sexual being. It would make sense, based on how disconcerting she found the story, even now.

Reece rubbed my arm. "I'm sure she'll come around. Parenting is hard. I worry all the time about screwing up Andi. I'm already saving for therapy, just in case."

"Maybe my parents should have saved for that instead of college," I teased. "Now I have to depend on Google to get me through."

"Google?" he questioned.

"Don't judge. I had a major breakthrough with Jenna today using the search engine."

"I have to hear this."

I made circling motions with my finger across his taut chest, telling myself not to rip his shirt off. "We found a great article about how to heal from childhood bullying. Jenna made me say my good qualities out loud. It was rough, but I made it through."

"I'd like to hear them." His hand moved up and began to caress my knee.

Oh, baby, he did things to me. "I think I've had enough therapy for today," I managed to say, between my heart skipping every beat. "Though later, I do plan to write a scathing letter to all my torturers and then burn it like the article suggested. That should be therapeutic."

Reece chuckled low in my ear, while his touch continued to drive me wild. He had no idea how close I was to ripping off his shirt again. "I can name some of your finer qualities if you would like?" He went from chuckling to sexy at Mach 10.

"What are those?" I tripped over my words. He had me under his spell. I loved it.

"Let's start with your skin." His hand ran the length of my calf. "I have never touched anything so silky smooth. Then there is the way you taste." His lips captured mine, his tongue immediately entreating me to let him taste every part of my mouth. I was more than happy to acquiesce.

My hands took their own liberties and ran up his chest and into his hair, imploring him to taste me thoroughly. He immediately complied and deepened the kiss. We were back on the hypersonic track. Regrettably, I pulled away, breathing hard.

He took my face into his hands. "You undo me, Josie Peterson. It is your finest quality."

I smiled, so touched. "I should probably go," I hated to say that, but it was getting late, and I had a hard time controlling myself around him.

"Please stay," he pleaded. "I want to hold you just a little longer."

"How can I say no to that?" I snuggled back into him and closed my eyes, reveling in how beautiful it felt to be wanted and treasured. I inwardly grinned, thinking I was one of Reece's treasures. It was either ironic or apropos.

"Thank you." He kissed my head.

"For what?"

"Giving us a chance."

"I feel like I could say the same thing to you. You know I'm still crazy, right?"

"I like your brand of crazy. It's one of your finer qualities." He didn't sound like he was teasing at all.

Oh, this man. Consider me branded for life.

Twenty-Eight

OCTOBER ARRIVED IN ALL ITS autumnal glory. The weather was cooling down, and the kisses were getting hotter. I was falling faster than the golden leaves on the trees. Best autumn in the history of all the seasons. With it came the school carnival. Guess who had the best booth ever? That's right. Moi. However, I couldn't get too excited about it in front of everyone, for fear people would see right through me and know I was having royal retreats with my Royal Highness as often as we could. Which meant I was exhausted. Late nights were pretty much our only option. Once, I'd accidentally fallen asleep while he was holding me on the couch. I'd woken up in a panic around five in the morning to zoom home to get ready for the day, before Andi woke up and saw her teacher in her dad's arms. That could have gotten awkward.

What wasn't awkward was when he'd said, "I knew you would have good morning eyes." I had no idea what that meant, so I'd asked him to clarify. He was happy to oblige. "They're eyes that say you are as happy to be with me in the dark as you are in the light."

I was happy to be with him anytime. If only I could. It was going to be difficult, keeping my feelings for him a secret for the next seven plus months. Like right now, as I walked into the gym and looked across it to find Reece and Noah setting up the photo booth in the corner. It took all I had to not go plowing through all the other booths and volunteers setting up the carnival and run straight into his arms. Although there was still a part of me that dreaded the thought of someone referring to me as the pirate girl when they made the connection between Recce and me. I was trying to come to terms with her. I'd even written my scathing letter and let Reece read it.

It was kind of embarrassing watching him read the tear-stained stationery I'd poured my heart and soul onto, detailing every pang of my heart caused by cruel words meant to cut. I spoke of my shredded soul and the privacy stolen from me. The toughest part was writing about how much I had loathed myself. I'd hated myself so much I went for three months without looking in a mirror, not being able to stand to even look at my face. During that time, Jenna came in clutch, doing my hair and makeup.

There was something about writing it all down that was cathartic. Admitting it happened and reliving the feelings, instead of suppressing them, was cleansing to the soul. After Reece read it, he took my hand and led me outside, where he flipped on his firepit. There, I watched all the hurt burn while Reece held me. We were still swimming to that shore together. The waters were deep and choppy at times.

My mom was still keeping her distance, as if she didn't know what to say or do around me anymore. Same went for my brother. I hated it, because I didn't know what to say either.

Then there was Nicolette. She kept threatening to leave rehab. She called Reece every time she was allowed to have her phone. He would beg her to stay for Andi's sake. Then she would say terrible things like he ruined her life and he never really loved her. She was still playing the blame game, which made me think she wasn't ready to get clean and sober. That scared Reece more than anything, given his own history. He worried for Andi's emotional and physical safety. I did too.

Andi was making great progress at school. Her math skills were improving each day, along with her social skills. I knew it was because she felt safe and loved at home. That, more than anything, contributed to a child's success. As teachers, we could do everything in our power to help a student, but it never compared to the influences inside the home.

"Your room-parent coordinator is yummy," Libby drawled, startling me.

I didn't even know she had approached me. I was too busy ogling my man. Which wasn't the best thing to be doing. "Uh, I guess so," I said, flustered.

"Right." She jabbed me with her pointy elbow. "You're telling me you haven't noticed that you have a four-alarm fire of a man doing your bidding."

"He's not doing my bidding. He's a volunteer for the school."

"Of course, darlin'. Whatever you say. But the pink in your creamy cheeks says he really melts your butter." She did a great impression of Dolly Parton, shaking her hips to the beat of her voice.

"I've gotten a lot of sun lately. You know, outdoor recess and such. And I've been helping out on the farm."

"Uh-huh."

"It's against the rules, Libby," my voice pleaded with her to drop it.

"I wouldn't let that stop me." She eyed Reece like he was fried chicken and he was finger-lickin' good.

"Have at him," I teased, but I really wanted to say, *"Keep your eyes and your hands to yourself, you cougar."*

She held up the sparkly diamond that graced her left hand. "Believe me, darlin', if I were younger and this ring wasn't around my finger, I'd hog-tie that man and show him some southern hospitality."

Great, now I was going to have to get that image out of my head. "Well, I better help set up the booth." I'd borrowed Dad's truck to haul over the hay bales and pumpkins. I wanted to see if Reece would like to help me carry them in. You know, since he was my Royal Highness and I would take any excuse to be alone with him, if only for a few minutes.

"You do that." She bumped me with her hip. "Have fun. By the way, I'm bringing my grandbabies to the pumpkin patch later today."

"Make sure it's after two. I'll be helping out here until then." It was the only Saturday of the season I didn't put a full day in at the farm. As a teacher, I was required to help with the fall carnival. I didn't mind. Especially not this year.

"Sounds good. See you later, darlin'." She walked off, swinging her hips.

I started to make my way across the expansive gym with a flurry of activity going on. All the room-parent coordinators and PTA volunteers were putting the finishing touches on their booths. Doors opened in just over an hour. Others, meaning Marilyn, felt the need to flirt with Reece. I was liking her less and less. How many times was Reece going to have to reject her advances?

I stood by the popcorn machine and watched the cringey scene unfold. Marilyn slinked over in her frilly checkered black-and-white apron, tied to show off her tiny waist. The aprons were a bit much. All the PTA board members and everyone running a booth were forced to wear one. This school was a little over the top when it came to these events.

Marilyn held up a masculine apron for Reece. "Look what we had made especially for you, as our token male room-parent coordinator."

There was nothing token about Reece.

Reece eyed the apron warily. "Thank you." He tried to reach for it, but Marilyn took the liberty of placing it right up against him, as if she were trying to see how it fit. But I could see behind her facade. She got very handsy, smoothing his chest.

That was it. No one else was going to touch or ogle him

today in my presence. I marched right over there. Noah smirked at me as I descended upon the ridiculous scene. Poor Reece kept backing up, and she just kept coming at him like a rabid vampire bat.

"Mr. Cavanaugh," I rushed to say. We had agreed to be formal in public settings, for fear that if we used first names, we wouldn't be able to hide our feelings for each other. He did say Josie awfully well.

Reece let out a heavy breath, as if relieved I had shown up.

Marilyn stopped attacking her prey, turned, and tsked.

I wanted to say *"Excuse me?"* but refrained. Even if I weren't dating him, this was not the place to be trying to pick up men. I did give her a sickly-sweet smile, though. "Sorry for interrupting"—I was, in fact, not at all sorry—"but I need help bringing in the hay bales and pumpkins."

Marilyn returned the fake smile. "You." She pointed at Noah. "You can help Ms. Peterson."

Oh, she was a piece of work. I had to hold back my diatribe. Thankfully, Noah came in clutch. "Sorry, I have to go pick up my wife and nephews." Bless him.

Reece took the out and sidestepped the psycho. Yes, I realized I had my psycho moments too, but Marilyn was a different brand. Like the scary kind, because she didn't know, or care, that she was insane.

"I would be happy to help you, Ms. Peterson." The corners of Reece's mouth ticked up, trying not to flash me his dazzling smile.

"Thank you."

Marilyn's eye started twitching. That couldn't be good. "Well, make sure to come find me afterward. I need help, uh, hanging some, uh, banners." Sure, she did. They'd strung up the lights and banners across the gym the day before.

Reece didn't respond to her, at least not verbally. His jogging away from her, to the sound of Noah chuckling, should have said it all.

I had to walk quickly to catch up to him, all while not looking like I was chasing after him.

Reece waited outside the gym doors in the cool morning, looking a little shell shocked. One would think he would be used to the overt attention. I was glad he wasn't.

I breathed in the air that was becoming more fall-like every day, trying not to accost him.

"Good morning." He gave me a sly grin. He'd already sent me a sweet good-morning text.

"Good morning, Mr. Cavanaugh."

"You know," he whispered, "I kind of like it when you call me that."

I rolled my eyes and walked toward the truck. "Why do all men love the boss and secretary fantasy?"

"Before you think I'm a sexist pig, I was picturing you as the boss." He wagged his brows.

I couldn't help but smile. "Stop. You're going to get me in trouble. I already had to stop myself from clawing Marilyn's eyes out. I swear, I can't take you anywhere," I half-joked. The man was a lady magnet.

He shuddered at the mention of Marilyn's name. "Thank you for saving me."

"I feel like I have to do that a lot."

"You're not jealous, are you?"

"No. I see the way you look at me." I was still amazed by it, but honored nonetheless. I had never had a man see me the way he did and like me for who I was, quirks and all. "Just don't look at me like that here." I grinned, but I was serious.

"That's going to be hard. You look beautiful today. The soft-pink sweater suits you. Everything suits you."

"Thank you." I stepped farther away from him before I kissed him.

He noted the distance. "Good call. I almost took your hand."

I shoved my hands in the pockets of my jeans. This was going to be a long school year.

We crossed the parking lot in a friendly fashion, not saying anything, but the sexual tension between us was palpable. My entire body was buzzing, wishing to be close to him. It was almost too much to bear.

"My mom is bringing Andi over soon," he said, as if he, too, needed something to take his mind off the unspoken thing we had going between us.

"I can't wait to see them."

We finally made it to Dad's old white Ford truck, with the farm's logo on the door. I so badly wished we were alone so I could drop the tailgate and accost him. However, I acted with decorum and casually let down the tailgate, trying not to inhale his spring-rain scent.

"Dang, that's sexy: a girl and her truck." Reece whistled low.

"Seriously, stop," I said out of the side of my mouth, though I really wanted him to keep going.

"You're not making this easy," he said, too close to me, making me shiver. I was getting fired for sure.

"Right back at ya, buddy," I playfully growled.

Reece chuckled and reached for a bale of hay. "By the way, Nicolette's parents are coming to the carnival today. They want to take Andi to the Aspen Lake street fair and keep her overnight."

"Oh," I said, a bit pitchy, while grabbing a pumpkin. "So, you'll be alone?"

"I hope not." He flashed me a seductive glance.

I was about to say something I probably shouldn't on school grounds, when a booming voice scared the living daylights out of me.

"Reece, my man," Mr. Nelson shouted from across the parking lot, sounding very chipper. I didn't even know he could be chipper.

I dropped the pumpkin on the tailgate and barely caught it before it rolled onto the pavement. Holy shiz, my nerves weren't going to survive this.

Reece deftly hefted the bale and dropped it on the ground in front of the tailgate. "Ken," he returned the enthusiastic greeting.

The two men walked toward each other. A bro hug ensued.

"So good to see you," Mr. Nelson patted Reece's back. "I wish more dads were as involved as you."

"It's their loss," Reece responded.

The men broke apart, and Mr. Nelson zeroed in on me, his happy-go-lucky attitude fading. "Good morning, Ms. Peterson." Heaven forbid he be personable with his teachers.

"Good morning."

"Is Reece being helpful?"

Oh, yeah. Very. Yep, I was so getting fired.

Twenty-Nine

THE CARNIVAL WAS FULL STEAM ahead, with the gym reaching near maximum capacity. The noise level was insane, given the number of excited children running from one booth to the next to see how many tickets they could win and cash in for prizes. With so many people in attendance, you'd have thought my focus would have been easily distracted away from Reece and Andi, but my gaze continually drifted in their direction as I played Cami's assistant at the photo booth.

Reece was oh so adorable with Andi as he and Molly took her around the carnival. He cheered her on as she did both the clown toss and balloon pop. I kept thinking maybe next year I would join the threesome and Reece could hold both our hands. Maybe then I wouldn't have to keep an eye on Marilyn, who kept slinking around him any chance she got. Not that every other female in the vicinity wasn't eyeing him like they wanted to trick-or-treat all over him. Even the married women stared a bit longer than they should have.

Between photo takes, Cami sidled up to me, noticing my line of sight. "I'm glad things are going so well for the two of you," she whispered. "You both deserve the happiness."

I thought for a moment. I was happy. Not like giddy happy, because that wasn't me, but this peace I had never felt before was creeping into my heart and soul. I knew I had a long way to go before I fully allowed it in, but Reece had helped me open the door. He'd given me hope that perhaps I could come to terms with my past, and even the pirate girl. He'd even offered to read the story with me, thinking it might help. I hadn't been brave enough to take him up on the offer. Yes, I had it memorized, but there was something about physically confronting it online and seeing what others had to say about it. That was scary and real. It would be like looking at old photos of my awkward teen self. I knew one day I would have to face her—and the story—if I wanted to continue to move forward with Reece. It was great incentive, as there was nothing more I wanted to do.

"Thank you," I whispered back. "And thanks for helping today. I think a lot of these people will be using your photos for family Christmas cards this year. It's not every day they get a famous photographer to take their pictures."

Cami grinned. "It's my pleasure. Now, back to work."

She and Noah were good people. I found myself imagining a future where the four of us would double-date. I enjoyed entertaining the idea. As I turned to help the next group of people, something caught my attention. Three people approached Reece, Andi, and Molly while they were at the pumpkin-decorating booth. I clutched my chest, as I recognized one of the two women in the group—Nicolette. I'd only ever seen her from behind a display, several feet away, but there was no doubt she was the beauty standing before Reece. I guess she decided to make good on her threat and leave rehab.

Even from a distance, I could feel the tension in the air. The well-dressed couple, who I assumed were her parents, appeared mortified. Their faces screamed an apology.

Reece drew Andi close to him, and Molly flanked her other side.

The beautiful Nicolette, with long raven hair and perfect cheekbones, wore what looked like a fake bright smile. "Baby, look at you," she spoke to Andi. "I missed you so much."

Andi wiggled free from her dad and grandmother, I assumed to run to her mom, but no—she bolted in my direction, weaving in and out of people. My instincts kicked in, and all I could think was to go to her. Without saying a word to Cami, I pushed my way through the crowd and met Andi at the ring toss. When she saw me, her eyes flooded with tears, and she ran straight to me, wrapping her tiny arms around my waist. "Ms. Peterson," she cried, while clinging to me.

I held her tight, knowing very well I was beginning to feel something deeper for her than the normal love I had for my students. It was as if I were meant to protect her. "What's wrong, honey?"

She didn't say anything, only tightened her hold on me.

Reece was there in no time, followed by Molly, Nicolette, and her parents.

I looked at Reece, worry etched in every crease of his brow, not knowing what to say. I knew too much about the situation and how he must be feeling. This was one of his worst nightmares—Nicolette not getting the help she needed and coming back to make his life a living hell. I wanted so badly to reach out and comfort him. I hated that I couldn't in that moment.

Reece gave me a pained looked before kneeling next to Andi, who was shaking in my arms.

Several people nearby came and went, glancing upon the scene. It was an all-around uncomfortable situation.

Molly gave me a knowing look as she stood apprehensively next to Nicolette's parents, who were grimacing at their daughter.

If her haughty expression was any indication, Nicolette seemed unfazed. How could she not understand the pain she was causing her child?

I narrowed my eyes at her and cast her a rebuking glare, holding back the mob of words I would love to throw at her. It didn't go unnoticed, and I soon became the focus of her attention. She looked me up and down and sized me up, and a spark in her eyes said she knew something about me. I wasn't sure what that was, but I had a feeling I wouldn't like it. She could scrutinize me all she wanted—all I cared about in that moment was making Andi and Reece feel better.

"Honey," Reece said gently, while stroking the hair he had so lovingly braided down his daughter's back, "why did you run away?"

I was sure he knew why, but he wanted Andi to own it. He wanted Nicolette to understand her actions, if that were possible.

Andi said nothing, but continued to tremble. I had felt like her so often, not wanting to confront those who had hurt me, especially myself. Until recently, I had never had the luxury of finding bravery in the strength of the arms of someone who cared for me. I knew I had to lend Andi that strength—a strength I didn't have for myself, but there it was for her, encompassing me, waiting to be unleashed.

Without releasing my hold on her, I knelt next to her. Probably too close to Reece, but it couldn't be helped, especially in the crowd. Although people were trying to give us space, they were also gawking.

"Hey, sweet girl. What's going on?" I used gentle tones. I knew from Reece that Andi longed to see her mother, but feared her as well. That was a lot of emotion to deal with for anyone, much less an eight-year-old.

Andi's gorgeous emerald eyes were wide with confusion. Her lips quivered, words trying to come out.

A thought came to me. "Can you picture the poster on the wall in our class that shows feelings?"

She nodded.

"That's good. Can you think about which pictures you would point to?" I often found children felt more than one emotion at a time, just like adults, and are capable of so much more than we give them credit for.

"Yes," she quietly squeaked.

"Can you tell me which ones you would point to?"

A single tear fell down her rosy cheek.

"Who is this woman, anyway?" Nicolette brashly interrupted.

The woman I was sure was Nicolette's mother shook her head as if embarrassed by her daughter's behavior. The father said, "Nicolette," with a voice of warning.

Reece whipped his head toward Nicolette, holding back what was sure to be a scathing glare. He swallowed down what I assumed were harsh words and responded, "This is Ms. Peterson, our daughter's teacher."

Nicolette rolled her gorgeous dark eyes. She was behaving as a juvenile, but I didn't mention it. I only wanted Andi to talk to me, to feel safe.

More tears began to fall down Andi's cheek, breaking my heart. I wiped them away, one by one, with my thumb. "Would you like to go somewhere else and talk?" I suggested.

Andi nodded.

"Okay, let's go to the classroom." I stood and took Andi's hand.

Reece followed suit. "Thank you, *Josie.*" He said my name so tenderly, there was no mistaking the emotion behind it.

Nicolette obviously caught it, judging by her sneer and the way her head ping-ponged between Reece and me. Then an evil glint lit up her eyes. "Josie Peterson," she said with an air of satisfaction.

I'd heard the inflections before and knew what was coming. There was no sense in bracing myself for it because it had never helped.

"Oh my gosh," she said like a true mean girl, "you're the pirate girl."

Everyone around us seemed to stop and stare. Or perhaps I only felt as if all the world were looking at me, as my temperature rose, and my heart rate increased exponentially. I was never getting away from the pirate girl.

"Nicolette," Reece seethed. "You're better than that."

She curled her lips in the most conceited manner, but then asked, "Am I?" as if pleading with him to know if she really was a better person. As if she wanted Reece to see that she was.

Andi, out of character and out of nowhere, stomped her foot. "Don't call Ms. Peterson names!"

A silence settled all around us. Reece and I shared a stunned glance before I looked down at my sweet Andi with her tearstained cheeks, doing her best to defend me. In her eyes I saw such courage and determination, it lent me some, as well as a good dose of reality. I should be defending Andi, not the other way around. Not only that, but I knew the way I responded would be an example to Andi, so it had better be a good one. The last thing I ever wanted was for Andi to think it was okay to let anyone push her around or make her feel as if she were less. The way I had felt for so much of my life. In that moment, I knew I had to own it. I had to be okay with the pirate girl, because the little girl whose hand I held in mine needed me to be. And I needed Andi to know that no one should ever tell her how to feel about herself. That she should never be defined by a cruel name.

I squeezed Andi's hand. "Thank you," my voice crackled with raw emotion.

Andi gave me that sweet smile of hers, calming my heart and soul.

I stood a little taller and faced Nicolette, who looked as if she might cry as she stared at her daughter's hand in mine. It was obvious she knew there was more going on here than just a teacher and her student and a parent-teacher relationship. She was aware she was losing something, and I knew it didn't bode well for me. But in that moment, I couldn't think about what was going to happen in my near future. I had to take a stand for Andi, and for all the children who would come into my life—those I taught, and with any luck, those I would bear—and for the girl I had abandoned in my past.

"It's so nice to finally meet you." I held out my hand, trying not to quake. I had to own this to show Nicolette that she hadn't gotten to me, so that I could show Andi that she never needed to run and hide. "I'm Andi's teacher. I am . . . the pirate girl."

Thirty

IT DOESN'T MATTER HOW OLD you are—getting called to the principal's office is never a good thing. Not that I was exactly called in. It was more like I was marched down the hall with Reece in tow, following a fuming Mr. Nelson, who was clearly on a mission I assumed included his recommendation to the board I be terminated. Remember Tad Fellows? It was possible my story might end up topping his. It was all a matter of opinion, I suppose. I could still hear Nicolette's shrill voice screaming, "I can't believe you are actually dating the girl who wrote that ridiculous story about you!"

Oh yeah, that had happened all of ten minutes earlier.

I was like a dazed zombie trailing behind Mr. Nelson to the stomp of his oxfords. The events of the last several minutes ran through my head like a montage of what felt like someone else's life. Because honestly, I didn't recognize the woman who had shown up inside of me. But I had to say: I liked her. I still couldn't believe I had owned up to being the pirate girl. It didn't mean I was automatically copacetic with that girl, but I had opened up the door for a reconciliation. That didn't sit well with Nicolette for some reason. It was like she needed me to cower under the name. I believe she thought it should have given her power, and I had taken it away. I was beginning to think she wasn't okay

248

with herself, and for some sick reason she needed me to not be all right. If that wasn't an epiphany. How many of my torturers were tortured themselves? How much power had I given them over the years? It was an unsettling thought.

But not quite as unsettling as what I was facing right now: I was ready to lose my job because Nicolette couldn't stand the idea that I had refused her more power. She'd sought her revenge by revealing that Reece was dating me—something she'd probably thought everyone would find ridiculous. Of course, she had only surmised this. She had no actual proof, but when she screamed it, I couldn't lie about it, not in front of Andi. I would never lie in front of a student, especially her. It was one thing to sneak around and her not have any knowledge of it, but this was different. And I couldn't deny it in front of Reece. How could I, after everything he had done for me? It felt like a betrayal to do so.

Reece took my hand as we walked down the hall amid all the gawkers. Might as well. You should have seen the way he beamed when he couldn't find the words to refute his ex-wife's revelation. I knew he wanted to on my behalf, to save my job, but on the other hand, he wanted to tell the world he was proud to be dating me. His eyes had implored me to know what to do, so I took matters into my own hands for once in my life. I looked Nicolette square in the eyes and said, "I needed new material for the sequel."

I wasn't actually planning a sequel, of course, but her spluttering was worth it. I believe part of her thought we couldn't really be dating and she would just be humiliating me when Reece denied it. Instead, her worst fears were confirmed: the pirate girl had taken the treasure she had so carelessly given away.

Why she had even come today, I had no idea. What was she thinking? Her parents had to practically drag her out while she hysterically bawled. Poor Andi stood horrified, watching her mother behave so erratically. I had told Reece just to stay with

Andi when Mr. Nelson demanded to see me, but Molly insisted he go with me while she attended to Andi in our absence.

With every step we took past every gaping stare from onlookers milling through the hallway, the adrenaline began to wear off. What I had done began to truly sink in. I didn't regret any of it, for Andi's sake, but . . . "How am I going to pay for my Turkish streaming channel now? And my mortgage," I lamented out loud, feeling as if I might lose it.

Reece tightened his grip.

"No more *Erkenci Kus*. I need to know if they get back together," I rambled, in my state of shock. I should have been more worried about food and shelter, but you must see Can Yaman for yourself before you judge me.

Reece slightly chuckled even though the poor man's worst nightmare had just come to fruition.

I suppose laughing was better than crying. Although I had a feeling the tears I had rarely shed over the years were bound to make an appearance when I got fired.

Mr. Nelson whipped his head back our way. "This is no laughing matter. You have put me in a hell of a position." He stared at our clasped hands and harrumphed before turning around to unlock the door leading to the administrative offices.

"We'll take you to court if we have to," Reece said, no holds barred.

I tensed at the thought of it. However, I admit to being turned on by Reece's sexy take-charge attorney side.

Mr. Nelson let out a sound of disgust. "Get in here." He waved us in.

The men had a cold staring match as we walked past my principal—potentially former principal. I hated that I had come between friends. Even more so, I cringed to think that by now my mother was sure to know that I was going to be losing my job because of Reece. I could hear the lecture now. Let's not forget the rumors that would be circulated about the rogue pirate and pirate girl coming together. Now I would have no choice but to own it all. For Andi and for every other kid out there who felt out of place, I had to. I think some therapy was in order, and not the Google kind.

Mr. Nelson flipped on the lights as we walked down the hall to my doom. I mean, it wasn't going to be all bad. I smiled up at Reece wearing that stupid apron Marilyn had given him and tried to tie for him. I'd had to step in as she eyed his butt, itching to grab it. Don't think I wouldn't have swatted her hand away had she given in to the urge. At least this way the Marilyns of the world would know he was off the market.

Reece leaned in and kissed my brow.

Mr. Nelson groaned behind us.

"Groan all you want. Legally you have no right to tell Josie who she can and can't date." Reece was apparently not going to back down.

"Get in my office." Mr. Nelson was up for the fight.

We all walked in to where it had sort of all begun. It truly began fifteen years ago, but this was the place where, despite my lunacy, Andi was placed in my care. I had no idea she and her father would help me to see life in a way no one else had.

I eyed the chairs I had moved apart. Without thinking, I moved them back together, even closer this time.

Mr. Nelson shot me an incredulous glance.

I already knew I was in deep trouble, so the fact that it bothered him that I was rearranging his office furniture without his permission didn't faze me.

Reece and I took our seats, clasping hands.

Mr. Nelson threw himself into his fine leather chair, rubbing a hand over his bald head dotted with beads of angry sweat. "You knew the rules, Ms. Peterson. Why would you deliberately break them?"

That was a good question, but there was an easy answer. I gave Reece an adoring smile. "Well, I mean, look at the man. Can you blame me?"

Reece returned my smile, just as adoringly.

"Hell," Mr. Nelson grumbled at the googly eyes Reece and I were making at each other.

A thought popped into my head—one of those you probably shouldn't say, but know you're going to anyway. "You only have yourself to blame," I accused Mr. Nelson. "I did tell you to put Andi in Aline's class, but you insisted she stay in mine."

Mr. Nelson's eyes widened to a frightening size.

I braced myself for his rebuke.

Mr. Nelson breathed out of his nostrils like a raging bull. "Ms. Peterson," he said my name like fingernails against a chalkboard.

It sent shivers down my spine.

"If you knew you had feelings for Reece, you should have disclosed those up front."

"I didn't realize at the time those feelings existed," I defended myself. More like I didn't know they would reemerge with a fury.

"Regardless," Reece jumped in, "she didn't have to disclose anything to you. That's a private matter."

Mr. Nelson pointed toward the door. "That private matter became very public today. I can't have domestic issues plaguing school grounds."

Reece leaned forward, eyes ablaze. "I apologize that my family is going through some turmoil at this time. I'm doing my best to handle the situation, but I can't control my ex-wife. You know damn well what I've done to help her."

Mr. Nelson's features softened. "And I admire you for it, but—"

"But what?" Reece interrupted him. "I can't be with Josie because my ex-wife takes issue with me moving on?"

"She's your daughter's teacher," Mr. Nelson gritted out.

"Yes, she is. And who did my daughter run to today when she felt scared? She ran straight to Ms. Peterson, because she knows Ms. Peterson loves her and will keep her safe. You're willing to let go of your best teacher because her biggest crime is that she's consensually dating a parent? How does that make any sense?" Reece challenged him.

Mr. Nelson pinched the bridge of his nose. "Reece," he sighed, "we cannot have situations like the one that just took place in the gym. Not to mention the problems it may create in the classroom."

"What problems?" Reece asked.

"Ms. Peterson may give your daughter special treatment or, worse, treat her poorly when things go south between you two."

"That's not going to happen," Reece was quick to say.

I was happy he thought so. "I treat all my students fairly; you know that," I stood up for myself. I was kind of getting good at it. "Besides, plenty of teachers at this school have taught their own children. How is that any different?"

"Andi is not your daughter," Mr. Nelson forcefully reminded me, though I was well aware of that fact.

"So, if she were, this would be a moot point?" Reece asked with a glint in his eye.

"She's not," Mr. Nelson iterated.

"What if she will be in the future?" Reece cast me the most meaningful of looks, sending shock waves through me.

I blinked and blinked, letting what he'd just said sink in. Did he just suggest that—

"Are you getting married?" Yeah, that. That was the suggestion I was thinking. Mr. Nelson sounded as shocked as I felt.

Reece lovingly tugged on a tendril of my hair. "Not today, but perhaps someday."

Some of those tears I thought I might shed earlier made an appearance, welling up in my eyes. I could hardly fathom the idea that Reece could possibly see me as his wife, and as a step-mother to Andi. But somehow a beautiful picture came into my head of the three of us snuggled up on the couch watching a movie and eating popcorn. It was pure bliss.

"Listen," Mr. Nelson sighed, "as your friend, I'm happy for

you. But as an administrator of this school, I have to do what's best for my students and faculty."

Reece glared at his friend. "Then you won't fire Josie. She is the best."

"It's not only up to me." Mr. Nelson let out a heavy breath. "The board will be notified and will make the final decision regarding your employment, Ms. Peterson."

I swallowed down my wildly beating heart. What had I just done? *You owned your life,* a tiny voice I had suppressed inside for years and years whispered to me. *Keep owning it,* the voice got louder. Oh shiz. I knew what I had to do. I had to fight for myself. I stood on shaky legs and wiped the tears out of my eyes. "Fine." My lower lip trembled. I closed my eyes and steadied myself, before reopening them to face Mr. Nelson again. This time a bit more confidently. "When will they meet?"

"I'm not sure," Mr. Nelson responded.

"Please let me know when. I plan to be there with my lawyer." I grinned down at Reece, who immediately jumped up and stood by my side, still willing to swim to the shore with me.

Mr. Nelson groaned and shook his head. "Please, don't—"

"Don't what? Stand up for myself? For Andi and Reece? I'm sorry; that's not an option for me. Not anymore."

Thirty-One

IN THE GLOW OF THE setting sun, I stared at Reece giving Andi a tractor ride where the barn once stood. It was the most beautiful sight. He was taking it slow, going in circles while Andi smiled. It was good to see her smile after the day's events. She didn't seem too worse for the wear after her mother's sudden appearance. Under the circumstances, Reece was keeping her close and wouldn't let her spend the night with her grandparents as originally planned. Her grandparents, who I learned were named Wendy and Gregory, were more than understanding. They wanted to protect Andi as much as anyone. No one was sure what to do about Nicolette. They all knew they couldn't change her or make her get help, as much as they wished they could. The focus now was on Andi.

"How are you doing?" Jenna joined me, taking off her pumpkin beret. The farm had just closed for the daytime events.

"Oddly, okay." I couldn't take my eyes off Reece and Andi. I felt as if I were watching my world right before my eyes. More than anything I didn't want to lose sight of it—of them.

"Do you think you'll lose your job?" she hesitated to ask.

I shrugged. "I don't know. Mr. Nelson didn't suspend me, so there's that. Just in case, we better watch the rest of *Erkenci Kus* this week." I laughed, but I was serious. That streaming channel wasn't cheap.

"I think you're going to be busy." She nodded toward Reece and Andi.

"Yeah." I bit my lip. I hadn't told her Reece had mentioned the possibility of marriage in the future. I was still trying to process that one. I had other things to get through first. You know, like saving my livelihood. Then there was the little—okay, big—matter of the entire town knowing the rogue pirate and pirate girl were an item. There was no going back now. I had to face the pirate girl and come to terms with her. There were two girls who were counting on me: the one on the tractor and the one inside of me, begging to be healed.

"I'm happy for you, Jo Jo."

"I'm happy for me, too." I smiled, thinking about how I could kiss Reece anytime I wanted to now.

Jenna snickered. "Looks like someone's going to get her freak on."

"By that, I'm sure you mean dancing."

"That's exactly what I mean," she said exaggeratedly. "Wink, wink, nudge, nudge, Bob's your uncle."

"Oh my gosh. Stop it. You know the sisters are nearby," I whispered.

The sisters had not weighed in on my situation yet, but no doubt they were in the vicinity, formulating what to say to me. The only reason they hadn't was because Reece and Andi had been with me all afternoon. Then Dad made a preemptive strike and gave Reece the keys to his tractor. That was as good as saying, *"Welcome to the family."*

Jenna looked around, trying to spot the elusive creatures we called our mothers. "I can't wait to hear what the sisters have to say about you 'dancing' with the pirate."

I rolled my eyes. "Maybe you should *dance* with someone."

"Maybe I already am," she said mysteriously.

I popped a brow. "Do tell."

"I will when the time is right."

I tilted my head. "What's going on with you?" We normally didn't keep secrets from each other.

"I'm good. I promise." She gave me a squeeze.

"Okay." I eyed her carefully to detect any lies. She seemed like she was on the up and up.

"Get over there," Kitty's voice unexpectedly rent the air.

Jenna and I turned to find Kitty prodding my brother toward me.

"Do it." Kitty shook her finger at Oliver.

Oliver hung his head and moped over my way. He was dressed pumpkiny in his orange polo shirt and ball cap.

"This, I have to see," Jenna spoke out of the side of her mouth.

I was certainly interested to see what Oliver had to say. We hadn't really spoken since the douchebag poll didn't go in his favor.

Oliver approached and kicked some rocks at his feet. "Hey, sis."

"Hey," I casually returned. "What's up?"

He slowly lifted his head. "Well . . . uh . . . I've been thinking a lot lately about stuff. You know, past stuff."

"Uh-huh."

"And . . . well . . . I've come to the conclusion I could have been a better brother to you."

"You think?" Jenna got snippy on my behalf.

Oliver flashed her a withering glance.

Kitty snapped her fingers. "None of that, Oliver."

I loved Kitty.

Oliver cleared his throat, while he plastered on a more docile countenance. "As I was saying . . . I'm sorry. Truly. I didn't mean to hurt you. I thought it would be a stupid gag among my friends, but it got out of hand, and I used you to impress people who should have never mattered to me. You didn't deserve that. I hope you can forgive me," he pleaded.

Wow. I was so taken aback by his apology, I wasn't sure what to say.

"You matter to me, sis," he added, while I searched for the

right words. Then he did something totally unexpected and drew me in for a bear hug.

I wasn't sure when we had actually hugged last. Maybe at his wedding? Whenever it was, it was a long time ago, and a hug was well overdue. I wrapped my own arms around him. "Perhaps there's hope for you after all," I said, muffled against his chest.

He laughed a rumbly laugh. "I'm getting there."

"Me too."

"Just make sure Reece treats you well."

I turned out of Oliver's arms and smiled at Reece, who I knew would treat me oh so well.

Andi called out, "Look at me!"

I couldn't wait to see her grow. To help her become who she was supposed to be. As I watched her and Reece, everyone else seemed to fade away—even Jenna. Eventually, I was left alone to admire the man who was wreaking havoc on my life. Oddly, I wanted to thank him for it. I mean, I might be singing a different tune if I lost my job. But at least I knew that if I did, I went out with my boots on and not cowering like I had been so good at doing in the past.

"They remind me of you and your dad." Mom surprised me. She was stealthy like that.

I hugged myself as the temperature dropped the farther the sun set below the horizon. I thought of all the tractor rides Dad and I had taken when I was a little girl and smiled. I always asked to stay out longer, just like I'd heard Andi ask Reece. Dad always gave in, just like Reece. "I miss those days." Days when I didn't know I could hate myself, and my biggest worry was whether Mom made brussel sprouts for dinner and how I was going to get out of eating them.

"I miss you." Mom tugged on my sleeve.

I faced her and noticed the tears welling in her eyes. "I miss you too, Mom." My voice cracked with emotion.

"I heard what happened at the school today," she mentioned.

"Are you upset I might lose my job?" I hesitated to ask.

"I'll start a protest at that school if you do." She gave me a crooked grin.

"Please don't." I could see the posters now.

"Oh, honey," her voice hitched. "I hope you know how proud I am of you. How proud I've always been of you. I didn't realize how bad you were hurting. How I hurt you," she blubbered.

"Mom." I hugged her, letting her bawl on my shoulder.

"I didn't know people were still calling you pirate girl and how much that affected you."

"I'm good at hiding my feelings."

"I should have been better at reading them. I'm your mother, after all." She clung to me. "The last thing I ever wanted was for you to hate yourself. I feel like I let you down in so many ways. I don't know how to fix that."

"I do."

She lifted her head with tearstained cheeks. "How?" she begged to know.

"Move on with me. Welcome Reece and Andi into our family with open arms."

She directed her attention toward them. "I hear he's a good man."

"He is. The best. I think you would really like him if you gave him a chance."

"I will." She nodded. "I promise."

"Thank you."

She took my hand and held on for dear life. "I'm sorry, honey."

"I know. I love you, Mom."

"I love you more than my life, kiddo."

I knew that.

"Why don't you and Reece take the tractor for a spin, and I'll take Andi to make some pumpkin sugar cookies."

I felt her forehead to check if she was feeling all right. "Are you sure?"

She swatted my hand away, laughing. "Go get your man."

She didn't need to tell me twice. "Yes, ma'am. By the way, Andi's had a hard day."

"I heard about that, too. Don't worry; I'll take good care of her."

"Okay. Save us some cookies." I ran out to meet Reece and Andi.

Reece put on the brakes when he saw me coming their way.

"That's some good driving there, cowboy." I winked.

"Did you see me steer, Ms. Peterson?" Andi was quite animated.

"I did. You did a great job. How would you like to make some pumpkin cookies with my mom?"

Mom came up behind me, giving Andi a big, grandma grin. "I'll even let you lick the beaters."

Andi's eyes lit up at all the possibilities. "Okay."

I reached for her and helped her off the tractor. In the process, I gave her a big squeeze. She hugged me back as tight as she could, and all felt right in my world.

"Come on, cutie." Mom held out her hand to Andi.

Andi took it and they were off, leaving only Reece and me.

"You want to go for a ride, cowgirl?" Reece drawled.

"I thought you would never ask."

Reece offered me his hand, and I took it. He pulled me up, and straight to his lips, where he rewarded me with a kiss. "I like this. Very much."

"Your shirt is so coming off."

"Well then, hop on, darlin'." He patted his lap, doing a great impression of a cowboy.

"Don't mind if I do." I settled right into him.

Once I was situated, he whispered low in my ear, "How about we drive fast and kiss slow?"

"Sounds perfect."

Reece threw the tractor in drive, and we were on our way to what I knew was going to be one of the best nights of my life.

"I'm proud of you, Josie," Reece said, above the noise of the engine.

"What a crazy day." I could still hardly believe it.

"You were amazing. The way you stood up for Andi, and yourself. Today, you reminded me of the girl in your story—Josie."

"She was quite a brave girl, wasn't she?"

"Not as brave as the woman who wrote her." He kissed my cheek.

From there it was a quiet ride out to the field. I thought a lot about the girl in my story and the one who wrote her. If only she knew it would all be okay. And more importantly, that she had the power to make it okay. Kind of like Dorothy from *The Wizard of Oz*. She had the ability to go home all along, by clicking her ruby heels. Not to say my problems would be as easily solved, but the solution always rested within me. It just took Reece to point it out. I guess that made him Glinda the Good Witch.

When we made it out to the back patch, there were a lot fewer pumpkins, but it was just as beautiful to me.

Reece killed the engine, and for a moment we watched the sun fade, leaving only a burst of orange in the twilight sky.

"Josie," Reece said my name so beautifully, "I think you should know I'm falling in love with you."

My heart got its freak on, like Jenna would say. We are talking major dance party. "I kind of got that from what you said to Mr. Nelson today."

"I hope I didn't scare you."

"No. It's a beautiful thought. But you know we need to get to the shore first? And even when we get there, I'll probably still be a little crazy."

Reece pulled me closer to him. "I sure hope so. I love your crazy."

"Thanks for jumping off the cliff with me."

"Anytime."

"You know, we are getting closer to the shore."

"I do," Reece groaned in my ear.

"I should probably check out your chest again to make sure it's primed and ready to go for all that sticky sand," I said in my best coy voice.

"It's good to be prepared for these things," Reece played along.

I could hardly contain my excitement when I maneuvered around and straddled him. Now facing him, I rested my hands on his stubbled cheeks. "I like this view much better."

"Me too." He nipped at my lip.

"Reece?"

"Yes, Josie?"

"I think there's something you should know," I purred.

"What's that?" he responded, just as sexily.

I told myself to be brave and own the very real feelings coursing through me. "I'm falling in love with you, too."

"That's excellent news." He grinned.

"Now . . . let's take off that shirt."

Thirty-Two

I WALKED UP THE SCHOOL steps Monday morning to the sound of my pounding heart. Mr. Nelson had called the night before asking to meet with me. Reece was due in court, so he wasn't available to come. Mom had offered, but I'd seen her supply of poster board and declined. I had a feeling she'd already made a slew of protest signs just in case.

I kept telling myself that no matter what, we owed it to the girl I had abandoned to own our choice. Then there was Andi. I smiled, thinking of all the Halloween movies we'd binged the night before while snuggled up on the couch. It was the perfect night, just the three of us. Maybe that's why I didn't feel as pukey as I thought I would. I was high on love. It was the best drug around. And like Reece said, according to the law, I had done nothing wrong. Not sure that would matter. Although, Reece did promise to subscribe to the Turkish streaming channel, so there was that.

I paused to steady my wildly beating heart before I opened one of the front entrance doors. I peeked through the glass and noticed the entire faculty seemed to be gathered in the foyer. I had seen a lot of cars in the parking lot, but I hadn't registered how unusual that was considering the early hour. My stomach sank, thinking they were all there to get a peek at the pirate girl before she got fired.

Gripping the door, I closed my eyes, begging myself not to let this derail me. *Triumphs, not tragedies. Andi. Me. The pirate girl.* I owed it to all three to walk in with my head held high. I let out a deep breath, opened my eyes, and flung the door open. I walked in to the sound of clapping and cheers. I paused, confused.

Aline pushed her way through the crowd and grabbed my hand. "There you are, querida."

"What's going on?" I yelled above the noise.

"We're here to support you."

I began to rapidly blink back tears. I was absolutely stunned, so much so, I had no words.

Aline smiled. "That's right. We're here to fight for you."

"I don't know what to say." I grabbed ahold of her and squeezed like heck. "Thank you." It seemed so inadequate, but they were the only words that came to mind. They had no idea what this meant to me. Not only were they fighting for me, but they were healing the girl inside of me who always felt unworthy of such loyalty or help. A new narrative was beginning.

"They mess with you, they mess with all of us." Aline sounded like she had joined a gang or something.

I laughed and gave her one more squeeze.

"We have your back, querida." She gave me a little push forward.

As I walked through the crowd, I received a lot of high fives and words of comfort and encouragement. My mascara was going to be toast at this rate, but it was the best feeling ever. Well, maybe not ever. I thought of Reece and the tractor. A shiver went through me. This was not the time to be thinking of all the wonders of Reece.

When I made it to the front office, I was met by a grinning Libby shaking her head back and forth. "I knew there was something going on between you and that fine, fine man," she drawled. "Darlin', let me know if you want to learn how to hog-tie."

Oh. My. Shiz. "I think I'm good. Thanks."

"You don't know what you're missing out on." She wagged her brows. "By the way, Mr. Nelson is waiting for you. P.S. He's a little peeved this morning."

I couldn't imagine him being happy about this show of support for me, especially in light of my rule-breaking ways.

I swallowed hard. "Wish me luck."

Libby patted my arm and walked toward the front desk. "You're going to need it."

"That's what I was afraid of." I turned and looked at all my supporters one more time, feeding off their energy. It filled me with courage and hope. Even if I lost my job, I would never, ever forget this.

"Go give him hell," Aline shouted, making everyone laugh, including me.

With that, I made my trek toward Mr. Nelson's office, wiping my eyes as I went, but holding my head up high. I was owning this day and my choice to be with Reece. The hall seemed longer—and shorter—than usual, all at the same time. By the time I reached his office, I felt like I couldn't breathe. I loved my job and, now more than ever, I loved the people I worked with.

Mr. Nelson sat at his desk, arms folded, waiting for me. "Come and have a seat. Shut the door on your way in." He nailed the intimidating tone.

I did as he asked, shaking while trying to look calm, cool, and collected. I sat in what was becoming my normal chair. I looked at the empty one next to me and smiled to myself thinking about how it wasn't that long ago that Reece sat there. How could I ever have thought that man was going to ruin my life?

"Ms. Peterson," Mr. Nelson's curt voice got me right out of my head. "I've had an interesting weekend," he complained.

I had too, but I didn't mention it. "How so?"

He scrubbed a hand over his face. "Let's see: I probably had over a hundred phone calls from past and present parents, threatening to pull their kids and funding if I even thought about firing you. Then two women called saying they were organizing a protest and they had local news station connections."

I pressed my lips together, trying not to smile. Oh, the sisters. I knew I'd seen marker on their hands the day before. But I loved them. And I had so much love for my students' parents—one in particular. I was amazed by all the love and support for me—Josie.

"Then," he growled, "your *lawyer* sent over a letter this morning, detailing your contract and spelling out how we have zero grounds to terminate you." A hint of a smile appeared on his face.

That's why Reece had asked for a copy of my employee contract. I was so in love. "That does sound interesting," I played it cool.

"So, Ms. Peterson, the board has decided . . ."

I held my breath and squinted, waiting for my fate. Ready to fight back if I had to.

". . . it would be in everyone's best interest if you remained employed here."

I let out the breath I held, while a happy dance ensued in my stomach. "I think that's a great idea."

Mr. Nelson let out a long sigh, and I dare say a real smile came with it. "You are the best teacher at this school, and I would hate to lose you."

"Thank you."

"Please take care of Reece." It was the warmest I'd ever heard him sound. "He's the best man I know."

He certainly was the best.

"I will," I promised.

"Good. Now go tell your fan club to get to work." All the warmth was gone.

I stood, hardly believing I was still employed, and loved, so loved. *Please love me,* a little voice inside of me pleaded. I would do everything I could to love that girl—the pirate girl.

"It was so amazing." I couldn't stop talking about it.

Reece pulled me closer on his couch and indulged me, even though he'd called me earlier in the day while court was in recess. "You're amazing. You deserved everything you got today."

"I'm just glad my mom and aunt didn't have to protest."

"Those women are something else." Reece had gotten a good taste of them over the weekend. Suddenly he was the crown prince around the farm. They fawned over him like everyone else, asking what his favorite meal was and serving him. Mom was so smitten with Andi. She was even helping Molly make her Halloween costume. She was going to be the cutest Priscilla Pumpkin.

"Yeah, they are," I agreed. "Anyway, tell me about your day. I feel like I've dominated the night."

"I like it when you dominate." He nuzzled my neck.

It was a good thing Andi was asleep already.

I tipped my head to the side to make sure he got all the good spots. "Well, Libby did offer to teach me how to hog-tie you," I teased.

Reece chuckled between gentle kisses pressed to my neck.

"Did you hear from Nicolette today?" I hated to kill the mood, but it was important for us to talk about her, especially given the scene she'd made at the school.

Reece paused, his warm breath dancing over my skin. "She's gone back to LA."

"I'm sorry."

"I can't make her get help. I tried, but she's not ready to admit she has a problem. She told me today she's going to stay clean, but we both know it's a lie."

"What about Andi?"

"Nicolette is now threatening to never see her again. She's claiming we all turned Andi against her."

"You know she only says those things because she's hurting and she wants to hurt you, too."

"I know that. But what am I going to tell my daughter?" he pleaded to know.

I turned to catch Reece's gaze. I loved that he wasn't wearing his patch. Don't get me wrong—I dug the patch, but I was honored he felt so comfortable around me that he went without it at home. I rested my hand on his stubbled cheek. "You are going to tell her that she is more loved than she will ever know."

Reece gently swept the hair off my shoulder with such a look of adoration. "I love you, Josie.

"I love you." I leaned in, my lips teasing his. "I was wondering if you would like a bedtime story?"

"Those are my favorite kind." He brushed my lips, barely taking a taste.

"I hope you won't mind if it's one you've heard before." I knew it was time, and I knew it had to be with Reece.

Reece leaned away just enough to peer into my eyes. "Does it involve pirates?"

I bit my lip and nodded. "And hot, sticky sand."

"Do we get to act out the parts?"

"I'm counting on it."

Thirty-Three

I COULDN'T BELIEVE IT WAS Halloween already. I felt like the month had breezed by. That's what love will do to you. I had to say, it was the pumpkiny-est October I had ever had. Long tractor rides marked by slow kisses, nights spent with Andi and Reece cooking and making fall crafts. Then when Andi would go to bed, the rogue pirate would come out and . . . well . . . let's just say it might be the only time I ever say something was better than the book. In fact, it was all pretty much perfect.

The end of the season meant another weird family tradition. I was almost embarrassed to have Reece, Andi, and Molly witness it, but I supposed it was best they knew what they were signing up for here. And I had warned Reece I was still going to be a little crazy when it was all said and done. He would soon find out how crazy the Peterson bloodline truly was.

At least I was coming to terms with the pirate girl. Reading that story with Reece was the best therapy around. Perhaps it was all the role playing that helped so much. But I was pretty sure it was that I saw Josie in those pages. It was more than beautiful that I got to show her dreams really do come true. And you know what? The girl in that story was pretty kick-butt. I hoped to be more like her.

"Gather around, everyone," the sisters called.

The daytime guests had all just left. But many would return to trick-or-treat around the farm. It was the last event of the season. Reece and I would take Andi around before we left for the Halloween Bash. Which was fabulously decorated. We'd set up last night, and Cami was so pleased with how it had turned out. My mom and his mom were going to watch Andi for us while we attended. Molly had been brave enough to strike up a friendship with my mom. Honestly, they got along quite well for Molly being sane and all.

Reece gave me a smirky, knowing look, as we walked toward where the old barn used to stand. He knew very well how I felt about this particular tradition. Andi held both our hands, and we swung our arms together in sync. Molly was on my other side, curious about the weirdness that was the Petersons. She was even wearing the pumpkin beanie my mom had given her. She was such a good sport.

The sisters were in the center, and we all gathered around them. Poor Jenna was looking downtrodden. She'd had a tiff with Aidan, the mystery man. I had finally met him, and let's just say he was kind of a curmudgeon but had a soft side to him. He was a total Mr. Darcy. I had proof of it in my pocket. He'd given me a check earlier today and swore me to secrecy. Yeah, that wasn't happening. After this bizarre tradition, Jenna was so going to find out about it.

When we all arrived, the sisters looked around at us and beamed, with their hands to their mouths, just bursting with pride.

"We did it!" they cried together.

It was kind of freaky how in sync they were.

Mom let out a sigh. "We just wanted to thank everyone for all their hard work this year. We couldn't have done it without you."

"We also wanted to let you know," Aunt D. took over, her voice full of emotion, "we fell short on donations, but . . . ," she tried to sound hopeful.

"Wait," I interrupted. "I have a last-minute anonymous donation."

Everyone jerked their heads in my direction.

"From who?" Mom asked.

"I said *anonymous.*"

Everyone snickered.

I reached into my pocket and walked over the cashier's check worth a hefty number of pumpkins. I handed it to the sisters. They held it delicately between them while bursting into tears. I had to hold back my own. I knew how much the money meant to all of us. I couldn't wait to tell Jenna the secret of who had made it all possible.

The sisters hugged each other and jumped up and down like teen girls.

The brothers looked on, smiling and shaking their heads.

I took my place, right where I belonged, with Reece and Andi.

Once the sisters got themselves under control, they both said in unison, "It's time."

Reece grinned at me, as I squirmed before the song had even begun.

The sisters hummed the note we were to start on before they led us in the pumpkiny-est song there ever was. Although it was sung to the tune of "Jingle Bell Rock." The sisters had once won a talent show when they were kids singing said song. And they kept the same dance moves to it, which we were all expected to do while singing. It was a total cringe-fest. But, if truth be told, I kind of loved it.

Petersons! Petersons! Family-owned farm
Pumpkins and corn
And hayrides and more
Cider and mazes and hayrides too
Look what the Petersons have for you!

Petersons! Petersons! Family-owned farm
The season is done
And the pumpkins all gone
We'll see you next year, so don't be too blue
Petersons are here for you!

What a fun time, is the fall time
To visit us at the farm
'Cause the fall time, is the best time
To see everyone arm in arm

Petersons! Petersons! Family-owned farm
Come back next year, oh please
We'll be here, just wait and see
Because That's the Petersons,
That's the Petersons
That's the Peterson farm!

Reece chuckled most of the way through it. Andi thought it was awesome and sang her little heart out. My mom had been teaching it to her . . . more like indoctrinating her. It was hard to imagine that grown adults did this sort of thing. But it was a Peterson tradition.

"Well, that was interesting," Molly said, when it was over.

That was one word for it.

"Now it's time to trick-or-treat," Andi squealed. "I can't wait to wear my costume."

"Should we go to the house and get ready?" I suggested.

"Yes!" She ran off toward my parents' place, down the dusty, well-worn path of my childhood. For a moment I saw myself at her age, flying and full of life. I would do my best to see that Andi always had wings to fly.

Reece, Molly, and I followed behind her, albeit more slowly.

Mom caught up to us. "I have a surprise for you two."

"You do?" I asked.

"I made your Halloween costumes."

Reece and I looked at each other. We had rented costumes and were going as Superman and Lois Lane. I really couldn't wait to rip off Reece's white dress shirt and expose him for the superhero he is.

"Mom, you didn't have to do that." I wasn't even sure when she would have found the time.

Mom looped her arm through mine. "I wanted to. I hope you love them."

"I'm sure we will. What are they?"

"Oh, you'll see," she sang.

I was more than curious now.

Our moms walked ahead of us, whispering conspiratorially as if Molly knew about the costumes as well.

"You know, I was really looking forward to seeing you in that tight skirt tonight," he groaned in my ear. "I thought we could play out the boss/secretary fantasy. I would play the part of secretary, of course."

"Of course," I purred, feeling all sorts of hot. I had to keep my hands to myself with witnesses around. "You know, I could wear the skirt and play your boss after the party," I said for his ears only.

"I love the way you think." He rewarded me with a peck on the lips.

We hustled to the house before things got too heated between us.

We walked in, and Molly took Andi to help her change, while Mom said, "Follow me." She led us back to my old room. Before she opened the door, she turned and leaned against it, smiling at our clasped hands.

It meant a lot to me that she had accepted Reece and had quit calling him the pirate, though I found out he didn't mind at all when *I* used the name. My mother did not need to know that.

"Josie, honey, I just wanted you to know that I read your story again."

"What?" I spluttered. It was one thing for me to read it again. It was another thing for my mother to. Especially because, wow, I was a very detailed writer. I could see why I got grounded. Holy shiz.

"It's okay," she said, in soothing tones. "I'm proud of you."

"You are?"

"I mean, you are very *descriptive*," she said it like she was dying inside a little.

Reece chuckled, but covered it up as a cough.

"I just want you to know that if you want to write a sequel, you have my blessing. I probably won't read it, but you should do what makes you happy. You're a talented woman."

"Thanks, Mom." I knew how hard that was for her to say. And if I did write a sequel, I would definitely not want her to read it. In fact, I would insist she didn't.

"I love you." She pinched my cheek.

"I love you too."

"Now, for the big reveal." She sounded so giddy. "I hope everything fits. Your mom helped me with your measurements," she said to Reece.

A look passed between Reece and me; we were more than interested to see what my mom had made for us.

She swung open the door with gusto, then pulled us in. There on the bed, two beautiful costumes were laid out.

"Oh, Mom." I could hardly believe my eyes. "They're gorgeous."

"Do you love them?" she was anxious to know.

I nodded, hardly able to speak for how much I loved them.

"They're fantastic, Lottie," Reece answered for us.

"I figured the world needed a rogue pirate and a pirate girl tonight." Mom kissed my cheek and flittered out, without another word.

"Thank you," I barely managed to say before she left the room.

Reece and I stood in awe of the cream dress, made to look

exactly how I imagined, and the cutaway coat with tails and burgundy cravat.

"I can't believe she did this."

"Does she know your breasts will be heaving in that dress?" Reece sounded pretty dang excited about the prospect.

"I don't think we should mention it. I'll wear a jacket when we leave."

"Good idea." Reece took me up in his arms. "Are you ready to be my Josie tonight?"

"She's all I ever wanted to be."

Epilogue

"I CAN'T BELIEVE THIS IS happening." I squeezed Reece's hand in the elevator, as we made our way up to the twenty-ninth floor. I had never even been in a building with that many floors. I had never been to New York until late last night. We flew in with Molly and Andi, after having Thanksgiving with my family. I mean, Reece had to see what the sisters' pumpkin pie was all about. It was well worth the red-eye flight.

"It's going to be great. As your attorney, I can tell you the contract is fair."

"What do you say as my boyfriend?"

He pulled me closer and whispered in my ear, "I say, I'm so proud of you, and I can't wait to act out all the new scenes you're going to write."

It was a good thing we were alone in the elevator. I was blushing from my head to my toes. "I am going to need a lot of new material."

"That's excellent news." He kissed my cheek.

I playfully pushed him away. "Now, stop. We're supposed to be professional."

"Cari is well aware of our relationship." He took my hand.

"Do you really think I can do this?" It was one thing to have my torrid teen story go viral; this was a whole other ball game.

"I know you can."

I squeezed his hand and tried to breathe normally. "Thank you, Reece."

"For what?"

"Believing in me. Helping me to love the pirate girl."

"That was easy. That girl was always you."

I loved that thought. I loved Reece, my very own pirate.

The elevator dinged and the doors opened. I looked at Reece, and then together we jumped off another cliff into some very unknown waters. But I had a feeling there was another sandy shore ahead, and I couldn't wait to reach it with him by my side.

The Engagement

"DASHING THROUGH THE SNOW . . ." MY students sang at the top of their lungs, while crowded around Reece and the keyboard he'd brought in for our class holiday party. Reece was, of course, singing louder than anyone, while his fingers danced across the keys. While it was adorable, I had to say I loved it more when he gave me private performances at his mom's house on the old upright piano. If that piano could talk, let's just say it would be applauding Reece's bare chest as much as I was. It was all done in the name of research, of course. It was a good thing my mother vowed not to read what Reece was calling my future masterpiece.

My first draft was due to the publisher in June. To say I was a ball of nerves was an understatement. While the research was fun, I worried if I could really write a novel. Reece was the most incredible cheerleader, constantly reminding me I could do this. I loved him more and more each day.

I smiled at my man wearing a Santa hat. He was the best Royal Highness to the Educational Professional, on top of being the greatest dad and boyfriend. Andi was right by her daddy's side, singing nearly as loud as her father. I loved to see her so happy and full of life. She and her dad were my life. I was looking forward to the two-week Christmas break, dedicated to just the three of us snuggled on the couch watching all the holiday favorites, while we ate cookies and drank cocoa. You know, between me writing and the after-hours research we would do once Andi went to bed. Reece was still the best pirate around.

The music and singing abruptly stopped.

"I think it's time we gave Ms. Peterson her gift." Reece flashed the children a conspiratorial grin.

I raised my brow, wondering what he was up to. He hadn't said anything about the children giving me a gift when we'd planned the class party together.

My students cheered and clapped their hands, before scattering to their desks.

"What are you up to?" I approached Reece at the front of the room, still behind his keyboard, wearing that illegal grin I loved to kiss off his face whenever possible. But definitely not at school. That might have thrown Mr. Nelson over the edge. Although, I had to say he and his wife, Denise, were a lot of fun to hang out with on the weekends. But he wouldn't want me to mention that. Or that fact that he knew how to play some serious poker.

Reece stood and swaggered my way. "So much," he said, as sexily as he could get away with at school.

I bit my lip. "Is that so?"

He reached for my hand. "Come stand over here."

I placed my hand in his own. It was right where it belonged.

He pulled me toward him, his first-rain-of-spring scent captured me and made me inhale deeply. "Just keep looking at me," he instructed.

I had no problem with that. I loved nothing more than to look at him. There I stood, admiring Reece's caramel eye that reflected me, and the stubble I ached to run my fingers across. Don't even get me going on his lips that I longed to be held captive by. I had to remind myself this wasn't the time or place for such activities.

Behind me, I heard my class giggling and flapping what sounded like posters. "What are they doing?" I asked.

Reece wagged his brows while pulling up our clasped hands and administering the perfect prince charming kiss upon my own.

"You are a tease."

"I'm only in love."

I never tired of hearing him say that. It still felt as implausible as the first time, but there was no denying the rightness of it. "I love you too."

"I'm happy to hear that. You can turn around now."

Reece spun me around, to find each one of my students holding up large pieces of cardstock colored in reds and greens. Each paper had a white letter on it. While I read what the letters spelled out, my students laughed and wiggled uncontrollably.

W I L L Y O U M A R R Y M E ? flashed before my eyes. I could hardly believe what I was reading. Then Reece dropped down in front of me, holding a small black velvet box. With bravado, he opened that baby to reveal a stunning antique diamond ring in a buttercup style setting. It was something straight out of my story.

"Marry me, Josie. Let's sail the high seas together for the rest of our lives."

"Please, say yes!" Andi shouted.

Reece and I laughed, before I could say, "I will be your pirate girl for the rest of my life."

Reece stood and tugged me toward him. "Is that a yes?"

"A million times, yes." I choked out with emotion.

Andi dropped her poster and ran our way. We wrapped her up between us while Reece planted a gentle kiss upon my lips. "I love you, Josie."

"Can I get a brother or sister now?" Andi unexpectedly asked.

Reece's and my eyes widened. Not that we hadn't talked about having children, it had just never been in front of Andi.

"I think that's an excellent idea." Reece winked.

"Yay!" Andi exclaimed.

Reece leaned his forehead against mine. "What do you say, my love?"

"I say, let's get this party started."

If you loved A Pumpkin and a Patch, please consider leaving
a review on Amazon.
Lots of love,
Jennifer

* * *

Check out Jenna's story, *Pumpkin Spice and Not So Nice*,
on Amazon.

If you enjoyed *A Pumpkin and a Patch,* here are some other books by Jennifer Peel that you may enjoy:

The Holiday Ex-Files (Cami and Noah's story)
The Valentine Inn
Christmas at Valentine Inn
All's Fair in Love and Blood
Love the One You're With
My Not So Wicked Stepbrother
Facial Recognition
The Sidelined Wife
How to Get Over Your Ex in Ninety Days
Narcissistic Tendencies
Honeymoon for One - A Christmas at the Falls Romance
Trouble in Loveland
Paige's Turn

ABOUT THE AUTHOR

Jennifer Peel is a *USA Today* best-selling author who didn't grow up wanting to be a writer—she was aiming for something more realistic, like being the first female president. When that didn't work out, she started writing just before her fortieth birthday. Now, after publishing several award-winning and best-selling novels, she's addicted to typing and chocolate. When she's not glued to her laptop and a bag of Dove dark chocolates, she loves spending time with her family, making daily Target runs, reading, and pretending she can do Zumba.

***

If you enjoyed this book, please rate and review it.
You can also connect with Jennifer on social media:
Facebook
Instagram
Pinterest

To learn more about Jennifer and her books, visit her website at
www.jenniferpeel.com.

Made in the USA
Monee, IL
29 September 2022

14928264R00160